Off Track

Off Track

C.P. Avis

Off Track

First Printing July 2019

ISBN 9781999467005

Cover Art, Book Design: C.P. Avis
Printed and bound in Canada

Published in Canada

www.cpavis.com

ISBN 978-1-9994670-0-5

*Dedicated to the County of Brant
where I found purpose and joy,
aggravation and inspiration.*

Prologue

The earth has its music for those who will listen.
— George Santayana

Take Highway 5 west from Toronto into Tecumseh County and drawers from history open and close one by one like the ascent and fall of the Niagara Escarpment itself.

The road is called Dundas Street West where it begins in the heart of the city. It hobbles through the struggling crime-ridden neighbourhoods of Parkdale, darts north across Bloor Street and meets a diamond of four railway lines at the Junction.

Near Keele Street one sees the vestiges of bleak Victorian scrapes, the foundries, the mills, the furniture factories, the meat plants, now subsumed by the frantic modernity of prosperity, all commerce and busy lives. It is at once an achievement and a loss. Just like Queen Victoria herself, the era was little understood, rarely appreciated, and substantially underestimated.

Horse paths become trolley rails and neighbourhoods, pioneer trails transmute into highways. Apartment flats over storefronts flushed the Irish, the Italians, the Poles into the many jobs that settled Canadians did not want. And a generation later those same immigrants drifted to the suburbs, started their own stores, and rented out the spaces above them to immigrants from another part of the world; poverty shifted.

Dundas is lured by the beauty of the Humber River as it soars through the valley west alongside the prosperous mansions and specialty delicatessens of Lambton and the Kingsway.

The neighbourhood changes ethnicity from the Italian, Polish, and Ukrainian — immigrants disparagingly dubbed DPs by the Anglo white majority of the 1950s: displaced persons, settling in west Toronto after the second World War.

Then wave after wave of new immigrants arrived in the 1980s and 1990s, those who took over the flats and the little bunglows of the DPs, the Arabs, the Sikhs, the Pakistanis, the Muslims, the Vietnamese, the Africans, who all came to the suburbs of the suburbs and moved their streetside stalls onto cement blocks with glass doors. Today the signs are cacophonous with colour and exotic lettering, the cooking smells drifting with the gritty gusts of urban winds, settling down around iron storm sewer covers and the bases of flyer-laden utility poles.

Dundas broadens to avoid being eclipsed by a tangle of transmission lines and soaring towers, becomes six lanes in heavily industrial lands where a ceiling of perilously low-flying jetliners ellipse and roar onto the landing strips of a nearby international airport. An ugly mesh of overhead wires bind roti, pizza, phô, and halal restaurants between strip malls and apartment towers that repeat in random combinations of what is nevertheless the same look for endless kilometres.

Small buildings begin to border box stores and sprawling urban amenities, and the asphalted multi-lane intersections so frequently lauded by urban transportation experts speed people to their destinations, excited and depleted at once by the dust and the noise and the hope of a tomorrow with more pay, and a vacation in the country.

At the Credit River, a marvellous height of land and a cushion of green, a serene Lake Ontario, gentle neighbourhoods. Here and there precisely measured landscaping, the sheltered lawns of half-hidden homes, an elbow of a park peeking out between the subdivisions and the strip malls. They are the soothing promises of serenity and fresh air that cannot be kept.

A roar of engines and exhaust and a knot of highway overpasses and cutoffs, malls and lined-up industrial shops then, just like that, the overhead wires are gone, Dundas Street on one side of the intersection and Highway 5 on the other, and it is the country.

The ascent up the Niagara Escarpment is slow, gradual, insistent.

The road is fast and smooth, the traffic signals are far-flung as the dark shadow of the escarpment fills the rear-view mirror. A sheep farm, a railway, another hydro corridor then suddenly and disappointingly there is congestion again. Billboarded subdivisions appear in mid build, the Longos and the Starbucks and the Boston Pizzas that cater to the affluent; crossroads with names honouring ejected aboriginal tribes.

After Oakville passes, there are fewer urban lies; there are real fields and barns and a long languorous view now and again, gangly belts of stores, gas stations, and bungalows on generous lots, the highway allowing arteries that crosscut south to Burlington and Lake Ontario.

Mount Nemo looms, sudden, improbable. Tiny, isolated churches built by the English at Confederation, only to be abandoned at the centennial. Gothic white, clapboards, an inn. A generous view of the lake, cool air, limestone outcrops; the clouds drift down to meet you. The road curves and a glance over a shoulder bids adieu to the land behind, aproning, misted.

Waterdown. Again, suburbs where none are expected, a town as annoying as a giggly teenager. Historic landmarks carelessly crowded by commerce, an abundance of mediocre chain stores, uneven asphalt abruptly halted by roadside concrete barriers. The stridency of the last coffee shops is almost forgotten but for the strewn garbage, the exhaust-spewing cars, the convenient drive-throughs.

Finally, there are nurseries and flea markets and antique stores and a raceway. Then, joyously, the promise of the land is kept: a swooping down over a shady gully that to the left, unbeknownst to those on the highway, drops sharply over a waterfall like a miracle, then south over the escarpment before sharing its current with a great lake.

The land begins to roll, the tiled fields and the fenced yards of horses and Herefords tilt away to farmhouses and stands of maple and lonely oak remnants from a long-ago forest, and Highway 5 finally abuts at the Grand River, the lifeblood of the frontier era of Ontario and the heart of the once-great, once-respected First Nations people.

But before the asphalt ceases and the gravel right-of-way touches the riverbank, Dundas Street-now-named-Highway 5 has traveled through a final set of stop lights, then follows the Grand River through the County of Tecumseh all the way to a mighty train bridge from whose height can be seen an orderly town built on the vestiges of a nineteenth century industrial settlement.

It rises at the juncture of the now-abandoned Grand Trunk Railroad and the Great Western Railroad, two spines that joined the far flung regions of a fledgling province to the bustling ports on Lake Erie and the great markets of the United States of America.

This little town of Waterford overlooking the Grand River is charming with its tree-lined streets and irregular lots footing narrow but picturesque Victorian homes, including one painted Delft blue with white trim and equipped with an office on street level and living quarters upstairs.

There, downstairs in the sunroom, on a plush yet firm couch overlooking a leafy backyard is where Kate Messenger likes to rest with a cup of tea to watch the birds.

And whenever she is not in the front office of the monthly newspaper *The Tecumseh Challenge*, where, unfortunately, she is usually found more often than not, this is where Kate will sit with her dog Alfred in her lap, listen to Chet Baker or Diana Krall or Oscar Peterson, and contemplate the day.

Chapter 1

Looking either up or down the river, from this Bridge, the prospect is a delightful one. Upwards, the river is seen glistening among the trees that adorn its banks with a line of silver, and the scene, while truly placid and quietly beautiful, has yet the wild liveliness of merely natural adornment. Looking down the river a view is afforded of a large portion of Upper and Lower Town.

— History of the County of Tecumseh, Vol. II,
by P. Martin Somerville, 1920

The old man could see two figures on the train bridge, and it frightened him. It looked like a woman and a man. They were arguing.

For Godsakes, he said to himself. *What in the world are they doing? At this hour of the morning.*

He sat motionless.

Leave me alone, the old man heard.

The man leaned into the woman. She shoved him away and yelled.

The old man was sitting in a wheelchair in the shade of the trees at the edge of a parking lot, a light shawl over his lap. He had a fresh bandaid on his forehead, as the result of a fall. The wheelchair was a relatively new thing, the consequence of that fall. The wheelchair had taken the place of an old plastic deck chair that he had secreted behind the building for his private morning ritual of greeting the dawn of every new day.

Before then, it had been the same scene through the branches every morning that summer — train tracks over an old cast iron high-level bridge that crossed the river, then disappeared into greenery.

The old man couldn't quite see the entire length of the bridge from his vantage point, and it was just as well. It would have been an unnerving sight. The bridge dropped down a fair distance. Some of the river was obscured but in its depths, the water was brown and turgid, half-heartedly masking unsightly dangerous objects.

Every day the old man had been content to watch the early morning light melt the gloom, then make its way through the treetops. If he was lucky, a blue heron would drift by.

But today, past the middle of August, on a Monday, things were horribly off track. And not only that, the train bridge was an active one, and the morning commuter was due.

The woman broke into an awkward off-balance run, stumbled, then steadied herself with a hand on a side rail. She glanced at the man behind her. He caught up to her and grabbed her. She clawed at him and began to scream.

Then — he hit her in the face with a closed fist. And quickly, a series of vicious blows to the head that drove her over the rail. There was a splash.

The old man sat as motionless as a block of stone.

Holding the rail with both hands, the man looked down into the river, then peered in the general direction of the trees that mostly masked the Penmarvian Retirement Home where the old man was sitting. Good. No one there. In a split second, he had whirled around and soon he was out of view.

Red shoes disappeared into the inkiness of raking morning shadows.

At the base of the slope that supported the railway abutment on the east side, a figure emerged from the shrubs and made its way into the river. It waded across and disappeared from view.

Purple martins arced through the air, chittering.

A short time later, the old man could see the figure making its way back to the riverbank, then walking beside the road that curved under the train bridge. Then it disappeared.

The old man squinted his eyes, but rays of sun were now piercing directly through the trees that bordered the rail trail. In the placid calm of the morning, he heard an engine fire up somewhere, then a vibrating roar as a pickup truck took off.

The morning sun's rays grew even stronger, and the old man's eyes began to water. He wiped them with the back of his hand. It was trembling.

Somewhere in the distance was the oncoming sound of a commuter train. Then just like that it was upon him, the roar and the clackity-clack and the dust, surrounding him in a suffocating envelope. A minute or two later and it was gone, his ears ringing.

A stout uniformed woman opened a side door of the adjacent old ornate building and poked her head out.

"Are you all right there, Mr. MacKenzie?" Then, to herself — "Tch tch."

She came over and steered the wheelchair behind some lilac shrubs. "I forgot, my dear, that you can't tell me these things. Here, that's better. You're in the shade now. I'll be back in a few minutes to come get you for breakfast. Now you just sit and enjoy this beautiful sunny morning, you lucky man. We haven't seen that sun very much lately, have we?"

The screen door banged shut and she was gone.

Huh, the old man thought. Lucky was not really the right word for him these days. He was shaky, and his head swam from vertigo. He could still walk, but it was tricky. In his mind was the thought that he would sneak off the premises in his wheelchair one morning, and somehow make his way to the shops downtown without getting hit by a car. It was possible. But then again, likely not. He sighed and his shoulders slumped.

The old man strained his eyes but try as he might, he couldn't see out of the shadows.

The whole thing had been very unsettling, and he shivered a little. *Truly terrible*, he thought. *That woman must have been very badly hurt. The Home should contact the authorities. The police should come.*

He felt panic rise up in his chest.

But how would he describe what he had seen? It would be impossible to tell them. He couldn't remember the simplest of words any more. And if he seemed upset, they would think he was making a fuss and would put him to bed.

Perhaps if he wrote it down, someone could decipher the shaky chicken scratch. But who would believe a sick old man anyway?

His heart ached. *God help me, it was difficult being eighty,* he thought. *Bloody awful most of the time.* He shook his head and closed his eyes.

The sun came up over the tree line, and from some distance the purple martins climbed higher and higher then passed right over the old man where he sat dozing in his wheelchair, head tilted, a raspy snore. Then they wheeled back to the river.

It would be a dastardly hot day along the Grand River in Waterford.

Chapter 2

Anybody can be good in the country.
There are no temptations there.

— Oscar Wilde

One could easily succumb to a certain complacency living in the country, where the roadsides were lush and green and one saw trees and fields and streams for miles and miles and heard only farm equipment and rustling leaves, where neighbours lent a hand and families and friends were loyal, and right and wrong were straight out of a country song.

After spending so much time covering store openings, new playgrounds, Women's Institute meetings, potlucks, and fundraisers, Kate almost believed it, too.

Not much happened in Tecumseh County. Running a newspaper in a town like Waterford was a dead dog of a business, a plodding compilation of snooze news day in and day out with only the rarest bit of manufactured excitement.

Some days Kate fantasized about taking last year's newspaper and running the same stories again, only substituting different names and places. Would anyone even notice?

She missed Toronto. At one time, her stories were devoured in the local daily and discussed on the subway, the radio, at city hall. She relished it. But the cachet of it was destined to be fleeting.

One day a freshly-minted college graduate with half her skills and twice her looks took her place, and Kate found herself out of a job.

Her mother advised she forget about being a career woman and instead, apply for a secretarial job. And on top of that, quit being so independent.

No, she thought. *I will work in my field. At whatever I can get. And to hell with them all.*

A different tack was required. She would start a small little newspaper in a small little town and try, just try to make a bit of money until the whole thing inevitably collapsed and she was forced to move on. Sure, her savings were lean. But perhaps if she was careful, they could be stretched out for a year. Maybe two. Then she would re-evaluate.

As for finding a mate, well, having never witnessed a matrimonial union that worked in favour of the female of the species, Kate had long ago concluded that despite the single-minded urgings of society, the institution of marriage was simply not designed for her benefit nor her happiness.

In the meantime, she didn't need much. Just the birds and the trees, the sky and the stars, and a roof over her head. And Alfred, her West Highland terrier, by her side.

The thought of her own newspaper was terrifying, and not a little bit thrilling too. *But surely it can be done*, Kate thought. *Surely it can be done.*

Newspapers. The entire concept was ridiculous when a person sat down and thought about it. Inventing and promoting a product completely from one's imagination, based on very little of material substance and selling nothing but ideas. Words prettied up with the flimsiest of artistry and founded on the efforts of someone who presumed they knew something.

Thousands of people had to be convinced they needed *The Tecumseh Challenge* in their lives, and how the hell would she pull that rabbit out of a hat?

God, it was hard to accomplish month after month. Especially for someone as misanthropic and fastidious and as damn irritable as Kate Messenger.

And now the whole thing had been going for ten years.

Really, Kate had not the slightest idea how.

Chapter 3

It was a trying time for business in Tecumseh County. A biting economic recession hung over the continent. Everyone was on the verge of going bust. No one was being hired. Salaries and benefits and over-regulation had throttled small business.

On top of that, a seismic shift was taking place in the newspaper world.

In the past, the odd newspaper had come and gone. But by the time the twenty-first century rolled around, the entire industry was in its death throes. With the advent of the internet, the conventional method of running a paper had been thrown out the window.

It was a calamity of intersecting misfortunes. Free on-line classified ads appeared on the scene, and hard copy newspaper classifieds took a nosedive. Then aggregating news websites sprang up, decimating the cushy subscription numbers of dailies and sending publishers into renewed panic. They were powerless to respond anyway, bloated and inefficient, stuck in their paternalistic hierarchies and spoiled from years of being the only game in town.

Readership and circulation numbers just weren't there any more. Something called email was a quick way to let customers know about upcoming sales. Advertising, the bread and butter of the newspaper industry, plummeted.

Things were clearly a-changing but most newspapers never really got it until it was too late. They were terrifying times.

In a key strategic blunder, desperate to keep readers at any cost, newspapers one by one built websites with free online news that strived to be more immediate and up-to-date than their competitors — although never as accurate or as thoughtful or as local as their own former hard copy coverage. Google, never usually a player in the scheme of things, was all of a sudden sucking a killing percentage off every ad. And by finally going online with free daily local, national, and international news, newspapers annihilated any remaining subscription revenue that might have come to them from their loyalists. It would never come back.

Soon the circulations of mighty daily newspapers matched those of the smaller weeklies and monthlies they had devoured in the past.

Collectively, it was a case of slow death on a grand scale — with each newspaper responsible for plunging the knife into its own chest.

The competition for the revenue remaining from the scant advertising left in the market was so fierce that it left anyone who didn't work seven days a week, choking in the dust.

Dailies and weeklies tottered on the brink of bankruptcy and were bought up at fire sale prices by shareholder-driven media conglomerates. The suits at the top cut back with a vengeance on serious reporters and scrupulous editors with years of experience and replaced them with sloppy layout artists in Mumbai and cheap internet marketing geniuses who favoured office interns and prepackaged generic news spewed by faceless writing services.

The Jack Olsens of the world were rendered expendable has-beens. Those close to retirement were dropped from the payroll post haste, reliving past glories with a tear in their eye and a cheap drink at the bar. They had heart attacks, lived out their final years on social assistance and beta blockers, and no one missed them.

Only the odd small newspaper that fought tooth and nail for its existence still carried on, sustained by the religion of discipline, ingrained barebones budgeting, and detail-conscious news gathering. They still knew how to please the locals. Those little papers, mostly ignored by the corporate boys, were still eagerly read by people at supper tables and coffee shops, more desperate than ever for germane here and now information.

The Tecumseh Challenge was one of those last holdouts. But it was never easy.

Kate's life was the monthly publication schedule. There was constant aggravation. Grief from her precious few advertisers, cheques arriving far too late, and phones slammed in her ear. There were all too many times when her work and polite inquiries amounted to just about nothing. On top of it all was the never-ending pressure of deadlines, story ideas, and photograph taking.

Days of non-stop writing melted into nights, the ability to sleep grew more and more diminished, and when finally print day arrived, she was at the end of her rope, an exhausted shell of a human being. Only then, when there was nothing, absolutely nothing she could do about it any more, did *The Tecumseh Challenge* go to print and Kate experience a modicum of peace.

A few days later, it would start again. The next cycle.

Sisyphus had nothing on her.

Chapter 4

The dream is unrelenting and unchanging.

Kate is in an elevator. She has the arm of the bad guy behind his back, a scrawny-limbed teenager, and she is bringing him to justice. You have assaulted me and you are going to be charged, she insists. He is hostile but for the moment, quiescent. He knows she is taking him to the authorities.

Three people step into the elevator and press numbers for various floors, and the button for Kate's floor is suddenly extinguished. It is all their fault. Angry, Kate asks them to press the fourth floor again, but instead they press all the floors and they stop every few minutes. The people eventually step off to their destinations until she is alone again with the teen.

No matter how often she presses the fourth floor it does not light. She presses and presses with her free hand then punches the button with her fist, then the elevator goes higher, and higher yet, and soon she is forced to release the arm of the teen in order to punch all the buttons, the emergency stop, the alarm, all of them. But it is too late. The elevator climbs higher and faster for what seems an eternity, then jars to a halt. Then just as suddenly, it releases and falls and tumbles head over arse, and she and the kid are twisting in the air with the cartwheeling elevator, turning and free-falling with its dead weight. It careens to the earth where it thuds to a stop, and just as the doors slide open, the young man slips out and is gone in a pounding of feet. She runs after him, shouting to all within earshot, stop him, stop him, he is a criminal.

But there is an elongated endlessly turning corridor, and he has long since disappeared, and she falls down in a heap on the cold, smooth marble floor and sobs. No one comes to her aid and she is not surprised. Bitter disappointment is a lump in her gut.

Abruptly she is in the elevator once again, and it is accelerating upward and not stopping at any floors, no indeed, not stopping at all until it almost hits the roof. Then it slows and halts with a shudder. But she knows what to expect, and when the motors click to reverse, it is plunging faster and faster and about to hit the floor. She shouts *no no no*, and the words strangle in her throat, and she cannot enunciate them at all. She is simply shrieking with her mouth closed and making ugly guttural noises like some animal caught in a trap.

Then she is awake.

Chapter 5

K ate lay in her bed, vaguely sensing her raw throat and sore jaw, her heart thumping against her ribcage. The pale first light of dawn painting the window frame yellow.

The mad beating subsided. The impact of hitting the ground was a memory slowly receding from her consciousness.

But she could still feel the collision. Her ears seemed to vibrate from the bang. In fact, it sounded as close as the wall right next to her head.

She lay still feeling slightly sick. There were the first faint twitters of goldfinches.

She remembered what faced her for the day. It was print day. And the paper was fully laid out. It was mere hours before the final pages needed to be sent, and there were still some truly vexatious knots to untangle. Time-consuming ones, too.

Time to get moving.

She groaned. Her head was sandwiched between pillows just like every morning at six thirty when the sounds of neighbours starting trucks, dragging garbage cans, setting off car alarms, slamming front doors, scraping ice, calling to children, letting out dogs, beeping horns, and a million other things, intruded into her slumber like a series of air horn blasts.

Only this morning, there was something persistently obnoxious yet somehow familiar now penetrating through six inches of foam.

Rattle. Ratteley ratteley ratteley rattle. Bang. Bang!

By the time she vaguely went down her list of familiar sounds (innocuous or menacing, worrisome or frivolous) she had clearly woken herself up and concluded that she was pretty sure but not a hundred per cent sure what it was.

It was always best to be a hundred per cent sure about everything in life.

Damn, she said to herself. That means I'll have to get up and see what the hell's going on.

Rattle. Ratteley ratteley. Bang. She groaned even louder. The noise made her teeth hurt, her brain hurt, her whole body hurt. She stifled the urge to jump up, to throw open the window, to lob something life-threatening.

I bet it's that pernicious demon next door, she thought to herself. *Doing the same stupid thing he's been doing every morning for the last month. Obsessive idiot. What the hell is wrong with him?*

Sam. She was sure of it.

She threw off the blanket, hauled herself up and out of bed, and staggered toward the window overlooking her driveway and the cement front porch slab of the house next door. Peered between the blinds.

But no, not Sam. It was his equally blond-haired, blue-eyed doppelgänger. So blond, as to look almost ghostly. Twenty-one-year-old Conner Hackett, Sam's brother, practising jumps on a flashy neon pink skateboard off the cement deck of the porch and onto the front walkway about ten feet away from her window. Dirty bare feet.

Just then, Sam, Conner's younger brother by three years, entered stage right. Bare-footed too. The banging and clattering multiplied.

Kate wondered if others shared her same agony over obnoxious noises. Perhaps it was all in one's attitude. Perhaps she had to learn to become more tolerant. Was it possible?

The thought briefly slid across the back of her mind then exited at the sound of another bang, dismissed as completely unattainable.

Sam threw an object in Conner's direction, narrowly missing his head. It hit the wall of Kate's house with the same thud that had terminated her dream.

"Get off my board jerk-off! Stop touching my stuff!"

Conner laughed.

"Why? You touch my stuff all the time, asswipe."

Sam disappeared in the house, then re-emerged shortly with a battered old black long board, tossing it at his brother's chest. Simon toppled to the ground on his rear, then uprighted himself.

"Asshole!" Simon threw the pink skateboard at Sam's head. "I don't want your shitty skateboard anyway."

The contest had stalemated. *Oh great*, Kate thought. *Now what?*

Ratteley ratteley. Bang! Ratteley ratteley. Bang! Conner and Sam traded jumps off the side of the porch onto the sidewalk, each outdoing the other.

"Wonderful," Kate muttered to herself. "Double the fun every morning."

For God's sake. Neighbours. I hate 'em. She exhaled.

Those two are just doing practice runs for the day when they would finally be hauled off to jail, Kate thought. Then finally — finally — she would be able to get eight hours sleep. She could hardly wait.

She threw herself back on the bed in disgust and re-stacked all the pillows over her head. Of course, it was impossible to get back to sleep.

She forced her mind to travel to the one thing that brought her to a steady state. The most recent image of a bird. A short-billed dowitcher she had tentatively spotted a few days ago. Slowly, the cloud of anger subsided. Perhaps it would be a good idea to get up early after all. The following night she could catch up on sleep. And the day after that she would return to the sewage lagoons in Glen Morris to get another look.

Gambatte. Keep on going. Still lots of time to deal with the paper.

Nevertheless, a tiny sliver of trepidation forced her to pick up the pace.

She had better get the garbage out. And the recycling.

She folded her legs in a lotus position, arms outstretched, meditating in the Bunkai tradition. *I am my own opponent. Discipline. Patience. Serenity. Breathe in. Breathe out.*

Alfred was stirring in the kitchen. He would need to go out in the backyard before he made a mistake on the old wooden floors.

She slipped on shorts, a T-shirt, and shoes. She plodded downstairs to the kitchen. She glanced out the window while tying shut a bag of garbage and noted the blue and white recycling bins at the side of the house. Cripes. The Hacketts had dumped stuff in them again. Their dirty unwashed fast food junk. Beer bottles stuffed with cigarette butts. *God.* She would have to sort through everything.

Why couldn't they use their own bloody bins? She wished she could find a better spot for hers but the side porch was just too convenient.

For both households, evidently.

"C'mon, Alfred," she said, as she opened the sliding doors to the back deck and stepped outside. Alfred slid out the door and carefully climbed down the wooden stairs to the lawn. Kate stood on the deck and enjoyed the shade of the elm for a few moments, noting with satisfaction that the potted geraniums looked lovely.

It was all that rain over the last couple of weeks. That, and the heat, had transformed the backyard into a greenhouse.

The early morning sun exposed the neighbour's open lawn where Kate's gaze was inevitably drawn.

Conner's mom, Moira the nutcase, was hanging a pair of jeans, socks, and an oversized black Mickey Mouse T-shirt on the clothes line. Apparently, she hadn't slept much either. Her yellowish hair was a complete mess; dark shadows underscored her eyes. She had scratches everywhere. She appeared to be suffering from a stupendously bad hangover, possibly followed by a fall, flat on her face.

Probably husband Stu, a.k.a "Mr. Charming," slugged her again, Kate speculated, *after yet another night of partying.* Moira probably gave as good as she got. She was built like a Mack truck.

"Good morning!" Moira called out and gave a perky little wave, knowing full well that the din of the skateboarding shenanigans had probably woken up half the people on the street.

Kate raised a hand robotically.

"What's so good about it," she said under her breath and went back inside to fix the same breakfast she had on odd days for as long as she could remember. Bananas and apples with homemade yogurt and honey. If she finished her breakfast with the last piece of banana together with the last piece of apple and the last spoonful of the yogurt, it was the most satisfying and perfect way to start to the morning. It could tilt the entire day into happiness.

The peel and core would be tossed into her high-efficiency rolling composter, imported from Sweden at great cost, but worth every penny. The output went into the gardens and produced the richest soil around.

The meal had a satisfyingly low glycemic index. Plus it was brain food. She would need it that day.

Chapter 6

Wolfgang Amadeus Mozart, Albert Einstein, Bill Gates, and Thomas Jefferson all displayed symptoms of Asperger's Syndrome. And, according to the experts, apparently more than one mass murderer as well.

Many people with the syndrome were known to have significant abilities in mathmatical, mechanical, or musical pursuits, or all three. The Nobel Prize had been awarded at least thirteen times to Aspies.

Aspies are idea persons; they certainly are not people persons. Obsessive or repetitive routines, intense concentration, minute attention to detail, awkward social relationships, and overheated reactions mark those with the condition. Or rather — plague them.

For with an Aspie, it is the world's continuous out-of-control sensual stimulation that wreaks the havoc and delirium of anxiety: lawnmowers, squealing children, whistling, basketballs, snowmobiles, car alarms. Cigarette smoke, laundry softener. Airplanes circling overhead, seadoos back and forth, leaf blowers next door. Crowds, movie theatres, celebrations, bright sunshine. People sneezing, visitors in the house, cramped spaces.

The list goes on and on.

Chapter 7

The computer — or "magic box" as it was fondly referred to by Kate — was stationed on a table at the back of the living room facing the window to the street. Kate sat on a stiff chair that kept her upright behind the computer. That way she could see if anyone was coming down the sidewalk.

It's always better to be aware at all times of one's surroundings. The immediate, the close, and the somewhat nearby. If possible.

Her hands ached from all the days of being propped up on a computer keyboard for hours on end. As she peered at the computer screen, mysterious semi-transparent objects floated between her eyes, her glasses, and the words, a product of her perpetually worn-out vision.

Most of the the time, her super-sharp hearing made up for her poor vision. Sometimes it more than made up for it. It amplified things. It was a bit of a curse, Kate sometimes thought. But she was okay with hearing everything that moved within fifteen metres. There were usually ways to divert all that information.

The Tecumseh Challenge was ready for its noon hour print slot. Everything was concisely laid out in that month's edition; the stories settled in their holes, the ads polished, proofed, and placed.

Readers would learn about all the things people were up to, their escapades, campaigns, failures, and accomplishments, easily comprehensible and imparted with simplicity, accuracy, relevance, balance, impartiality, insight and — most important — proper grammar.

It was a delicate juggling act and one that required concentration, especially in the days prior.

Much time had been spent combing through county council's committee agendas, correspondence, and minutes. In those dry staff reports, couched with a mishmash of legalese, bromides, and white lies, were nuggets that blossomed into provocative tales of botched tasks, uncertain outcomes, inept performances, trouble ahead. The stuff that people loved, just loved, to read about.

Ten or twenty interesting stories were fashioned about what the neighbours were doing with their properties. Or how the new arena was progressing or not. How the community services department was handling a new dog park. The fundraising plan for the outdoor pool. A new subdivision just outside the town boundary and the ensuing complaints. The gun club squabbling over parking with the church next door.

These might appear inconsequential to some people, but they always seemed to affect someone somewhere. Every edition brought comments and emails from her readers, thanking her or cursing her for bringing attention to their issue.

Kate tried not to take any criticism personally. Love it or hate it, people read the paper and that's what counted. Hundreds showed their appreciation by paying for a volunteer subscription, a veritable and astonishing army of citizen readers. Those were the people Kate worked for. Not the haters.

It made up somewhat for a trying lack of paid advertising. And allowed more money to be put against her perennially outstanding printing bill.

She sighed and booted up the computer. It wasn't too early to head to email just in case there was late breaking news.

Ha ha. What a thought. Wouldn't that be something. In Waterford.
Clicked on the inbox.

Something from the local police. She clicked on the message.

FATAL FALL AT WATERFORD TRAIN BRIDGE
WATERFORD POLICE DEPARTMENT |
Posted on 2001-08-23 | Print View

(Waterford, ON.) –

At approximately 9:00 a.m. on Wednesday, August 22nd, 2001, Waterford Police received a 9-1-1 call for a body in the Grand River in Waterford. Officers responded, along with members of the Tecumseh County Fire Department and Belleview EMS.

The victim was pronounced dead at the scene by Coroner Jay

Sakamoto. Police are continuing to investigate the incident and to locate next of kin. The Tecumseh County Fire Department and Belleview EMS assisted with the recovery of the victim from the river.

Another Media Release will be issued when more information is available. The incident is being investigated by the Waterford Police Department.

The investigation is continuing, and any witnesses or anyone with information regarding this incident are encouraged to contact Constable Leonard Kowalchuk at the Waterford Police Department at 519-447-1000.

- 30 -

"Holy guacamole," Kate said aloud, then sat back in shock. She leaned forward again and stared at the screen.

Incredible. A body. In Waterford. She would have to tear up the front page and execute a redesign. It normally would have ticked her off no end.

She began to type. Finished a short blurb. Tapped her fingers impatiently, wishing there was an update on the identity already. Where was her phone?

"Hello, composing?"

"Yup." It was Steve.

"Hey there, Steve. Could you hold off on the front page for a few hours? I've got to chase down a late breaking story." The words seemed quite unnatural coming out of her mouth.

"Yeah."

"I'll send the rest of the pages now and give prepress a head start."

"Yeah, thanks. We'll move you to seven o'clock tonight."

"Super. Thanks."

She glanced at the clock. Nine.

A few last complications were sorted out. A couple of ad proofs with the final okay. A quote was double-checked against an interview she roughly remembered from four months past. The name of a contributing photographer was ascertained from a source, and anchored with the correct spelling of the last name. Super important. Payment for a classified ad (payment in advance only). Confirmed.

Kate crossed them all off her mental list. Good.

Page one was separated, and the other pages sent to composing. *I'm going to get out of here*, she thought. Just for a minute. *Let this sit in my skull.*

Kate took Albert around the block, hoping that by the time she got back, there would be another police report with some details.

Progress was predictably slow when one had a Westie on the end of a leash. As always, anything vile on the ground was much more important than forward progress.

That morning, there seemed to be a never-ending succession of vile things on the ground, and Kate grew impatient. She tugged at the leash. Albert planted his feet solidly on the ground and refused to budge.

Totally self-obsessed. Just like people. She blew air irritably out of her mouth.

Then wondered if dogs thought humans were equally as tyrannical with their incessant stream of demands.

Well, we are. We need to be in control. Of everything. Always. We don't care that the universe is so much bigger than just us. Or at least, most the time. But sometimes we do. At least, I do.

She forced herself to relax. Peace, joy, serenity, she whispered herself. Her meditation mantra.

An unusually late Baltimore oriole called from the tree tops.

Huh. That was interesting.

Kate's nerves were momentarily calmed.

Soon, she had successfully weathered a good long wait. As soon as they were home, it was straight to the inbox. Surely it would be there by now. There was a twinge of anticipation.

There it was.

POLICE IDENTIFY VICTIM IN GRAND RIVER, the email was titled. She tsked. The police. Everything always had to be in caps. It always meant she had to retype everything instead of just cutting and pasting. Another irritation she could live without.

She clicked on the email.

Waterford Police have identified the deceased as Julie Rose Crawford, 39, of Waterford. No foul play is suspected.

If anyone has information about this incident, they are asked to contact Constable Leonard Kowalchuk at the Waterford Police Department at 519-447-1000. Or to remain anonymous, call Crime Stoppers and you will be eligible for a cash award.

Kate's eyes widened. Julie Crawford? That Julie Crawford? No, it couldn't be, was all she could think as she stared at the computer screen. Could there possibly be another Julie Crawford?

She went to the website of *The Belleview Daily Journal*. There it was, already on the header. WIFE OF WATERFORD CLOTHIER FOUND DECEASED IN RIVER. A picture of firefighters hauling something out of the river with the William Street bridge in the background.

Her head spun a little.

Oh my God. Julie. How could it be?

Poor Emma and Sarah.

She steeled herself and tried to concentrate. The news was the news, and it must proceed post haste.

Kirk Steele had already interviewed Marshall Crawford and posted the story. *Damn it,* Kate thought. *If I had a police scanner, I'd have had that story by now too. And a photo. But I can't afford a scanner.*

She reminded herself that one didn't need to gather breaking news when one was a mere monthly. No one expected it, and she couldn't fulfill it on a regular basis in any case with a staff of one. Besides, a police scanner was a mortgage payment.

Julie's husband had been devastated. "'I don't know exactly what happened,' Marshall said. He was in tears," Kirk wrote. "He covered his face with his hands and said Julie hadn't been herself lately."

Oh no. Poor Julie.

What in the world had happened?

Chapter 8

Drugs are all around, if you really start looking. People both young and old. Some had jobs, some didn't. Some I'd seen before downtown or at the liquor store, or the school, walking the sidewalks at night.

Life is all about who you hang around with.

It all started with them. At the end of the day I got a big coffee for the night, and there she was, the first girl, behind the counter in that tight little black skirt. Chatty. Skinny eyebrows pencilled onto her forehead like a porn star. Big boobs. They looked pretty good in those T-shirts she wore.

I had a feeling about her. Laughing and playing with her hair and looking through her eyelashes. And those boobs.

Once in a while I'd get a free sandwich. And the questions. Innocent enough but I thought you know, just fishing around for information that girl. Do you live in town? Do you smoke cigars? she asked me. Do you ever go out at night? Yes, yes, and depends. Depends on what, she said. I laughed.

One night after the coffee shop closed up, she showed up at the back door with a girlfriend. Looked like her, too, except blonde. And I thought, hmm. "C'mon in, girls," I said. "I could use some excitement in my life." They laughed.

I had started on the Jack Daniels already. So we're all talking and joking around and I'm being my usual lovable self and kind of wondering what they wanted, you know. Then the one girl pulled out a joint. I was already kind of drunk. So I got stoned on weed that night too.

Then they both took their clothes off.

In real life, her boobs were kind of stuck onto her ribcage like water balloons.

The other one had real boobs but saggy. She went down on her knees and undid my fly. The coffeeshop girl rubbed her tits all over my face.

A few days later they were back. They called a guy somewhere, and for $250 he drops off a couple of grams of crack. Cream coloured. I paid. They're looking at each other and grinning. They want me to try it.

From out of her purse one takes a bit of brillo, sticks it in a glass pipe, and breaks off about a tenth of the stone. They walk me through how to smoke it properly. I wasn't sure I was even going to do it, to tell you the truth. I'd heard a lot of stories. I'd seen some bad things. But then for some reason I thought — *I'll try it just once. I don't want to die without saying that I tried everything.* I was pretty sure I could do it and come out okay on the other side. So I sucked on the end of the pipe like they told me.

As I held the smoke in for a ten second count and exhaled, I'm thinking I don't feel anything except a little excitement, not bad or pleasurable either. There was about a ten or fifteen second delay.

Then — I could never have believed what happened next. A complete rush. Amazing. Like nothing I'd ever felt in life. Nothing.

I realized right then that yes, there was a heaven on earth. And I wanted more.

There was enough crack for two more hits after that. I felt great, a huge increase in energy. Then I got a little crazy wanting more and more, but there wasn't any left. They actually had to calm me down because I was getting out of control. They gave me a couple of Valiums and that helped. Then they took their clothes off again, and it was the same thing as last time, only longer. I couldn't stop, man. I really couldn't.

It was incredible.

Afterwards when they left, I just sat there and and shook my head. Completely stunned. I never felt so good in my whole damn life.

I heard crack was a dangerous drug but you know what? It changed me forever. I was grateful to those two little whores. They showed me something I never thought was possible. Not even in my dreams.

I did it a few more times. Then as time went on, more and more.

I thought I could fight it. I thought I could fight anything.

But crack steals your soul.

Chapter 9

FROM/DE: Waterford Police Department
DATE: August 24, 2001

COMMERCIAL BREAK AND ENTER - DUNDAS ST. E. |
WATERFORD POLICE DEPARTMENT |
Posted on 2001-08-30 | Print View

(Waterford, ON.) –

On August 24, 2001, members of the Waterford Police Department
(WPD) responded to a commercial break and enter at Waterford Auto
Parts on Dundas Street East, Waterford.

The investigation, thus far, has revealed that the culprit(s) attended
the business during the early morning hours. Once on the property,
the culprit(s) trespassed, accessed the storage area of the business
and stole approximately $6,000 worth of vehicle tires, car parts, and
wheel covers.

Residents of Waterford are reminded to immediately report suspicious
vehicles and persons to police by calling 9-1-1.

If anyone has information about this incident, they are asked to
contact Constable Leonard Kowalchuk at the Waterford Police
Department at 519-447-1000. Or to remain anonymous, call Crime
Stoppers and you will be eligible for a cash award.

- 30 -

Chapter 10

"**D**rugs and crime go hand in hand," Kate wrote for that month's Challenge editorial.

"It's startling to tally all the local crime incidents connected to a proliferation of drugs in Tecumseh County.

"Decades ago, marijuana and alcohol were the drugs of choice. Today, pharmaceutical companies have entered the addiction marketplace.

"Some say this is an unintended consequence of prescription use, but others claim it is a deliberate marketing ploy, that addicts like the predictability of legal pills, and business has capitalized on that.

"The use of mood-altering painkillers like Xanax and Valium have led to the abuse of opiates like oxycodone, percocet, and hydromorphine. When those drugs don't work any more, doctors then prescribe morphine and fentanyl. And when patients are abruptly cut off from their prescription drugs, they head to the street for heroin, crack, crystal meth, and cocaine. The results are debilitating losses to our society. Families and communities become plagued with mental health problems, rampant crime and theft, and social breakdown. Individuals suffer from abuse, self contempt, and prostitution, and resort to violence in order to feed drug habits.

"Our small towns have been left in shambles. Our families have been broken by overdoses, incarceration, sudden death, and wasted lives. Our businesses have suffered the effects of lost productivity and stolen goods.

"Countries like China say the answer is blanket bans, severe criminal penalties, and ruthless condemnation and enforcement. Sweden, which has one of the lowest drug usages in the western world, has a drug policy that has strong prevention and treatment services, as well as strict police enforcement.

"Maybe the answer for small town Ontario lies somewhere in the middle."

Chapter 11

A familiar-sounding bell chimed in a back room as Kate walked through the front door of Marshalls Mens Apparel. She had a feeling of trepidation.

It was crucial that she get a photo of Julie. She had considered calling Marshall first but kiboshed that in favour of coming down in person. Harder to refuse her that way.

She stiffened her jaw and her resolution.

It was still and muted within the cool, air-conditioned space. The starchy scent of brand new fabric drifted through the room along with a faint undertone of cigars. Neatly pressed matched sets of shirts and ties lined a shelf. Full-length mirrors reflected antique display tables and stacks of lightweight wool sweaters. All year round, as it were.

Her thoughts hurtled back to a similarly sunny warm day, almost ten years ago.

* * *

Kate had never actually met Marshall, an important businessman in the community, but was well aware of who he was.

She had spent the better part of a day cold-calling and introducing herself at all the shops on Grand River Street North in Waterford, the heart of business in Tecumseh County. Most were disinterested at best. They all enthused about *The Waterford Reporter* or how easy it was these days to use email to publicize their sales and special promotions. Why pay to advertise when the internet did it for free?

It was pretty darn hard to argue with that. In the meantime, Kate had noticed that Marshalls Mens Apparel was a regular advertiser with *The Waterford Reporter*, more so than anyone else.

In true salesperson form, she thought she might convince the owner, Marshall Crawford, to split some of those advertising dollars with the competition — her.

Marshall Crawford was head of the Waterford business association and she needed to get on his good side. She hoped she could convince him with her best public relations tactics and ad salesmanship to support *The Challenge*. It would be great if he did.

On Grand River Street North she loitered on the sidewalk for a few moments, her eyes fixed on the Marshalls Mens Apparel doormat with its printed store logo. It lacked apostrophe "s." As in "Marshall's Men's Apparel." Appalling grammatical blunders. Tsk tsk.

She screwed up her courage and pushed open the door.

Marshall was finishing up with a customer's alterations.

"Hello."

He glanced up. "What can I do for you today?"

"I'm with *The Tecumseh Challenge*. The new paper in town."

"Oh yes."

"Have you read it?" Kate waited for a response. Usually, they were complimentary.

"Yes." He placed a final pin inside the pants waistline. "Okay, John. That looks like it. Thanks for coming in. We'll deliver them to your house when they're done."

Kate stepped back from the middle of the aisle to give the customer lots of room to get by. He nodded and left through the door.

"Yes, I read your paper," Marshall continued, head down. "Were you the one who wrote that article on the church parking lot?"

"I did. I write all of the news articles. My contributors write all the service club reports." She hoped he would acknowledge all the free publicity she gave to volunteer groups. None of the other papers gave them anything.

"Well, the president of the rifle club is a good friend of mine. And he didn't like being called a liar in your article."

This was not going the way she wanted and her heart sank. She pricked at Marshall's tone and took a breath, scrambling to retrieve the article in her head. It was almost lost in the whirling cloud of deadlines, edits, victories, and defeats of the first few months of running a fledgling newspaper. But she recalled the gist of the article. She summoned her training and put her mouth into gear.

"I don't remember all the details of the article. I write quite a few. But

I can tell you that I definitely would not have called anyone a liar."

"You might as well have. Here. Here's the article." Marshall pulled out a clipping from his desk drawer. A few sentences were emphasized with a thick underline.

Kate took a few moments to peruse it, then thought once again. "Yes, I remember now. All the information came straight from the staff reports."

"Why did you have to stir the pot?" he said. "Why can't you just leave things alone? You know what they say about not kicking a pile of shit? Well that's what it's like in Waterford. We don't disturb things that shouldn't be disturbed. We mind our own business around here."

Kate paused. *Control your breath.*

She chose her words carefully. "Well, in the first place, all the reports are public information, so I'm not the only person to have read them. Secondly, it's not because I want to stir the pot. It's because there's useful information or a useful example, and it's instructive to other residents who might be thinking about making the same mistake."

A slight eye roll.

"Thirdly," she continued, "thirdly, it doesn't pay to not follow the rules. It will cost the gun club more now than if they had done things properly in the first place."

Marshall shoved the article back in the drawer. "What can I do for you today? " His blue eyes were flat.

Right. He couldn't care less what I have to say. Not much point in asking for advertising, is there?

"I just wanted to introduce myself to all the local business owners and drop off a rate card." Kate pulled a sheet off her clipboard. "Here you go. And here's the latest copy of *The Challenge*." She left both on Marshall's counter. "Our rates are the cheapest around," she said. "And I give the best service."

"I advertise only with *The Waterford Reporter*."

"Okay. Well, if you change your mind, here's where you can find me." She pointed out her email.

"Right. Thanks for dropping by. You have a good day," he said, striding towards the door of the shop and waving her through. Kate was forced to stumble outside onto the sidewalk.

She was dismissed. The glass door practically slammed against the back of her head.

Yikes. *Now that was a complete waste of time,* she thought, rubbing the back of her head where it seemed to need comforting. She stood gathering her senses, her eyes drawn once again to the doormat. Marshalls Mens Apparel.

"It's possessive," she said aloud. "Not adjectival."

Goon, she thought as she headed back to the office.

I am so totally screwed.

* * *

In the following years, Kate came to learn that at one time, half the women in Waterford had a crush on Marsh Crawford. Blond hair, prematurely grey at the sides, and piercing blue eyes that went straight through you. Mischievous smile, strong chin, deep voice. Wore a suit better than any other man around, and all those suits came from his store. Usually, he was on his way to a hockey game or a drink with the boys or a round of golf. He was buddies with the police chief, the fire chief, and the local bar owner. Good-looking, affable, sociable — the formula for a very popular guy in a small town like Waterford.

The back door opened, and there he was once again, sliding a pack of cigarillos into his breast pocket. But this time, the first time in quite a while that she had seen him, he looked different.

"Hello, Kate," he said in a hoarse voice. He was nattily dressed in a blue polo shirt, white chinos, and fancy red canvas boat shoes as befitting the owner of a posh menswear shop. But in every other way he looked awful. His face was lined and drawn, his eyes shadowed and sunken. Julie's death had obviously hit him hard.

Off to one side from another rear door, a young woman entered the showroom. The girl had dead straight long black hair, a push-up bra, and high heels.

Kate had worn high heels once too, when she was younger and more foolish. But never the push-up thing. She considered it an instrument of torture solely devised for the pleasure of the opposite sex and worn only by dupes.

She wracked her brain for the identity of the woman but unlike the push-up bra, nothing popped up.

Kate politely nodded a greeting in the woman's direction. It was ignored.

"I'm so sorry for your loss, Marshall," Kate said. "What a terrible tragedy."

Was that the correct thing to say?

"Thank you," Marshall said. Kate watched his expression intently, afraid to miss a cue. She noticed he seemed to have a bit of a fat lip. And was that a bruise on his cheekbone? She pulled her gaze away and admonished herself.

Stop staring. He probably fell down somewhere. Not looking where he was going. Who could blame him? He was probably on medication. He had a lot on his mind.

"What can I do for you?" he said. Not a hint of emotion.

"I'm really sorry to bother you." She stood a little straighter and forged ahead. "We're running a piece on Julie, and I was hoping you could help us with a little bio and a photo." She knew that he had already given an interview to *The Journal*; she was banking on him giving her one too. She had her pad and pen out.

"Sure, all right," Marshall said, and Kate smothered a sigh of relief. "What would you like to know?" he continued.

He gave some basic information and Kate scribbled it all down.

"Do you happen to have a photo I could use?"

"Let me take a look in the back," he said, and his gaze briefly swung over to the woman before he went into the back of the store once again. Out of the corner of her eye Kate could see her leaning over the far end of the counter, examining her long black nails.

Marshall emerged in the doorway near the woman. "Do you know where that photo is of Julie?"

"Yeah, they're all in the desk drawer," said the woman. "I'll get one." She disappeared into the back. Marshall shuffled through some paperwork at the cash register.

"What a terrible shock it all must be," Kate continued. "I'm so sorry."

"They found her near the train bridge. She was suffering from depression for quite some time."

"Yes, I read that in *The Journal*," Kate said, surprised that he was offering the information. She drew some courage. He really didn't seem angry with her at all. What a relief.

"That's so sad. She must have been suffering for a long time." *I had no idea,* Kate thought, *that she had depression.* "I never noticed before. She used to pop down to my house for tea with the girls when they were babies."

Marshall paused. "You two were friends?"

"Not close ones," Kate said. "A few years ago, when she first moved to town. I live on High Street. She lived on Jane Street. Er, that is, you both lived on Jane Street, but I only knew Julie when she was at home alone. That is, when you were at work. I mean, I guess you weren't home during the day, and she was at home with the kids. I saw her on my walks sometimes."

Oh why do I try to explain things. Just shut up already.

Marshall appeared to not notice. "She loved the outdoors, especially the Waterford Cemetery with the great view."

"Isn't it wonderful there?" Kate piped up. "I've been there a few times looking at some birds at that spot," she added, feeling suddenly ridiculously confessional. "Not far from the river."

He paused again. "Actually," he said, "she loved to see the river from the train bridge."

Now that was curious. "The big cast iron trestle bridge? You mean she went up there?"

"Yes, we both did. The access is pretty easy to find. A lot of people go up there."

"Really? I'd be afraid to."

"I've been walking the trails around here for years," Marshall said. "The view is tremendous off the bridge. One of my favourite spots in the whole county, actually. I often took Julie there. She loved it."

That's a lot of personal information. Maybe he's finally warming up to me.

"But what about the trains?"

"The trains …"

"Weren't you worried about the trains using the bridge? Wasn't that dangerous?" Kate said. Wasn't it obvious? People so often chose to ignore the obvious. She, on the other hand, was forever hard-pressed to not blurt out the obvious.

"I've been there a lot. I know the train schedule off by heart. Everyone does. Every hour, on the hour, rush hour morning and rush hour night. An extra freight train at night."

"So plenty of time."

"Plenty of time."

Kate continued. "But still ... a bit scary."

"Not at all," he said firmly. "There's plenty of warning when a train is coming. You can always hear the whistle from the junction a few minutes before it crosses the bridge. And anyway, if you get stuck, there's a couple of safety platforms at the side. I've been there. No problem."

"Oh," Kate said.

"Yeah, a lot of high school kids take the bridge as a shortcut," he said.

But they're high school kids. And you're not.

"The scenery from there would be lovely at this time of the year." She awkwardly shifted her weight. "I'm sorry, Marshall. That bridge is probably not something you want to think about right now."

"It's fine," Marshall said. "Julie would have wanted people to know how much she loved our beautiful town." He moved, restless. Kate felt her window closing.

"I'll miss Julie," Kate said. "She was a special person." Her heart swelled. She struggled for a moment.

Get a grip, Kate. Plenty of time later to feel emotion.

"Yes." He paused, then glanced toward the back room.

"Look, I've got some things that need my attention. Phone calls, forms, arrangements. I'm sure you understand."

"Of course," Kate said, relieved for the interruption. "I better go write this story so we can go to print. Sorry again, Marshall. Thanks for the information."

"Tiffany," he called out. "Did you find that photo yet?" Tiffany emerged from the back holding a photo between a fingertip and a thumb. It was a headshot of Julie, her hand up against her hair which curled fetchingly on her shoulders, pink lipstick. An unusual necklace around her neck. A pewter or maybe a silver dragonfly. It looked oddly familiar but for the life of her, Kate could not remember why.

"Thanks," Kate said. "I'll bring it back in the next day or two."

"Don't bother," he said. "If there's anything else you need, just give me a call." He walked her to the door and closed it behind her. A soft click.

Ah, she said to herself. *That was so much better than the last time.*

She was out on the noisy main street again where the hustle and bustle and roar of the traffic was a comfort. The notebook was slid into her bag, and in her mind, the story lede was already falling into place.

Now what was wrong with all that.

Nothing. Nothing at all. I'm obsessing about nothing. As usual.

A prick. A flash. A memory. She could hear a voice in her ear.

You worry about nothing all the time. What's the matter with you? You're such a strange little girl.

"The body of a hometown business woman, community volunteer, and mother of two was discovered in the Grand River. Julie Crawford, 39, who operated Marshalls Mens Apparel with her husband Marshall, was found dead on Aug. 22. Julie left behind ..."

The sentences were all coming together.

Chapter 12

The summer was beginning its decline by the third week of August, into an ever-increasing cycle of longer nights, shorter days, cooler evenings.

The shorebirds must surely feel it too, Kate thought as she watched them through her scope at the Glen Morris sewage lagoons.

It was a week before things would start to get crazy in the office, and Kate knew she would need something to sustain her through the trying days ahead.

The Glen Morris lagoons were a thorn in the side of the municipality, but Kate considered them a wonder and a blessing. They were one of the last vestiges of the historic 1950s sewage system, an old-fashioned storage, filtration, and evaporation set-up that was good enough when the county was still in its infancy, but had long since outgrown its usefulness and efficiency.

These days, the province mandated municipalities to mothball their lagoons, to install state-of-the-art piped sewage systems with huge complicated mechanized treatment plants that monitored bacterial levels and everything else, and were manned by a small army of technicians on call twenty-four hours a day.

Thus the Glen Morris sewage lagoons became a mostly abandoned facility, only occasionally used as an overflow valve by cities upstream, and by a small number of rural properties still stubbornly hooked in. The lagoons were full of washouts and cracks and eroding banks: impossible to rigidly control and monitor the way things needed to be in the year 2001. And they had a tendency to empty into the Grand River, too.

Pond corners were built up with smelly algae composed of billions of bacteria-eating single-cell microorganisms called diatoms, plugging outlets, coating the sandy banks, and producing endless headaches for personnel struggling to meet standards.

Kate loved it. Algae clustered in clumps were food for migrating shorebirds already heading back to their winter homes in South America. Birds were drawn from every direction, and Kate was never sure how. Could it be the smell? Avian scientists claimed this was impossible, that birds did not have much of a sense of smell, but she suspected otherwise. How else could they know where to find these hidden places, miles inland, some distance away from watercourses, surrounded by trees, buildings, civilization.

Birds were obviously on the move. Most birds are intrinsically nomadic, and only sit still long enough to hatch offspring and see them fledge. The rest of the time they are journeying or preparing for journeys, fattening up for long flights, showing youngsters the ropes, stubbornly moving south or north to warmer or about-to-be warmer grounds.

They are assailed by the changes in wind, in the strength and length of daylight hours, the quality and quantity of their food, and they act accordingly, propelled by an instinct that is older than civilization, more fundamental than any need a mere human being could understand.

After all, they were quite simply creatures of the air, the sun, the stars. And that was why Kate loved them so.

She trained her scope on a particularly shorebird-rich section of the complex that boasted a long protective sandbar curving around a pond corner. Recent weeks of torrential rains had raised water levels and eliminated much shoreline, concentrating the birds in areas of thick sloppy mud sheltering a treasure trove of juicy worms and grubs.

Tiny hunched-over silhouettes belonged to least sandpipers; the slightly bigger, more elongated shapes belonged to semi-palmated sandpipers. Here and there a lesser yellowlegs poked a head into the slop, up and down, up and down, hinged at the neck, crying its long drawn-out reedy complaint.

But wait, what on earth was that stocky, bigger bird, just sitting and staring, twice as big as a yellowlegs, six times the girth of a sandpiper, long straight heavy beak about two-and-a-half times the length of its head. A white line of feathers ran over a dark eye line, its round ball-like head crowned with a dark cap. It preened the leading edge of its flight feathers.

Surely it was the short-billed dowitcher of several days ago.

Then, just like that, it began a forceful selective poking into the mud, probing and confident, a jab at a different angle with just the slightest pause to feel around, thorough and quick, then onward to the next spot. As it moved into water, Kate could see its legs bending repeatedly, twice for every poke of the beak, its head often dipping below the surface. She studied its movements, its silhouette, its technique. Her ears strained to hear it call, but it was silent with the concentration of searching. Then it startled, taking to the air for a short distance before landing once again and resuming feeding.

Had that cheerful strong three and four-note peeping complaint belonged to the dowitcher? *Perhaps.*

She made a mental note then stored away the sound to research, and to savour, later.

She whipped out her camera with its extra-long telephone lens, brought the bird into focus, clicked the shutter multiple times.

At home, the photos would be processed, contrasted, and filed away for future reference and enjoyment, the memories rushing back, the smell, the sights, the sounds.

A curative for all that ailed her.

Chapter 13

The exact cause of Asperger's Syndrome is unknown. Although research suggests a genetic basis, there is no known genetic cause and brain imaging techniques have not identified a clear common diagnosis. There is no single treatment, and the effectiveness of particular interventions is supported by only limited data. The mainstay of management is behavioural therapy, focusing on specific deficits to address poor communication skills, obsessive or repetitive routines, and physical clumsiness.

Most children improve as they mature to adulthood, but social and communication difficulties persist somewhat. Childhood desire for companionship can become numbed through a history of failed social encounters.

Individuals with Asperger's Syndrome, most of them males, experience difficulties in the basic elements of social interaction, including a failure to develop friendships or establish shared enjoyments or achievements with others, poor success in showing others items of interest, a lack of social or emotional reciprocity, and impaired nonverbal behaviours in areas such as eye contact, facial expression, posture, and gesture.

— Dr. Gerhardt Mansbrugh,
Asperger's Syndrome: A Pathology;
Humboldt University of Berlin, 1967

Chapter 14

K ate's antique dining room table held various carefully arranged piles: books, a jar of pens, a printer and a scanner, a box of cue cards, a calculator. Stale editions of the Berliner-style 150-year-old *Waterford Reporter*, and the century-old *Belleview Daily Journal*, a broadsheet. *The Tecumseh Challenge* was tabloid-sized — the baby of the bunch in more ways than one.

Her antique wooden chair had two pillows, and arms covered with rubber strips wrapped with duct tape — protection for forearms and wrists that needed to be bandaged, iced, and heated regularly. All from working on the computer, day and night, weekends and holidays.

Her left elbow always ached. *Why the left*, she always wondered.

Against one wall sat a four-drawer filing cabinet with supplies, files, packets of photos, and a radio perched on top. Near the window, a high-backed chair and a corner table with a small television, used only to watch the news. In front of the bare brick fireplace lay Alfred's dog bed on the bare wooden floor. Facing the fireplace at the other side of the room, a couch.

Julie had sat on that couch.

There was nothing else in the room. No adornment, family photo, nor figurine. *I like it like that*, she thought. People don't need to be surrounded by endless needless meaningless junk.

The room was spotlessly clean.

Julie's story was swiftly typed, spell-checked, edited, and set on the front page. Then another series of clicks, and it was off to the printer's FTP site. Composing would fit it onto the body of the paper, the plates would be burned, and the web press would print the whole thing that night.

Maybe she would beat *The Waterford Reporter* for once, Kate mused. But she doubted it. Chelsea Darling would likely have come and gone by the time Kate had arrived at Marshall's store. Chelsea would have made the most of the situation.

Kate rubbed her eyes, stretched, and stepped onto the front porch. It was a strange feeling to enjoy the outdoors after so many fourteen-hour work days. The sun felt good on her face. She looked up and down the street, then nearly jumped out of her skin when with a tremendous roar, an engine fired up in her driveway. A beat-up GMC van with flashy chrome wheel covers pulled out, gravel spraying everywhere. The driver was a thin young man with a buzz cut. At the same time, the front door of the adjacent house slammed shut.

Oh no, not again. Her hand went protectively to her beating heart. *Damn them,* she cursed. Sam and Conner's friends eternally coming and going. And as usual, parked in her driveway, which was conveniently located alongside the Hacketts' front door.

For Pete's sake, she muttered. The Hacketts had their own driveway, even if it was off to the other side of their lawn. Why the heck did everyone have to park in Kate's driveway all the time? How many more times did she have to complain about her driveway being blocked?

She made a mental note to address the issue yet one more time. Or maybe not. Despite the necessity of being able to use her driveway at all times, talking with the neighbours was so stressful.

Avoidance. The best solution. Often the only solution.

She sighed.

"C'mon Alfred," she called out. "Let's go for a walk."

Chapter 15

The old abandoned Lake Erie and Northern Railway had once travelled the fifty-one miles from Port Dover to Cambridge with tobacco and fresh produce from the rich agricultural areas of Norfolk County to the CPR mainlines, and thereon into the most populated parts of Ontario. Summers, the electric railway had transported that same population south to Lake Erie's welcoming beaches and fish fries.

The iron railway lines were built on beds of rough Grimsby limestone aggregate infilled with the debris of transportation caught by old cowcatchers: anthracite coal from Pennsylvania, sand from the wetlands of Lake Erie, creosote from the wood spur lines of Cambridge.

In the spring of 1955, the last passenger train took a farewell trip to Port Dover and back to Cambridge, passengers enjoying for their final time the romantic feel of flanged wheels, air whistles, and trolley wires. In the 1980s, the last diesel freight trains rumbled through. Then the rails were pulled up, leaving behind their beds like so many ribbons criss-crossing the crust of southern Ontario.

— A Twentieth Century History of Ontario Railways,
by Stewart Alfredson, 1993

Chapter 16

THE LAKE ERIE AND NORTHERN RAILWAY COMPANY

(ELECTRIC, Gauge, 4 feet 8 1/2 inches.)

— A.D. MacTier, President, Montreal, Que.

Providing an Unexcelled Freight and Passenger Service.

Stations and Miles from Cambridge.—Glenmorris (6.7 miles), Waterford (13.3 miles), Belleview, Ont. (21.1 miles), Mount Pleasant (26.1 miles), Oakland (29.4 miles), Scotland (36.7 miles), Simcoe (43.6 miles), Port Dover (51.1 miles).

Leave Cambridge for Port Dover †7 05, *9 05, *11 05 a.m., *1 40, *3 05,
*5 10, *7 05, §9 20, †10 15 p.m. Returning, Leave Port Dover †6 15, *9 00,
*11 00 a.m., *1 00, §3 05, *5 00, *7 00, §9 05, §9 45 p.m.
* Daily; † daily, except Sunday; § Sunday only; x flag stations. *Eastern time.*

For Freight and Passenger Rates, apply to agents of Can. Pac. Ry. or connecting lines.

— *Advertisement, August 1931, The Cambridge Tribune*

Chapter 17

Kate found herself at Preservation Park very early the next morning, in the newer part of town where a far-sighted developer had built a subdivision beside an old farmer's field, a forest, and a series of wetlands. The area was laced with walking trails that joined the arterial rail trail along the Grand River, stretching from Lake Erie to Cambridge, the roadbed of a once vast and thriving railway network.

Kate always felt good at the end of the month to be shutting down the computer and to be shutting down the constant nagging stream of emails and press releases too for a short interlude.

It felt even better to escape the office entirely and head outdoors where there was sure to be a thrilling adventure in nature.

Kate was dressed in special birding garb: long sleeves and long pants, cleverly vented along seams and folds. Size large, to fit her gangly frame. Baggy around the waist and hips, and most comfortable.

Mosquitoes were still biting hard, and would be until the first frost; the flies were tortuous. There had been much rain in the previous weeks and disease-carrying deer ticks had secreted themselves in the undergrowth.

Kate plonked a wide-brimmed hat on her head, fixed the chin cord in place, tossed the strap of a pair of binoculars crossways across her chest, and carefully shut the car door without undue noise.

Her hat doubled as eye shade and handy squasher of bothersome stable flies, with their black-banded wings and their seemingly unlimited capacity to stalk and torment. She had a special trick when it came to the whiney little demons. When they landed on the back of a temporarily hatless head, she would press them into the tangle of her hair, crush them with the hat, then shake them out, dead. A satisfying way to dispose of a seemingly indefatigable enemy.

After half a dozen or so of the flies met their demise on the back of her head, the rest seemed to get the message and avoided her the rest of the day. If her hair was a bit buggy, it would all wash out in the shower when she got home.

Such were the somewhat icky but rather unavoidable habits of a dedicated birder.

It was a special time of the year. The first of the fall's passerine migrants were passing through on their way to warmer climes in Central and South America.

Kate hadn't seen her feathered songbird friends in a quite while. In spring, most of them did not stick around but headed north to the Boreal forest and the more isolated parts of the province to bring up their young, far away from the disruptive ways of human beings.

At this time of year, they mostly wore only the faded versions of their beautiful springtime multicoloured plumages. But still, Kate was thrilled to see them. Happiness and melancholy permeated her thoughts simultaneously. It would be more than seven months before she would see those creatures again.

She turned and immediately faced one of her favourite trees in the county: a wide lazily spreading mulberry tree with the last of its sweet juicy purple fruit dropping onto the gravel lot. There was quite a commotion amidst its leaves. A cornucopia of birds was gorging on fruit and didn't much care who was watching.

Kate spied the taupe and beige colouration of warbling vireos sporting a hint of their tell-tale white eyebrow. A blue-headed vireo was now mostly grey but still could be easily identified by its white spectacles. A Baltimore oriole was charcoal and cinnamon instead of black and orange, the edges of its primaries still edged in white. Its long, sharp, black beak and underlying curve were a dead giveaway. A mostly mustard yellow female hung close by. Not a single bird emitted more than the faintest of tweets or chirps, their idiosyncratic mating calls shelved for another year.

She stood in place, staring through her binoculars for as long as she could before her arms finally succumbed to numbness. What a joy it was to see the birds behaving so naturally and without fear.

The first warblers were already moving through as well. A male redstart had lost its electric orange highlights in favour of yellow and was bopping from branch to branch, squeaking away, seemingly oblivious to Kate's presence. She admired the bird for several minutes, following its playful antics under and over a branch and between leaves, legs splayed, upside down then right side up, trying to grab a berry at just the right angle to avoid being steamrolled by the bigger birds.

The redstart had it over the others, nimble and energetic, gaming the whole process so that it ended up with the juiciest berry at just the right time and place.

What a delight. Kate couldn't get enough of the frolicking creature. Always, there was one Highlight Of The Day and Kate knew that later on, she would bestow that moniker upon the redstart.

Finally, the sun coming straight at her over the tree line was too much to bear and Kate headed to the comforting gloom of the nearby walking trail.

Inside the forest, leaves were already dropping from yellow birches. They were always the first to die off.

The woods were almost impenetrable but Kate knew where to go. She hurried to the boardwalk, where there were likely to be some puddles off to one side, and tried to be as soundless as possible.

Sure enough, a small but veritable lineup of songbirds was waiting their turn to jump into a puddle. Kate hid behind the thick trunk of a thick blue birch and focused her binoculars on the ground between the puddles and the shrubs. Three grey catbirds were duking it out for first dibs, hopping to the edge of the mud, dipping their beaks into the water then jabbing and swiping at their competitors, darting back to the shrubs, then back again to the water. Finally, they sorted it all out, and at once, all three jumped into the puddle a safe distance away from one another, spreading their wings, soaking it all in, splashing water over heads and bodies, sinking down for another soak, then finally exiting and landing on a nearby branch to shake off and dry off.

Kate was beside herself, a huge smile plastered from ear to ear.

All of a sudden, there were the sharp cries of danger calls and as one, birds lifted off the ground and from nearby twigs and hurtled into the deepest, shadiest parts of shrubs and into the highest part of the forest ceiling. A pair of dog walkers sauntered through, chatting and laughing, their off-leash Briard crashing through the underbrush.

Kate groaned.

She kept her place against the tree trunk, nodding hello. They glanced over without bothering to acknowledge her in her camouflage-patterned birding gear and strolled ahead, immersed in conversation.

No point in making eye contact with another human being, is there?

She shook her head at their retreating figures. Hopefully, they weren't trail regulars, but in her heart she knew they likely were.

The Briard bounded back, goofing around with the ball and trying to entice Kate to toss it into the bush. When there was no reaction, it set out into the undergrowth once again to cause as much commotion as possible.

Kate returned to the parking lot to consider her options. It would be at least ten or fifteen minutes before the birds settled down again. By that time there could be even more dog walkers. Was there any point in sticking around?

The other end of the route aimed almost directly into the sun. There was about a kilometre of open stonedust trail before she hit any substantially treed area. She decided to take her chances, and slid a water bottle into her knapsack.

The first part of the trail was partially shaded by shrubs and offered good cover for more denizens of the thrush family: robins and a brilliant pair of bluebirds: azure blue and cinnamon orange. Kate's eyes feasted on the variety of shades of blue in their feathers. She tracked them through her bins as long as she could before they finally got wind of her and swept away.

Willow Street bisected the trail and Kate met it on the other side. The sun was getting high in the sky and a pair of stable flies performed their tortuous dance, incessantly circumnavigating the space around her head, drawing energy from Kate's hapless swatting, occasionally coming in for a long whining nip.

Soon there was open landscape and a blazing sun beating down. She walked faster, ignoring the parched chicory, the fluffy white asters, and the black-eyed Susans that skirted the path up to a wall of trees, a dragonfly or two whizzing by. It was uphill until Portland Street and Kate puffed and mopped her brow. Finally, she reached the shaded underpass of the train bridge and paused to recover from the heat.

Something else had had the same idea. The cheery bubbling song of a house wren sprang from the tangled depths of a buckthorn. Kate's eyes adjusted to the gloom, and she whistled back a reasonable facsimile of the same song. After a minute or two, the petite bird popped out of the undergrowth and onto a branch, puffing out its chest, beak wide open and tail cocked. Taking up the challenge, it replayed its message at the top of its lungs, hitting a high note that made Kate's ears ring. She grinned.

She veered right into the welcome shade of Portland Street and followed it uphill to its terminus at a small gravelled parking area where it was deliciously cool. Off to one side was the narrow lane leading to the historic Waterford Cemetery.

She was always drawn to the cemetery and its breathtaking view of the valleys, creeks, and hazard lands bordering Green Lane and the Grand River. She walked to the edge of the grass where a tall obelisk marked the location of Hiram Capron's final resting place. Nearby beckoned a deep sturdy bench shaded by a spreading oak.

She slowly circled the tall stone. Hiram Capron. Born Feb. 12, 1796. Died Sept. 10, 1872. *Hoc oppidum condidit.* This town founded by.

Julie had loved to visit the cemetery.

Did she come here first before she climbed the shallow rise to the train tracks that led to the bridge? Kate wondered. *This spot may have been the last place Julie had paused to rest.*

Kate peeled off the knapsack and fell onto the bench, exhausted. She unscrewed the top of her water bottle, took a long swig, then poured the rest over her head. She lay back on the cool metal and stretched her arms along the top. A welcome breeze sprang up, drying her perspiration.

Julie drifted through her mind.

I'm sure she said she hated heights.

A few inches away on the other side of the fence within the grasses towered a bamboo-like six-foot tall stem awkwardly branched with whorls of angular dried-out sticks. *What an odd-looking plant. I wonder why I never noticed it before.*

She grabbed her binoculars for a closer look. It had obviously died off. Some stems ended in curious beaked seed capsules about the size of a walnut, sharp ends peeled open.

She went for a closer look and pledged to remember to identify it when at home on her computer. Was there a way to break off one of those seed pods?

The chain link fence was an easy climb. She waded through the tall grasses, and gently spread open a pod to ensure there were seeds. They were the size of a sunflower seed, brown and ovoid, flat, ridged, and irregularly shaped. The whole thing went into her pocket. On the other side of the fence, she leaned over to pick up her knapsack, and there on the ground were the same seeds. Indeed, she had been stepping on a few where she had sat on the bench, now that she took the time to look.

The route back to the car was noticeably less arduous, and when she met up with the two women and the Briard again, this time they nodded and said hello. The dog, thankfully, was too exhausted to jump up. It trotted along, swaying its headful of tawny hair cut neatly around its eyes.

The sun had moved to one side, the gravel path was mostly downhill, and she returned to the heat of the parking area feeling the breeze. A wood thrush skulked about in the dappled shade of a sycamore tree. Pulling up her binoculars, she admired the bird's darkly spotted breast, easily discernible against splotchy, greyish green tree bark.

An altogether successful excursion by any measure, Kate decided, and now it was more than time for an early lunch. She congratulated herself for getting the better of the ordeal, and wiped the sweat off her face with a handy damp cloth she kept just for that purpose in a plastic bag on the front seat. She took to the road.

George Harrison's "My Sweet Lord" came on the radio, and she improvised "sweet fall migration" in place of the chorus. What a wonderful time it was to be in the woods!

At the office, she surveyed seed photos on the net, discovering that hers were from the extraordinarily rare American Columbo, *Frasera caroliniensis*, a member of the gentian family. The plant was monocarpic, taking twenty or thirty years to bloom and come to seed before dying. And that was right when Kate had come along.

How do you like that. Isn't timing everything in life.

She celebrated the day's outing with a cup of victory tea, chilled orange pekoe with honey and milk, and sat overlooking the back deck with Albert, while Etta James played in the background.

Chapter 18

"I don't think there's an addendum," Pete said, absent-mindedly rubbing his three-day's old beard as Kate slid into her seat. It was close and musty in the Waterford council chambers.

It was the first Tuesday of the month and the emergency council meeting was right on time.

"Okay."

Kate switched on her laptop. Pete shoved on his Clark Kent eyeglasses and woke up his computer by tapping at the keyboard.

She reached out and riffled through the thick slab of the agenda.

"Thanks for holding on to this for me," she said to Pete. Even though she was precisely twenty minutes early, there was nevertheless a strong chance someone would slip their hand into the media desk and grab her agenda. A member of the public. Or, more likely, the other media. Some reporters had no shame.

"No problem. How did you like *The Waterford Disorder* this week?

"Ha."

Kate had just seen a copy of the most recent edition. She was a bit surprised to see the declining number of ads. But Marshall's was still there, bigger than ever.

There was the front page story about Julie Crawford, complete with an interview of the fisherman who had found the body, a neighbour of Chelsea's, naturally. There was the same photo from Marshall, in colour and blown up five times original — Kate could even spot the milgrain-bordered diamonds in Julie's wedding band. WATERFORD MOURNS MUCH LOVED MEN'S STORE OWNER IN TRAGIC DEATH. JULIE CRAWFORD FOUND WITH VITAL SIGNS ABSENT IN GRAND RIVER.

Oh my God, Chelsea. DEAD. i.e. the woman was found DEAD in the Grand River.

"Did you read that story? What a soap opera," Pete said.

"Yeah. And she quoted Kowalchuk saying it was suicide. Actually, they didn't release a cause of death. And if it's suicide, they generally don't mention it."

Pete shook his head. "I didn't get the lowdown on the cause of death. I assumed suicide, but I didn't put it in the story."

"Same here."

"That *Reporter*. Do you read it?"

"Only because I have to."

"How does she get away with it? Doesn't head office care?"

"It's a mystery. You know, I don't know why they don't just get rid of Chelsea completely and do a straight dump of all the *Journal* stories. Save the expense of Chelsea's salary."

"Because she's probably sleeping with the boss."

"I never thought of that."

Pete raised an eyebrow. "Yes, you did."

Chuckles.

Kate and Pete Steckler were seatmates at the back of the council room at the smallest media table; the lower tier for the barely recognized and the second-rate, far away from the door to the snack bar, the conference room, and the restrooms. Pete was the newly hired civic reporter for Belleview radio station CKTC and ten years younger than Kate. Some days it felt like a lot more. But most of the time it was okay.

All the reporters were at their usual spots in the room, Chelsea Darling right across the aisle at the "preferred" media table beside Kirk Steele, the short, stocky, senior reporter for *The Belleview Journal*. Kirk's hand was already upending his cropped blond hair, anxious about something. It was always something. Being the only daily newspaper reporter in the room was a heavy mantle to bear.

Chelsea got to sit beside "the most important media" guy in the room and share the aura. She also got to share the almost continuous head cold that besieged Kirk, who had a nasty habit of perpetually wiping his nose with his fingers, thus bringing to his face almost every conceivable germ that existed within arm's length and incubating them even further before releasing them into the universe.

A living nightmare.

Kate kept a wide distance and compulsory hand wipes in the drawer.

The weekly paper *The Waterford Reporter* and *The Belleview Daily Journal* shared the same parent company, Annex Media, which did cartwheels in order to corner the local market, and did. The two newspapers gobbled up most of the only ad revenue left in the newspaper world: all the local flyers, all the real estate ads, the lion's share of the municipality's regulatory notifications of zoning changes, environmental assessments, and road work, and all of Tecumseh County's discretionary ads for county-wide events. Occasionally, the county threw a bone in *The Challenge*'s direction, just enough to keep her alive.

It stuck in Kate's craw because *The Reporter* and *The Journal* were two prime examples of how low newspapers could go — a skeleton staff providing the skimpiest of coverage and mainly canned newswire content with the odd amateur photo thrown in for local effect, plus plagiarized stories from all the other media around.

If Kate hadn't maintained her invaluable roster of local in-depth coverage and a nigh army of subscribers, *The Tecumseh Challenge* would have been out of business a long time ago.

In the meantime, the most important media guy in the room was having trouble arranging everything on his desk, finding all the reports in the agenda, and logging into his computer. He shuffled his papers, squinted at his laptop, and dug through his briefcase for a pen. Finally, he jumped to his feet and strode out the door at the other end of the council chambers to grab a quick coffee from the snack bar without paying. It would be his fifth of the day.

"When I read your last paper I noticed that you didn't get an interview with the roads superintendent," Pete said. "About that big project on Misener Road West. Stonewalled?"

"Yeah, totally. The story of my life."

Because *The Tecumseh Challenge* was owned and operated by a single person — Kate — she was constantly being rebuffed by municipal staff. And there wasn't a damn thing she could do about it. She didn't have the clout that a huge corporation like Annex mustered.

"And you? How come you rated?

"Hah," Pete said. "Our ad manager knows his wife."

"No fair."

Pete grinned.

All were waiting in anticipation for the first delegation on the agenda.

The Ontario Provincial Police had begun to aggressively lobby small municipalities all over the place for policing contracts and now seemed to be targeting Waterford. They already patrolled Tecumseh County — all the land outside Waterford. And now they were aiming for the jewel in the crown.

Maybe they thought adding to the existing contract would be a slam dunk. But the Waterford Police Department had something entirely different in mind.

In the audience were some uniformed members of the Waterford Police Department: The balding, red-faced, pot-bellied, slightly nasal Chief Bill Pound, the swarthy Staff Sergeant Johnny Grimaldi, and constables Leo Kowalchuk and Dean Schmidt. All four sat on their chairs arms crossed, knees apart. Eyes watchful and none too friendly.

Kate pointed them out to Pete. He stopped texting his new girlfriend and nodded.

"They look pretty intense."

Kate concurred.

Two OPP officers had made the trip from Orillia to give a power point presentation to council. They sat in the back corner of the room, trench coats draped over the two chairs separating them from the rest of the packed chamber room. They needed the protection.

"I haven't heard from Tiffany yet," he said. "Maybe I should call her again. What do you think?"

Kate presumed this was a rhetorical question and continued to type.

"God, I can never get a hold of her with the first text. What is it with women?"

"What do you mean?" Kate asked, grudgingly. She would have preferred to just not know. Male-female relationships were a quagmire as far as she was concerned. The less she heard about it all, the better.

"Especially in the mornings," Pete said, turning to Kate. "What is it about mornings? Are all women too busy to use the phone? Too much preparation going on? Tell me, I'm really curious." He looked like he really needed to know.

Kate appraised his expression and decided that yes, he really did want to know.

"Well ..." she said slowly. In her case, she always answered the phone, no matter what time of the day or night. It could be a customer wanting to know something.

"Some women. Maybe she's getting ready for work."

"She works at a restaurant. It doesn't open till ten."

"Maybe she's prepping inside before it opens."

"But wouldn't she at least answer the phone?"

"Maybe her hands are too dirty to answer the phone."

He looked unsatisfied. "I'm going to drop by in the morning and see what's going on."

Kate didn't quite know what to say. Then: "Maybe you shouldn't do that. People usually don't like surprises."

He looked startled.

Here I go again. Why oh why do I interfere? I only get blamed when things go bad.

"Council is now in session," Mayor Edison Bywater called out in an official mayoral tone. "At least I am pretty sure we're back. If we're not, we will be momentarily." He glanced around the semicircle of ten desks surrounding him, the Chief Administrative Officer, and the clerk on the podium, then pointedly at a councillor's desk, the only one still vacant.

"Washroom break," someone muttered. Councillor Fred Terryberry finally slid into his seat mumbling "too many beans." There was a brief, hysterical all-round chuckle. Bywater banged his gavel simultaneously.

"I just love doing that," Bywater muttered loudly as if to himself.

It was precisely what they expected from sixty-six year old Mayor Edison Bywater, the gangly, white-haired chief elected official presiding over twelve thousand residents in the countryside of the County of Tecumseh, in villages and hamlets with names older than most could remember, and in the town of Waterford itself, population seven thousand, which housed the somewhat dignified and pseudo-stately council chambers. Adjoining the chambers was a beehive of staff offices for several departments, a convenient way to connect the worlds of the somewhat impermanent with the overly permanent — the elected officials and the gainfully employed municipal staff, respectively.

The reporters rolled their eyes when they heard the gavel comment and waited for things to get cracking.

Six councillors sat at the table, each representing their own unique constituency. Councillor Herb Pickett of Waterford took on the concerns of all things military. The stocky and short Councillor Arnold Biggar was a staunch Waterfordian and a pompous protector of the status quo.

Councillor Marjorie Cleghorne, a retired nurse, had been stubbornly re-elected from Maple for decades despite a regrettable penchant for incompetence. Councillor Ivan Popowich, a quick-tempered farmer, represented the tiny community of Maple and environs.

Councillor Fred Terryberry was a hoary old retired farmer from the village of Scotland who, according to the grapevine, took on the job because no one else would. Councillor Mary Chang, a relative newcomer to the area, was a middle-aged accountant from Mount Pleasant.

Mayor Edison Bywater lived just outside of Waterford on a goat farm run by his wife Susan, a fetching misplaced flower child twenty years his junior.

Pete had given the group the moniker The Sexy Seven.

Kate dubbed them The Satanic Seven.

"Good evening ladies and gentleman. The council of the County of Tecumseh is now in session," announced Bywater. Beside him at the podium sat the pot-bellied Chief Administrative Officer Fred Bouchard, and on the other side at her computer Clerk Janice Stapleton, tall, short-haired, efficient, wearing winged cat's-eye glasses and steeped in the knowledge of all things paper-based and archival. She tapped away at her computer, compiling the official set of minutes.

"Welcome members of council and guests, some of whom will be speaking. I hope everybody has been doing their duty these last few nights. And that is requesting and praying for a dry spell, which we so desperately need before our crops rot in the fields."

Farmers in the audience nodded their heads in agreement. The fields needed to be dry and hard for heavy combines and tractors to execute the fall harvest, set to happen any day now.

"Approval of the agenda. There is an addendum report on the new green bin program. Are there any additions requested by members of council? None tonight. Thank you very much then. A motion to approve the agenda. Councillor Pickett, seconded by Councillor Cleghorne. All in favour, opposed, carried. Declaration of any pecuniary interests by members of council? None? If not, then we'll move along. We have one request to speak tonight listed under delegations. What is council's wish regarding that request?" He nodded at the councillors, looking for a gesture.

"Councillor Biggar moves that we grant permission to the delegation to proceed. Seconded by Councillor Terryberry. All in favour, opposed, carried.

"First delegation is Superintendent Don Pearcy and Inspector Roger Kapoor from the Ontario Provincial Police. Please come forward to the microphone and proceed when you're ready. Welcome."

As the men rose from their seats, Clerk Stapleton fussed around the speaker's platform, plugging in a laptop, moving electrical cords, and rolling down an overhead screen. She nodded at the CAO who stood manning the dimmer switch on the other side of the room.

Pearcy, balding and muscular, took the podium while Kapoor, a large, bespectacled, tan-skinned man, rounded the horseshoe of councillors' desks, handing out stapled sheafs of paper — copies of the presentation for present and future reference — to each person. He walked to the back of the room and pleasantly surprised the press corps by handing a copy to each reporter as well.

Pete licked his index finger, made a checkmark in the air, and grinned. Kate raised her eyebrows in return. Kissing up to the media. That could take a person quite far in life.

Kapoor dropped off three copies, which the CAO allotted to the mayor, the clerk, and himself, and joined Pearcy at the podium.

Clackety clackety clack. Four sets of reporter's hands began typing at four laptops. But not before Kate heard, "Paki. He's a Paki." She craned her neck above the crowd to see who on earth could be so incredibly ignorant and saw a man snickering into the ear of his wife. Pete rolled his eyes. Kate made a mental note of the face.

The two men were no strangers to council. They had appeared on previous occasions to deal with various issues with the OPP's patrol units in the county outside Waterford.

There had been the reconciliation payment that came in January, always more than a million dollars. There had been the announcement of the new forensics building in Kitchener. New search and rescue equipment, then, an addition to the canine team, and the creation of the Emergency Response Team. There had been a slim year-end statistical report on calls, occurrences by type, and hours worked.

Sparse on information, Kate had noted. And what information there was was mostly unverifiable. She never reported on it. It was better, however, than the report from the Waterford Police Department. Non-existent.

"Thank you, Your Worship," Pearcy began. "The Ontario Provincial Police would like Tecumseh County Council to consider our force for an all-encompassing cross-county service including," he paused and glanced up for emphasis, "the town of Waterford.

"We have a proven history of effective policing in rural areas and small towns with seventy signed contracts across the province.

"The OPP have taken care of the majority of the square mileage of Tecumseh County for the last decade. We're no stranger to this area. We have sixty years of computer data on calls outside Waterford."

The superintendent laid his presentation on the podium and began to click away at the control for the overhead monitor. A map appeared showing the OPP-patrolled areas of the county.

"To fulfill our proposed contractual coverage of Tecumseh and Waterford, the Ontario Provincial Police will form a brand new detachment in its current building near Belleville, naming the new detachment the Waterford-Tecumseh County OPP."

He detailed the composition of the new force and its auxiliary and clerical staff. Hours. Zones. Headquarters. Public access. Dispatch. State-of-the-art communication system. Back up towers. Public complaints process. Media office.

On the podium, Clerk Stapleton typed away in a frenzy. Ditto for the four reporters in the room.

Pearcy lifted his gaze for a moment, then down again at his notes.

"Our force is weaponized with the latest model of the Sig Sauer

P226, a reliable and powerful semi-automatic used by enforcement personnel across North America. It outperforms the WPD's Smith & Wesson model 66 .357 magnum wheelgun in all categories."

Pound and Grimaldi twitched.

"We can provide specialized no-charge services from experienced OPP officers from our western region detachment in London, and a head office in Orillia dedicated to forensics, canine, drug enforcement, anti-rackets, illegal gaming, child pornography, behavioural science, explosives, collision reconstruction, and water search and rescue. No extra cost, all included in our package."

Eyebrows raised in unison across the room.

Finally, it was police chief duties, contract negotiation procedures, recruitment, and victim assistance.

"We also offer free service from western region officers patrolling the two provincial highways who could be diverted into the community in an emergency."

A chart flashed on the screen.

"Our estimated cost for year one of a five-year contract would be $3.85 million plus $153,000 for 24-hour access to the police station. A one-time start up cost of $116,000. Transition time six months. A five year cost of $20.4 million. Plus some unknowns: some settlements with Waterford Police Department officers could stretch over two years.

"The numbers don't include equipment that could be sold from the Waterford Police station, or increases in wages and benefits, or inflation.

"The Ontario Provincial Police are confident that Waterford will be pleased with the service we do provide and can provide. We are proud of our professionalism and of our record in the rest of Tecumseh County. Thank you for your consideration tonight of our proposal."

He turned to the mayor. "I can answer any questions you may have," he said. "Now or later."

The lights came back up. The clerk stood at the podium and clicked off the projector. Murmuring swelled in the audience.

"Thank you, Superintendent Pearcy," the mayor called out over the buzz. "Questions on the presentation."

The hand of every councillor but one shot up.

"Councillor Biggar."

"Through you, Your Worship." Arnold Biggar nodded at the mayor. His family stretched back over a hundred years in Waterford.

"Thank you, Superintendent Pearcy, for that informative presentation. And all the details. As a realtor and therefore the owner of a small business, I always believe that numbers are important, but that sometimes there's more to the story. When I go back to my constituents here in town, they're going to want to know in a nutshell what the Ontario Provincial Police has to offer. Can you tell me in short, and I do mean short, why you think we should hire the Ontario Provincial Police for Waterford?"

"We shouldn't," somebody said. A few guffaws from the audience. The gavel banged.

Superintendent Pearcy paused for a second. Then bent down to the microphone.

"Councillor, we are a modern police force with modern facilities at our disposal. I don't want to disparage our brothers and sisters at the Waterford Police Department whatsoever." Someone in the audience made a skeptical noise. "They do an excellent job with the resources they have."

Kate glanced at the audience and the five members of the Waterford police force. Stone-faced.

"But we are well financed, well resourced, and highly trained. We presently provide services that the WPD have to contract out for. That has ramifications now and down the road, for case management, costing, and labour."

Kate blinked. She had never heard it put quite that way before. She racked her brains for the implications. Did it mean that the Waterford Police had problems when it came to getting the services they needed to solve cases? Delays? Or maybe improper handling of evidence. Or maybe they would hesitate to pay for some fancier crime fighting or crime solving equipment or personnel. Or maybe there was a complete failure to gather evidence because they couldn't afford it or didn't have the proper space. She glanced at Pete, but he apparently hadn't noticed. Across the aisle, Kirk and Chelsea were immersed in conversation.

"Councillor Pickett." Herb Pickett, a retired rear admiral with a perfectly trimmed Hitler-like moustache, lived in Waterford.

"Mr. Mayor, through you to the presenter. Inspector Pearcy. The OPP charges a lot for its services and municipalities have no control over what they have to pay. Salaries are set to match the highest paid police force in Ontario, which is the Toronto police force, and municipalities are dictated to by head office. I don't like that. At least here with the Waterford Police, we can negotiate salaries. The captain steers the ship."

"Hear hear," someone yelled from the audience. "That's the gist of the matter," someone else called out.

The mayor rapped his gravel once again. "Please," he said. "We cannot have any interruptions from the audience. Please. Inspector Pearcy, if you would." He nodded at the officer to respond.

"That isn't completely true. You can always limit the number of officers you want to hire."

Murmuring.

"Yes Inspector," Pickett continued. "But doesn't the detachment commander know best how to fight crime? Doesn't he tell council the number of men he needs?"

"Or women," Pearcy added. "The numbers of staff are negotiable. With your police services board."

Kate wondered about that. Surely, police unions dictated that officers needed to work in pairs in each sector of the county and the town. The county's insurer would want to rely on best practices, or else the county would be left vulnerable and rates would go up. The commander would define the patrol sectors probably based on what was taking place now, and that would be very difficult to change except upwards. Of course, the police services board would lean upon a seemingly endless supply of taxpayer money to fund whatever was needed. Pickett could be right.

"Councillor Cleghorne." Cleghorne, even though she lived in Maple, sat on the Waterford Police Services Board simply due to the fact her husband was a retired police officer.

"Mr. Mayor, I don't see how we can even entertain the idea of replacing the Waterford Police Department with high priced OPP officers because where would these men and women go? We'd be stuck having to pay hundreds of thousands of dollars in severances, we'd have more unemployment in Waterford and Tecumseh County, and we'd have a lot of unhappy people suffering through no fault of their own."

Three councillors abruptly leaned forward in their chairs, raised their hands, and called out. "Point of order, Mr. Mayor. Point of order. Point of order."

The mayor was right on top of it. "Councillor Cleghorne. Do you have a question of the presenter?"

"Yes. Yes, Mr. Mayor. I do. My question is, why does the OPP think Waterford needs to hire them in the first place? We have a perfectly adequate and capable police force."

A dozen people in the audience stood up and clapped. Kate groaned. Pete grinned.

Bywater pounded the hammer. Chelsea Darling bounced up from the press table and positioned herself at the side of the room with her camera. It flashed a dozen times like a short-circuiting neon sign.

"Mr. Mayor!" Councillor Popowich leapt to his feet. "Mr. Mayor, Councillor Cleghorne is not asking a real question whatsoever. She is making a statement. Mr. Mayor, we need to be able to debate this issue without making accusations or assumptions or presumptions or wildly inflammatory comments or what have you. We must be able to move this issue along and make rational, reasonable, logical decisions, not ones based on emotion or partiality or anything else. Please, Mr. Mayor. We need to have some sort of reasonable process here that makes sense."

"Here we go," Kate muttered. "Total chaos." Pete grinned again.

"Mr. Mayor," cried Councillor Cleghorne. "I *am* making sense. I resent what Councillor Popowich is saying. Someone has to ask the hard questions and that is exactly what I am doing."

"Mr. Mayor!" Councillor Popowich was on his feet again.

"Mr. Mayor." And now it was Councillor Mary Chang from Mount Pleasant. "Can we please return to the discussion?"

"Yes, councillor," said Bywater, sighing. "Councillor Biggar."

"Thank you, Mr. Mayor. Through you to the presenter. Inspector Pearcy. We control the budget of the Waterford Police Department by looking carefully at which services we can do a good job with, and which services we'd be better off contracting out. For instance, having a fully stocked crime lab, properly equipped, is a very expensive proposition and that's why we contract with the Belleview Police. Our coroner is also on contract from Belleview. Our vehicles are purchased only on an as-needed basis, and we get a discount at our local car dealership, who has supplied us for years. My question is, can we control our expenses with the OPP by choosing which sorts of services we need, which ones we don't, and where we can buy equipment. I am assuming the answer is no. Thank you." He sat down.

Pearcy and Kapoor conferred in muted tones. Kapoor approached the podium.

"Councillor, I have been the manager of OPP supply and services for eleven years. Our process is that we consult with local detachments and police services boards and find out what their needs are before we finalize contracts for supplies and services. This may take some time but we work within a large institution, and we work diligently to meet everyone's requirements. So based on that, our contracts become province-wide. We use the tendering process. We get discounts based on bulk purchasing, fleet vehicles, that sort of thing.

"With regard to choosing services, there is no opting in or opting out of any particular service. I understand that Waterford may not need search and rescue for instance. But the costs are spread out over a total population base that stretches across Ontario. We're talking about several million people here. In the end, the costs to individual municipalities would only be a very negligible part of the budget. On the other hand, other municipalities are sharing the cost of services that Waterford might use, such as river rescue watercraft. I hope that answers your concerns. Thank you."

There was some nodding in the audience.

Cleghorne's hand shot up.

"For a second time. Councillor Cleghorne," the mayor called out.

"Through you, Mr. Mayor." Cleghorne patted her hair as if to put herself back in order.

"Superintendent Pearcy. Regarding the hours of the detachment building. You said that the OPP don't actually need a 24-hour accessible police station. Our citizens in Waterford now have 24-hour access to police right at the building. Are you saying that your police building will be open to residents only from nine to five? Business hours?

Doesn't crime take place during all hours?" She sat down abruptly.

Mutterings in the room.

Pearcy regained the podium. "Yes, councillor, I totally agree. First of all, the WPD employs a buzzer service after 5 p.m. right now."

Cleghorne was about to say something, then decided against it.

"The OPP would provide the same service as presently exists. Residents can press the buzzer after hours and connect with dispatch."

Cleghorne rose to her feet. "Yes, but the Waterford Police have an actual police officer in the building at all times."

Pearcy responded. "Dispatch could connect directly with the shift supervisor at any time through our mobile response system."

"Is the shift supervisor a police officer?"

"Yes."

"Next question," the mayor called out. "Councillor Popowich."

* * *

The exchange about station hours and response troubled Kate. She wondered how hitch-free the OPP's mobile response system actually was. Tecumseh County was full of hills and valleys, especially in Waterford around the Grand River. In the end, both police forces would use the same signal towers and encounter the same obstructions. It seemed unlikely that the reception would change much depending on the actual equipment within each police car. But it could. If council was really on their game, she thought, they would ask for a third party consultant's study on the communications ability of both forces.

"They would never think of that. Or maybe they don't want to," Kate mused out loud.

"What?" said Pete.

Kate shook her head, mute.

Popowich was up on his feet. "Through you Mr. Mayor. Inspector Pearcy, the OPP already have their own dispatchers, administrative staff, communication, and human resources personnel. That means five part-time and five full-time employees from the WPD would be out of their jobs. And I haven't even broached the topic of unemployed WPD officers. Do your figures account for the extra settlement costs?"

"To answer your question councillor, severance costs differ with individual municipalities," Pearcy responded. "They can be negotiable to some extent. Without having access to actual employee contracts, I can't say what these costs would be. So no, these costs are not included in our figures. On the other hand, while severance costs are a one-time event, yearly employment costs for those ten people currently in the WPD administrative staff are ongoing, and with us, the municipality would no longer have to cover these employment costs from year to year. So in the end, there would likely be some savings."

The rest of the session was taken up with questions about the more prosaic aspects of the deal. Would the WPD vehicles suffice for the OPP? Was there a cost for new ones? Transitioning. Uniforms. Supplies.

Finally the questions petered out. "How would council like to deal with the presentation from the Ontario Provincial Police?" called out the mayor. "A motion to receive and a staff report?" he suggested.

Stapleton was already typing the motion into the minutes.

Councillor Chang raised her hand. "Seconded," Popowich called.

There was a lull in the proceedings accompanied by the noise of an audience growing increasingly impatient. The mayor glanced at the room. "I now call for a ten-minute break." He banged his gavel.

Kirk Steele gathered up his pad and pen, ready to jump for the interview. Pete gathered up his tape recorder, gestured at Pearcy and headed over, Chelsea and Kirk hot on his heels. At the front of the room. Kirk elbowed his way in front of Pete despite the latter being a good six inches taller. Pete turned around and seeing Kate's sympathetic head shake, gave a roll of the eyes.

Kate didn't want an interview. She would gather comments later without the other media listening in.

She logged out of the text program, shut down the computer, and closed the cover. In the council chambers, she never just put her computer to sleep. You never knew who might want to take a peek at what was being written.

She stretched, rose from her chair, and grabbed her purse.

Time for some oxygen.

Chapter 19

Faint whispers of wind marking the end of the summer languor caressed Kate Messenger as she leaned over a steel balustrade and tried to pick out the edges of the Grand River.

After Kate had fled the chambers for air, she had headed down Grand River Street North for a minute or two, then across to where a streetlight illuminated the concrete paving stones of a narrow downtown parkette stuffed between two tall Victorian buildings — a gap marking an opening to the charming Grand River.

The parkette was hard to find unless you knew exactly where it was, sandwiched between Green Heron Books and John M. Hall Linens. Kate approached the sound of the water, liquid silver where it caught the moon's reflection, then inky and churning noisily through the weeds and the abandoned bicycles, the worn detritus choking the river. The water was high and fast after weeks of late summer rains.

Leaning out on her elbows, she stretched out her aching lower back and peered into the shadows. Something landed on her face, and she swiped at a cheek. Midges.

She looked upwind, taking in the water and the rank odour of rotten debris, and had to strangle a breath.

Much of the water was treated sewage heading south down the river from Cambridge, about twenty-five kilometres away. But some of it was untreated sewage, the direct result of the heavy rains and the ensuing overflow from Cambridge's wastewater treatment plant, a common occurrence within the province despite many a municipality's distress.

The odour was normally rank vegetable rot with top notes of detergent and ammonia and the odd occasional wrenching stink. When Cambridge's out-of-date sewage treatment plant couldn't handle the load of effluent, the smell was mostly rotten stink with just the odd top note of detergent. Repellent.

Privately, Kate loved the river's awful smell because it drew birds in for miles around, especially ones that were migrating south and north. For them, rot and sewage were a beacon for insects like flies and juicy worms that would sustain them for the days and weeks of their voyages south. The river was a north-south highway, making their exhausting journeys just that much easier.

It took a moment of facing away from the breeze and the stench to get back her breath.

Then something moved in the shadows outside of the overhead light. There were steps behind her.

Kate whipped around, blinded by the streetlight, and froze, unable to make out who it was. She knew the person could clearly see her, though.

How could I let myself be vulnerable? What a mistake.

He moved forward under the beam of the streetlight, and there he was, a tall lanky guy with a buzz cut, carrying a briefcase.

It was one of the officers from the council meeting. Her heartbeat level descended. She let out a sigh of relief.

The man let Kate's eyes adjust, then: "You're with the press, right?"

"Yes," she said.

"Sorry," he said. "Didn't mean to scare you. Leo Kowalchuk. Constable. Media officer for the Waterford Police Department."

"Shouldn't sneak up on people like that. Although now that I think about it, the briefcase didn't look too dangerous."

He laughed. "Don't worry. I'm not armed."

"I thought you guys were always packing."

"Ha ha. That's just the movies."

She wasn't completely surprised it was Kowalchuk. During the break at last month's meeting, she had seen him head off in the direction of the parkette, fishing for the pack of cigarettes in his pocket.

Why do people smoke, she thought. A slow but certain self-imposed death. *Human beings are completely senseless.*

"Kate Messenger," she said. "*Tecumseh Challenge.* Armed only with the facts." They shook hands.

He laughed again. "Ah yes," he said. "It's good to put a face to the name finally. That's what emailing does. You never get to meet people any more."

He gestured at the empty parkette. "Usually, there isn't anyone here."

"Yeah," Kate said. "Thought I'd come down for some air."

"Me too."

They both stood awkwardly beside the steel balustrade and looked down upon the river. Kowalchuk refrained from going to his pack of smokes. A small act of consideration.

Suddenly a small but resonant beeping sounded overhead.

She pricked her ears, peered upwards. Kowalchuk noticed too, and followed the tone. "I wonder what that was?" he said. "Maybe a tree frog."

Kate was surprised he even knew what a tree frog was.

She squinted into the dark sky but could not make out much beyond a faint silhouette. Something flying, erratic. Were those white blotches on the undersides of wings?

"It looks like a bird, actually," she said. The noise persisted.

A short silence. "You know, I think you're right. Where I grew up in Guelph we used to walk downtown at night with my parents and hear that sound. Dad said it was a special kind of hawk that flew at night. A nighthawk or something."

Kate raised her eyebrows. "Yeah, it's probably a nighthawk," she said. "A hawk hunting at night. Normally hawks hunt during the day."

"Hunting? I don't know about that," he said. "How can they see anything at night?

She glanced over at him. "Echolocation." She peered back at the sky again.

No response. Then, another beep. Another pause.

"Echolocation," she repeated. "Like a bat. Or a whale."

"Yeah. I think I know what you mean. Like chimney swifts."

"Yeah. Are you a birder?" she asked. She did not say birdwatcher. But he did.

"Sometimes I go birdwatching," he said. "My dad and I used to do Pelee every spring. Then he got sick."

"Oh, that's a shame. I bet he really misses it."

"Yeah, he did. He passed away last year."

"Oh, I'm so sorry," Kate said.

"Yeah. Thanks."

The beeping continued. There was another awkward silence.

Better get to the point.

"I got the press release about Julie Crawford," Kate said. "Did they pull out the body just below Penmarvian? I saw the photo in the Journal."

"Uh, yeah, north of the bridge."

She squinted, looking up river to the William Street bridge.

"You were there?"

"Yeah."

"Must have been awful."

"Not pretty. She'd been in the water for a while."

Kate mulled this over without comment. "Marshall said she'd been depressed for a long time. Did you tell *The Waterford Reporter* it was suicide? I thought you didn't release a cause of death."

Kowalchuk grunted with no real meaning. Then: "Actually, that's true. I never said that. That was an inference made by that reporter."

"You should ask for a retraction. Otherwise people will think it's official."

"Maybe. I'll talk about it with my boss." A second or two went by. "I really can't talk about the case any more," he said. "Sorry."

"I understand. I just thought I'd mention what Marshall said to me. I thought it was a little strange. I knew Julie."

He glanced over at her.

She pressed on. "She wasn't the type to commit suicide. She had a lot to live for. Two small children. She really loved those girls. She wouldn't just abandon them like that. It just wasn't possible."

Nothing. Then: "Well, we don't ever really know why people take their own lives, do we?"

"So there wasn't any suicide note."

"I didn't say that," he said. "But not everybody takes the time to write a note."

"Julie would have."

If that's what actually happened to her.

No comment. Then: "We don't consider it an active case any more."

"Really," Kate said, turning to face him. "Look. Don't you think it's more than a little strange that a young woman would choose to commit suicide by jumping off a train bridge? I mean, that's not a normal thing to do. Don't you think? There are a lot more convenient ways to take your own life. Pills. Or slicing your wrists."

Kowalchuk grimaced.

"I understand where you're coming from. You're upset about your friend. But there was no foul play suspected. Maybe the bridge had a symbolic meaning for her."

"Yeah," Kate said. "She hated heights. What's the symbol there?"

The breeze picked up, amplifying the smell of the sewage. In the moonlight, Kate could see that Kowalchuk was trying to decide what to say.

She pressed on. "When you say there was no foul play suspected, what you really mean is that you didn't find any evidence of foul play. But maybe you didn't look hard enough."

Kowalchuk gave her a look. "I don't know what else I can tell you. I can see you feel strongly about this."

"I do," Kate said. "I always do when it matters."

Another pause.

"Look, if you feel you have useful information, call Crime Stoppers," he said. "Or, if you're not afraid to testify in court, here's my business card." He pulled out his wallet and fished out a card. "Business number, cell, email."

"Okay." She paused. "I'm sorry to put you on the spot," Kate said. "I don't normally get involved in police investigations. I know you people have your job to do."

"Yeah," said Kowalchuk. "That's all right. But like I said, if you feel you have some solid information, don't hesitate to get in touch."

"I will. Thanks."

"Well, maybe I'll be getting back to the chambers," he said. "It's kind of stinky out here."

"Yeah."

"Nice chatting," he added. He broke away with some relief, Kate felt, and made his way to the light of Grand River Street North.

Awkward. But entirely necessary.

She waited a few moments to catch the beeping sound again.

There it was. As she stared up into the sky, she saw it silhouetted against against the moon, yes, a dark outline with long sharply pointed wings. And were those white spots on the undersides of the wings? Surely. A quick flap or two, then it was gone. A nighthawk. Distinctly.

She hurried back to the council chambers and things wrapped up abruptly. She and the other reporters gathered up their notepads and pens, computer satchels, and purses, and were soon in the parking lot.

"Bye Kate," Pete called out.

"See ya," she returned.

*   *   *

On the way back home she decided to head north on Grand River Street North to a high point of land across from the Waterford Fairgrounds. She drove by the high school where some shadowy figures huddled over lit cigarettes in the doorway of the school entrance. They glanced up furtively as she passed by, then dipped back to their discussion, intent. Druggies, Kate thought. They're everywhere.

She parked the Audi, opened the car windows wide, and peered at the night sky. The stars twinkled intermittently, a breeze blew from the north. Almost immediately, Kate heard what she had come for. The tiny night-time peeps of migrating songbirds, catching the wind. Every minute or two were the almost imperceptible chirps of hundreds, maybe thousands of birds flying overhead, exchanging calls with their fellow travelers, flying by the light of the starry sky, navigating by the constellations and the moon and the smell of rivers and trees, soybeans and corn.

Safe journey, my friends, she murmured. *Safe journey.*

Chapter 20

K ate wrote the story the next day in her office.

OPP PITCH POLICING PLAN, the headline read.

Hmm. Alliteration. Perhaps improper. Flippant. She typed: OPP OFFER POLICING TO WATERFORD. Simple and to the point.

She pondered the wording that would best describe the situation.

"Superintendent Don Pearcy contended that the Ontario Provincial Police was better equipped and trained to handle policing throughout the entire county including Waterford. The OPP could literally outgun the Waterford police force, offering more equipment, more officers, and better options for covering a variety of law enforcement situations." That was the crux of the matter.

She called Pearcy and WPD Chief Bill Pound, got comments, and incorporated them into the article.

"'We do very good work for the town of Waterford,' Pound said. 'I don't know why the OPP wants citizens to pay millions of dollars more for service they don't need, based in a big city a hundred miles away. WPD officers are rooted in community, historically, economically, socially, in every sense. We contribute a lot to Waterford. We belong here, not the OPP.'

"In an interview, Pearcy said that the OPP used the results of an internal study, comparing towns with similar populations to Waterford. 'We have numbers comparing incident types and numbers of investigations, crimes and convictions, calls for service, public complaints, that sort of thing,' he said.

'While the WPD did an excellent job with the resources they had,' he continued, 'the OPP could do even more.' He did not specify exactly what 'more' was required."

Her editorial would supplement the front page article.

"The Waterford District Police have a long and storied history in town," she wrote there. "But even the finest products have their 'best before' dates.

"The study relied upon by the OPP must have offered enough convincing evidence to spur the force to make its offer to Waterford County council.

"An arm's length third-party investigation of the capabilities of both forces wouldn't be a bad idea.

"The regrettable thing is not the process taking place, but rather the forum, the things that still remain hidden. If our present police force is lacking, then it should be an issue aired and examined in the open, not merely hinted at, kept secret and locked away in a report."

There's no hope that that will ever happen. But at least it's being said.

"We must remember that not all change is bad. Open minds and clear heads are what it's all about.

"The numbers will tell the story. Let's see them and come to the proper conclusion about which police force is the right one for Waterford."

She switched on the radio. "The Ontario Provincial Police hope to replace the Waterford Police Department with their own men."

Ouch, Kate thought. That should be officers, Pete. Not men.

She listened to the rest of the broadcast then clicked it off. Went to the websites of the competition.

OPP Make First Move In Waterford, headlined *The Belleview Daily Urinal*.

OPP vs Waterford Police, shouted *The Waterford Contorter*. The article referred readers to a double page spread advertising feature titled, We Support Our Waterford Police. Chelsea had solicited advertising from dozens of local businesses who touted their support.

That was completely unethical, Kate thought. Slimy rock-bottom journalism. Any business not appearing in the advertising feature would be condemned as opposing the WPD. And those appearing on the page would hope to curry favour with them.

It was disgusting. Misleading. Divisive. Sensational.

Another Chelsea Darling masterpiece.

She shifted to *The Journal's* editorial. "Everyone should support the WPD," it read. For what reason? "The Waterford District Police has been vigilantly serving the town for decades. These people know what they're doing. They've been at it a long time."

Oh my God Kirk, Kate thought. Diligently, not vigilantly. Diligently.

The other media were hell-bent on portraying the issue as a rivalry. Kate sat back in her chair. What good that would accomplish? Not much, even if it were true. Better to show overall that a slow and steady hand was needed at the keel of things, and merely imply the rivalry in the body of the story.

Newspapers did more than just report the facts, after all. They helped nudge the direction of public discourse, whether they admitted it or not. Why not nudge it in the most helpful direction possible?

She reached down and rubbed Alfred's head, flipped the switch of the CD player, and clicked on Martha Argerich — Bach's Partita No. 2 in C minor. It was a stretch from jazz but nevertheless, she adored it.

That woman could really bang the keys, yet at other times, have such exquisite nuance.

Kate crossed her arms behind her head, closed her eyes, and listened to the first movement, the Sinfonia. Her favourite. *Magnificent,* she said to herself.

Tears pricked her eyes, the rapture swept her away, and she almost forgot that she had to write six more stories that day.

Chapter 21

It was a pleasant early summer day when Kate first bumped into Julie at Marshalls Mens Apparel. The year 1996.

Kate hadn't been there in quite a while. She stared at the door mat, and glanced up at a new backlit old-fashioned awning and a matching sidewalk sign. Still — no bloody apostrophes. Marshalls. It should be Marshall apostrophe "s" and Men apostrophe "s". As in possessive. Men's apparel belonging to Marshall.

The old stone building with its ornate brickwork, cornice, dentils, and big glass windows was one of about a couple of dozen nineteenth century restored storefronts lining Grand River Street North. Shop on the ground level with apartments above. Very small town Ontario.

Kate steeled herself that day in 1996, pushed open the glass door and a bell tinkled somewhere in the back. Mahogany tables sat beside an old ivory-faced grandfather clock. A plush carpet muffled her footsteps while she located the counter.

Banned ivory. Made from the tusks of critically endangered elephants. Tsk.

Spotlights beamed down on linen jackets and Oxford button-down shirts, silk ties, and trench coats. An air conditioner pulsed while the faint smell of whiskey-tipped cigarillos drifted through the air.

A back room curtain slid open to reveal a woman close to Kate's age. Kate was struck by her appearance. A delicate lilac blouse accentuated her best features. Her nose was straight and fine, her lips full. Her curly auburn hair was so voluminous, her figure so shapely that she could have been a movie star.

She greeted Kate with a smile and a hello.

"Hello, I'm Kate Messenger. I'm with *The Tecumseh Challenge.* Would your store like to run an ad in our upcoming summer sale feature?"

"I'm not sure," the woman said hesitantly. Her forehead crinkled.

"Marshall isn't here right now. Could you come back in a few hours?"

Despite her looks, the woman did not exude the confidence of one who had an exclusive membership in the Club For Beautiful People. In fact, it seemed almost the opposite.

Well, Kate thought. *I can't come back.* Who would? Who had time to stop by in person anywhere these days, never mind make a repeat visit.

"How about if I just leave my card?" Kate fished out a business card and slid it over the counter with the latest edition of the paper.

"I own *The Tecumseh Challenge*. Did you just start working here?" she asked. "I haven't seen you here before." *Maybe too forward.*

"I'm Julie." Didn't seem to take offence at all. "I'm new in town. Pleased to meet you," she said and held out her hand. Kate shook it politely. Limp and small.

"How do you like Waterford?"

"I like it. It's a little different from where I'm from but I like it."

"Where are you from?"

"St. Catharines."

"That's pretty far from here. How did you find this place?"

"Oh, a church friend of my parents knew Marshall. They told me about the job."

"It's great you got a job in this recession," Kate said. "There must have been a ton of other applicants. Do you have a diploma in retail?"

Julie flushed.

Darn, that was prying. Stop it.

"Well, no, I just have high school to tell you the truth. But I have sales experience."

"Well, I hope you enjoy living here. It's a pretty town."

"Yes, it is. I moved into an old house on Jane Street on the weekend. The neighbourhood is really lovely."

Kate knew exactly where that was. It was on Waterford's Posh Hill, as it was dubbed by the locals, not far away from her own home actually. The neighbourhood was full of stately Victorian homes, treed and shady.

"The Burt's house?"

Julie looked surprised. "How did you know?"

"They advertised their place for rent in my paper last month." Kate smiled ruefully. "I guess they'll be pulling their ad now."

"Oh, that's too bad."

"Not a problem, that's what the paper's for," Kate said. "I'm glad they found a nice tenant." *Oops. Perhaps too presumptive.*

"Don't you just love this old town?" Julie said. "Full of interesting places and history."

"It is," Kate nodded. "I love it. The parks are nice, too. And the river."

"Do you ever go to that beautiful old cemetery on Portland Street near the river? It's just around the corner from here. I like going there early in the morning when it's quiet and no one's around. It's so peaceful and lovely. It helps me think." She smiled a little. "Sometimes I go to cemeteries just to look at the graves," she continued. "Sounds crazy, but I love them. And I learn so much. A lot of the streets around here are named after those old families."

"Actually, you're right," Kate said. "I've been at that cemetery myself." She was rapidly warming up to Julie. Sincere. Not vain and self-centred the way most good-looking people could be. "There's some pretty good birding near the spot where Banfield Capron and his sister Jane are buried," she continued.

"Isn't that interesting," Julie exclaimed. "Jane Capron. That's who my street is named after."

Kate grinned. "Hiram Capron, their dad, founded this town in 1829."

"Is that so." Julie suddenly glanced at the clock. "You know, I hate to cut things short but I really should get back to work. I've got an order that needs to get done. "Marshall should be back any minute," she said. "If you want to wait I'll just slip into the back and finish up a few things. I hope you don't mind."

"No problem. But I think I'll get going," Kate said. "I have a couple other people to see. Please tell Marshall I dropped by. Here's the flyer for the special we're running. Nice meeting you. And good luck with the new job."

"Thanks," Julie said. "It was nice meeting you too."

As Kate slipped out the front door and the little bell tinkled in the back of the store again, she knew exactly why Julie got the job. There were lots of men in town who needed an outfit for a special occasion. Who cared whether Julie was or wasn't the most astute appraiser of men's fashion needs. They would soon be beating a path to the place just to lay their gazes on such a lovely creature.

And she was nice, too.

She didn't blame Marshall one bit for hiring her.

Then in a few months — for marrying her.

The local men rejoiced. The women were sick with envy.

Two little girls were born within the space of a couple of years.

Chapter 22

Here, the doctor said. Take this to the pharmacy. Two weeks supply. It'll help take the weight off your shoulders.

Finally, I thought. There was hope. You have to do what the doctor says, Mom always told me. It's for your own good. In the meantime, God will look after all of us.

Well, sometimes. Thanks to the doctor's prescription, I floated in a big pink shiny cloud day after day. It was so wonderful. I didn't know I would love that feeling so much. It meant everything to me. Xanax made life so much easier. Better. Happier.

It was finally bearable to be stuck at home every day. Waiting for him to come home for supper. It was so hot in that old house. No air conditioning, you see. That's the thing about those old Victorian homes. They look nice and all, but there's not enough hydro for an air conditioner. Just old wiring and knob and tube and a mouldy layer of dirt in the basement.

He liked to say the house stays cool enough during the day. Yes, that was true. Until about three o'clock. Then the sun dropped to eye level and fired up the whole street, the old bricks heating up and retaining it way into the night. You could warm your hand on the outside wall at one o'clock in the morning.

Those hot summer days were so foggy. Sitting on the back deck under the patio umbrella with the kids, eating watermelon. Moving the seats around the little metal table so that everyone had some shade. Listening for the sound of his car, listening and waiting and drowsy in my chair, I would doze off and the sun would burn my face into a red mask. Mama, mama, wake up, I would hear. Little hands tugging at my arm.

I'd be in bed before it was dark, unconscious really, and he would come in the door and in the oppressive heat of the night head straight to the girls' rooms. Wake them up. Then it was hard for them to get back to sleep. In the morning, I would let them sleep in.

But I couldn't. My eyes would pop open in the middle of the night, and I would be shocked wide awake and thirsty. He'd be asleep beside me in the bed, snoring. I'd get up and check on the kids. They would be blissfully unaware, and I would watch them with envy. Why couldn't I sleep like that? Never could get back to sleep.

Oh dear, the doctor said, scribbling quickly on his pad. That doesn't sound very good. Here. Here's something to help you sleep. Call me if you need anything else.

I was so relieved. Another solution. Doctors know everything. Thank you, doctor.

But it didn't last very long. I still couldn't sleep. One Ambien became two Ambiens. Then three and four. And then I started getting shaky and sweaty if I didn't take the Xanax. One Xanax became two Xanax. Then more.

So began the pattern of my life.

One day when it was back to the doctor again, he said maybe you should get off the Xanax. There could be dangerous side effects like memory loss. Headaches. Blackouts.

Those doctors, I said to myself. They didn't know everything after all. Why did he give it to me in the first place? I wanted to phone Mom and tell her how much I hated doctors for not giving me the medicine I needed.

No more Xanax? What are you saying, doctor? How will I be able to get through the day? It will be impossible. It will be hell all over again and this time, no way out. That's the way I felt. But I didn't say that.

What I did say was, actually, doctor, now is not really a good time. Things are still pretty hard for me. I don't know if I can cope. And the girls. They need me. Please, doctor. Please.

I started to cry. If you give me one more prescription, I will wean myself off, I promise.

A look. He wrote another prescription. But this is the last one he said. You will have to cut back. Completely.

Completely? Okay, I will. Thank you doctor. I promise.

As soon as I was out the door, I couldn't remember one single word he said about anything. Even the side effects. I guess I didn't really care. I probably should have.

What I did remember was that look on his face. Disapproving. Skeptical. I couldn't bear to see that look again. That was awful. I didn't deserve that. I'm not that kind of person. I'm a good person.

So the next time, I just went to see another doctor.

Chapter 23

In the morning, Kate woke to the sound of an engine revving, over and over.

What in the world, she thought. Was there a motocross tourney gearing up beside her house?

Oh my God.

She groaned, placed her feet on the cool wooden floor and shuffled to the window. She wedged a finger between two slats to reveal Stu and Moira's two boys gunning Conner's super-charged extra-wide white pickup truck in her driveway, the contents of a toolbox scattered all over the Hackett's front porch. The plate read MFKR 001.

Nice. A swear word for a licence plate.

How could he even afford a truck?

Sam was sitting behind the wheel turning the throttle over and over while Conner adjusted something in the engine with a wrench, exhaust clouding the morning sun and staining the air grey. The noise reverberated and echoed in the space beside her house like a series of explosions. Sam jumped out of the driver's seat with a curse-embellished exclamation, leaned under the hood, and returned once again to jump on the gas pedal.

Why? Kate muttered. *Why my laneway? Why beside my house? What's wrong with your own bloody driveway. Oh wait, it's already full of your own junk. So let's spread it over to the neighbour's property now too.*

Kate gritted her teeth with the same thought she had every morning.

Yet another day of being woken up too damn early by some tomfoolery from the neighbours.

When would those two finally be hauled off to jail?

They were getting too old to lecture. As a matter of fact, they were on the verge of being downright menacing. Who knew what they were capable of these days.

She heaved a sigh. One day she would move to the country, far away from everyone and everything and their stupid gas engines.

I'll take Alfie up Banfield Street. Try to enjoy the day.

It was not the usual route, and it was out of her way. She didn't know the people there. She hoped she wouldn't bump into anybody.

It was a nice old street, lined with maples and elms, and Kate was glad to stretch her legs. During the day it was quiet and she could gaze at the ornate Victorian homes and study their details at leisure, secure in the knowledge she would not be accused of staring.

Or be stared at.

She rounded the corner to Jane Street, and when she approached the Burt's house, she saw a woman on her hands and knees in the front garden. She hesitated. The woman's hair was pulled back and her face was devoid of makeup, but she was still lovely. She carried extra weight and looked tired. It was Julie, without a doubt.

On the porch was a bassinette and a stroller. Both were filled with tiny occupants.

At the sound of footsteps on the sidewalk, Julie turned her head. It was too late for Kate to turn around.

"Hello there," Julie said casually. Kate paused.

Talk to her. Just for once. Give someone a chance.

"Hello, Julie. Remember me?"

She looked quizzical. "Oh yes, you're the girl from the newspaper. Was it Kate?"

"Yeah, Kate Messenger." Kate pulled up on Alfred's leash. He tended to wander to the nearest tree at every given opportunity. It would not be a good thing if he peed on Julie's front yard.

Julie got to her feet. "Yes. Messenger. I remember that name. Is that really your name? It's sort of perfect for a newspaper lady." She brushed off her hands and smiled.

Kate laughed. "Actually, my real name is Visnyk but no one could ever spell it. So I anglicized it when I got out of university and it's so much easier now. I live a few streets away from here."

"Really?"

"High Street."

"Sure, I know where that is. Do you have an office in town too?"

"No, just my home office on High Street. It's convenient. How are you doing these days, anyway?"

Alfred shook off the leash, and stared up at Julie with his coal black eyes. Between parted black lips emerged the tip of a little pink tongue. He panted slightly.

"Well, I'm at home with the babies. Oh, what an adorable dog you have," she said. "Is that a West Highland Terrier?"

Kate was surprised. "How did you know?"

"We used to have one when I was growing up in St. Catharines. Do you want some water for him? Wait. I'll get a little dish."

A fellow Westie lover, thought Kate. *How do you like that.*

Julie climbed a set of wide shady cement stairs and disappeared into the house, emerging momentarily with a bowl.

"Here you go." She set down the water on the front walkway.

Alfred made a dash for it and frantically slurped away, much of the water ending up on the scraggly fur around his black lips. Then he pulled back, shook himself hard enough to send water flying in all directions, sat down, and scratched behind an ear with a hind paw. Julie laughed, putting out a hand to shield herself.

"Whoops, sorry about that," said Kate. "He can be a bit messy." *Darn. I should have been more considerate.*

Alfred stood up, nudged forward in Julie's direction, and shook himself out again before straining at the end of his leash.

"Don't I remember." She bent forward and scratched Alfred behind the ears. He, of course, loved it.

"What a cutie. Would you like to meet Emma and Sarah?"

"Sure," Kate said. Then thought, *whoa, what the hell am I thinking? Now I'm in for it. Babies are such a pain in the ass.*

Julie motioned for Kate to come onto the porch.

There was newborn Emma, swaddled in a pink sheet, lying in the shade, the lines of her tiny eyes pressed shut, little cheeks flushed. Sarah, already more than a year old, dozed in a stroller, head tilted sideways. Her hair curled all over her head in the softest light brown curls.

They already look like Mom, Kate thought. *Beautiful.*

"They are so precious," she said, then thought *of course they're all precious when they're asleep.* More quietly: "I won't wake them up."

"That's okay," Julie said. "They're both good sleepers. Would you like to come in for a tea?"

"No, thanks. I need to get back to the office. The emails are probably piling up by now."

"Well, first sit here on the stoop for a few minutes before you go," Julie said. "You can't work all the time." She was half joking but half serious too. Kate was slightly taken aback. She laughed, then acquiesced. Maybe it was a good idea to take a break.

"Okay."

It was a lovely afternoon and it was nice to sit and relax. Julie wasn't a big talker. The two of them admired the freshly leafed trees and the emerging hyacinths.

"Nice garden," Kate said. "How do you like this place?"

"It's pretty good. Marshall decided to keep on paying the rent here after we got married. He loves the area. He didn't think living above the store downtown would work out very well with children. "

"Yeah."

"And I didn't like the height of the store building anyway. Looking out over the river makes me nervous. Especially with the kids being so small."

Alfred settled onto the walkway, dropped his head between his paws, and sighed, eyes closing. His sharp tail lay straight out behind.

Julie got up to check on the babies, ensured they were still sleeping in the shade, adjusted the sheets slightly, then rejoined Kate on the stoop. She held her chin on one hand and stared into space. Her wedding band glinted silver in the sunlight.

"That's a beautiful ring," Kate said. "Silver?"

"Platinum. It's an antique. It's Marshall's great-grandma's ring. The top is diamonds. Orange blossoms on the bottom. See?" She pointed beside the milgrain detailing. "I love jewellery and old things out of the past. I never take this off. It means so much to me."

A minute or two went by.

"I wish I knew more people here in this town," Julie said. "Not many people stay home during the day."

Kate glanced over. Julie might have been fishing for an invitation to come over to her house, but Kate was just not the sociable type. Nothing personal. She just didn't like people there. She liked everything in its place, undisturbed.

"But you must meet a lot of people at the store," she said sympathetically. "Marshall has a lot of customers."

"I know," Julie said. "It's just that right now I'm at home with the children all the time. It's a little hard to meet people."

"Maybe you can bring them to the store ..."

"No, that wouldn't work very well. I'm breast-feeding," Julie said.

"Oh. Of course," Kate said, slightly embarrassed and realizing she was not the world's biggest expert on baby procedures. "Well, that's probably the best thing for now. I'm sure you won't regret it later when the kids are big and strong and growing like weeds."

"I know, that's right." A pause. "No kids?"

"None. But a few nieces and nephews."

"That's nice."

Alfred coughed a little. Kate felt she should probably get going. It had been quite an unusual feeling to sit on the step and have a friend in the neighbourhood.

An agreeable feeling.

"Marshall hired a new girl for the store," Julie said. "So I guess I won't have to work there for a while."

"That was a good idea. Give you some time off."

Julie didn't say anything, and Kate felt she had said the wrong thing. Again. She mentally kicked herself.

"Look, if you're passing by my house on High Street, drop by," Kate said, regretting the words even as they were coming from her mouth. She probably shouldn't get involved with one of her customers on a personal level in any way, even if she did feel a little sorry for her. It could conflict with business.

But then another voice said, on the other hand, technically speaking, Julie wasn't a customer. And neither was Marshall, of course. He never advertised, not even once.

What was there to lose?

"Twelve High Street," Kate said. "A yellow brick Victorian two-storey with an Audi in the driveway. Afternoons are best. Knock at the front door. The doorbell's broken," she said. "Permanently. Is tea okay?"

"Sure," Julie said. "Tea is great."

"Okay. Well, then. I guess I'll be getting back to the office," Kate said. "It was lovely chatting with you."

It really was.

Julie stood in her driveway and held up her hand in the universal gesture of goodbye.

Kate took the sidewalk to Banfield Street, turned left at the first corner onto Warwick, then made her way over to High.

Why would she invite a woman with two crying babies into her home in the afternoon when she was right in the middle of work, Kate chided herself. Especially someone who had all the time in the world? Lord knew, she didn't.

The whole thing was impossible. What was she thinking? She wasn't the social type. She didn't have time to exchange pleasantries with the neighbours. She wasn't even interested in the neighbours. Usually all they did was complain about her articles, anyway.

Sam was sitting on his front stoop with a friend when Kate walked up the driveway. Why was he not in school?

When she got closer, he was careful to put his hand out of sight while he and the friend looked at each other and guffawed. She proceeded straight into the house, ignoring both them and the fetid odour of marijuana.

Ha ha, very funny. Be even funnier if I called the cops, wouldn't it.

But of course, she didn't.

The image of Julie waving goodbye wouldn't leave her. There was something a bit melancholy about her, Kate decided while sipping a cup of chilled tea with honey. Perhaps she needed someone to talk to every now and then. After all, her family lived pretty far away.

She settled down to the computer once again, reviewing all the work she had wanted to get done that afternoon. She still had time.

Of course, if worse came to worse, Kate told herself, she didn't have to answer the door.

Chapter 24

A few days later Kate found herself at her desk scanning pages from the competition.

The Belleview Daily Journal, usually chock full of immaculately presented ads and articles, was looking somewhat alarming lately. Local news articles were stretched in ungainly ways to fill rather vacant-looking pages. Ads were few and unnaturally large. The paper was made up of only a dozen and a half pages in its entirety, and maybe four or five original pieces. The rest was stuffed with filler off the internet and irrelevant stories from affiliate papers.

She flipped to an item written by Kirk Steele titled WEEKEND EVENT WILL HIGHLIGHT ADDICTION ISSUES FOR TEENS. The lede: "Fun activities for teens will be part of a local focus on National Addictions Week."

For God's sake, Kate thought. *National Addictions AWARENESS Week. Well, I hope those teens enjoy themselves while they celebrate addictions from coast to coast.*

And the next page — WATERFORD SUBDIVISION POISED TO EXPAND. A paraphrase of last month's *Challenge* story, the sentences rearranged.

Huh. At least he had the decency to reword the headline, Kate thought. She threw the paper over the edge of the desk in disgust.

What about *The Waterford Contorter?* Would they be able to show their big brother how to properly write articles? Of course, that was ridiculous.

At the top of the front page blazed the headline: TEACHERS STRIKE IDLE KIDS. *Whaaa?* Kate thought. *No, it couldn't be.* That was incredible. Did they press assault charges? She scanned through the article: an interview with local elementary school children affected by a teacher walkout.

She groaned in agony. Turned a few more pages to the big grocery store ad. Highlighted in a box: "Ground beast: 99 cents per lb."

"Argh! Chelsea! Don't you proofread for crying out loud?"

Give it one more chance.

On the next page, a headline caught her eye. The article featured an upcoming tour of a local tall-grass prairie reserve and an interview with the organizer. "The tour is not suitable for dogs, but if they have to come, they must be leased," wrote Chelsea Darling.

"*'Leashed'* not *'leased'*! Oh, I completely give up." She threw *The Reporter* at *The Journal*'s jumbled heap and together they embraced in a messy courtship of incompetence.

She glared at the pile of newspapers then glanced at her own front page. The date was from two months ago. She had forgotten to change the date again. Again!

She buried her head in her arms.

There was a sufficient recovery period, then, "gambatte," and she raised her head. She gathered up *The Journal* and *The Reporter*, reassembling the pages on her desk. Was there anything she could use? Anything at all?

She skipped all the vanilla cake and went straight to the important stuff — the ads from the municipality and the bureaucracies. The local institutions would quite often agree to advertise in the Tecumseh paper if they had already advertised in the others. Equal treatment, or covering their butts, it didn't matter. It was the result that counted.

There were a few retail ads too, although she hated to even bother. Not only was it a constant struggle to get stores to advertise, in the long run, it was hardly worth it. They rarely paid their bills on time, they always needed chasing down for the smallest amounts of money, and the time Kate spent dealing with them was only time lost from dealing with more reliable customers or from researching and writing good articles.

There was an abrupt knock at the door.

She jumped, then immediately realized who it was.

Panic.

Answer the door or not? She glanced at the list of stories that needed to be written. There they were, all the source documents, neatly stored in a file on her computer labelled "raw stories." If she got five or six stories done that day, she could perhaps take the next morning off and go birding at the walking trail beside the Grand River ...

The knock came again.

Gaaaah. She had so wanted to see whether there were any warblers nesting along the creek that fed the river. They were easy to find. All you needed to do was listen for the super high-pitched, continuous rasp of baby birds that was detectable even during the most raucous morning hours …

Another knock.

She sighed. *Okay Kate, just this once,* she told herself. *Wipe off the grumpy work face and put on the happy neighbourly sociable face. If you have one. And if you don't have one, find one.*

Try hard.

She got up from her desk and went to the door.

"Hello there," Julie said, holding a baby against her shoulder which was draped with a small towel. "I hope you don't mind."

Kate smiled. "Come on in," she said. "Nice to see you. Have a cup of tea with me. Keep your shoes on," she said, looking down at Julie's white Keds.

She surprised herself by feeling genuinely pleased to bring out a cup of fragrant hot chamomile tea and a plate of homemade cookies to her guest. If the dishes were mismatched, her guest didn't appear to care.

Julie sat down in the high-backed chair by the window and breastfed Emma a late lunch. Kate felt a little uncomfortable. Wasn't quite sure where to look.

"Where's Sarah?"

"Oh, she's asleep in her crib. The neighbour is watching her."

Emma reached up and grabbed Julie's ear.

"Ouch," she said, holding on to her ear. "There goes my earring. Darn things are always loose." She pulled something into her hand and gave her breast back to Emma.

Kate said nothing and retreated to the kitchen, pretending to fiddle with some plates. When she returned, the soft warm scent of baby milk had filled the room. Julie had reassembled herself and was hooking the errant earring into her ear.

"Is it in?" she said. It was. It was a silver earring in the shape of a heart and where the two curves met, a tiny diamond. "I'd hate to lose it. They were an anniversary present."

Alfred lay on his dog bed near Kate's desk and let out a long sigh.

"Herbal tea is so good for the baby," Julie said. "She'll get a nice nap this afternoon."

Soon Emma had settled in for a sleep. Her tousled head fell back against mom's arm and China doll lips pursed and pressed, pursed and pressed together.

"Julie," Kate said, a thought striking her. "Let me take your picture with the baby. Something for you to keep and remember. Babies grow up so fast. And the light is so nice right now."

"All right," Julie said. "How's this?" She bent over Emma and nuzzled her with her nose. Kate snapped the shutter a few times, then brought over the camera so that Julie could look through the previews. The photos showed a lovely soft-skinned woman bent lovingly over her smiling baby.

"Nice," she said.

"I'll email them over to you in the next couple of days," Kate said. "By the way, how's the garden coming along?"

"Well, there's quite a bit of weeding that needs to get done. Old houses always have old gardens, you know. Especially ours. Things have pretty much gone wild for a long time," she said. "But it's nice to be outdoors."

"Yeah."

"How about you? Do you have a garden?"

"Yes, I do a lot of gardening when there's time," Kate said. "I like to feel the earth under my hands."

"That's for sure." She took a sip from her cup. "Do you run the whole newspaper from here?" She looked around the sparsely furnished Victorian dining room, at Kate's piled-upon desk, her computer and filing cabinet.

"Pretty much. Everything's done over the internet these days. It's so different. The phone is quiet most of the time."

"You know, my dad used to work for a newspaper," Julie said. "*The St. Catharines Standard.* He was the editor for a while. And he did a lot of the hard news too."

"Really!" Kate said. "How long?"

"Oh, about twenty years. Then he retired and became a minister."

"Huh. Well, that's better than most newspaper people. Usually they just become alcoholics."

Julie laughed. "How true. Actually, my dad still visits at the Salvation Army. There are a couple of guys he knew from the old days living there. Down and outers."

"I'm not surprised at all. Poor guys," Kate said. "You still can't get a job in the business these days. Not that you'd want one."

Julie shook her head. "I know it's not easy running a newspaper," she said. "My dad used to tell us stories about it. The late hours. Weekends and holidays. Always having to re-do pages at the last minute. Setting new type. It was a horribly stressful job. He was glad to hand it over to a younger guy with more energy."

"That's my dream too," Kate said. "To have a real life again some day."

Julie laughed.

Emma stirred and mewed and Julie gave her a kiss on the cheek. Alfred raised his head and stared. What sort of alien creature had entered his domain?

Julie chatted about mundane things, the kids' nap schedule, her chores for the day. She needed to go downtown to drop off papers for the family's life insurance. Marshall said it had to be today. It was important. He didn't want the policy to expire.

"Well, I should be going," she said. "Time for this one to get her diaper changed." She stood up. "Thanks for the tea."

Julie eyed the room to find a place for her cup and saucer. There really wasn't one. The place wasn't set up for guests.

"Here, let me take that," Kate said. "Why don't you take these cookies with you? I really don't eat cookies. Maybe Marshall can have them with supper."

Julie paused. "Oh, Marshall doesn't get home till late."

"Please, take these and have them yourself," Kate said. And, before she could think twice, "And come back any time. Except the end of the month. That's my busy time. Final deadline."

"I know all about it," Julie said as she stepped outside with Emma. "Dad was the same way."

"Bye for now," she said over her shoulder as she brushed aside Emma's downy hair. "It's home for you now, young lady." She took the sidewalk, kissing Emma's forehead.

Well, Kate thought as she closed the door. *Now that wasn't too bad.*

Sort of quick and pleasant, actually. And that baby was adorable. A baby human being. Just wait till she figures out where she is. She'll want to go right back where she came from.

Kate stood at her desk. Still enough time to finish off her stories. Maybe she would be able to see those nesting warblers after all.

She sat down, straightened out some papers, and resumed typing.

Baby smell lingered in the room for quite some time. Every once in a while Alfred would lift his head, stare at Kate with a strange look, then settle back to the floor.

"Tell me about it," Kate said.

He closed his eyes with a long malodorous exhale of breath.

Julie visited a handful more times that summer. Then ... nothing.

Chapter 25

WPD INVESTIGATE BREAK AND ENTER TO WASHINGTON
STREET RESIDENCE
WATERFORD POLICE DEPARTMENT I
Posted on 2001-09-03 I Print View

(Waterford, ON.) –
 Members of the Waterford Police Department were called to attend a residence located on Washington Street in Waterford at approximately 1:00 p.m. on 31 August 2001 in response to a break and enter.

 WPD officers conducted their investigation and found that unknown person(s) gained entry to a residence sometime between 7 a.m. and 12:50 p.m. on 31 August 2001. Once inside thieves stole a knife collection, antique lighters and cash. The total value of all items taken is approximately $2000.

 The Waterford Police Department is asking for assistance from the public in locating and identifying the suspects and suspect vehicle in this case.

 If anyone has information about this incident, they are asked to contact Constable Leonard Kowalchuk at the Waterford Police Department at 519-447-1000. To remain anonymous, call Crime Stoppers and you will be eligible for a cash award.

- 30 -

Chapter 26

His lips tasted light and sweet with the sugar of youth. And his skin. Oh my goodness oh oh oh. Soft, and smooth as a ceramic vase. Blond hairs everywhere. Blue eyes you could drown in.

Wide eyes locked to wide eyes. Fingers to skin and hands to flesh. Lips to lips.

How could I know there would be no escape after falling into that abyss?

How did it start?

For months he had been paying me little visits in the back of the store where I did the books. Poking his head in the door. Would you like a coffee or tea? Can I get you a donut? Do you need anything next door? No, I'm okay, thanks. No thank you, I'm not very hungry. I'm good for now, thanks.

It was a day when spring was turning into summer. One of those days when the sun was shining and lovely. I ate my lunch at the little table beside the river. He showed up at the back door, came outside and said, "Do you want to see what I found?"

He was a big guy, but still, he managed to look small and hopeful and vulnerable, begging me with his eyes.

For some reason I said okay. Maybe I shouldn't have.

It's over there, he said, pointing down near the side of the river.

"Where?" I stood up.

"Come over here," he said. He guided me over a short grassy hump and to a big flat rock at the water's edge. His hand was big and calloused, with squared-off fingers. When he touched my elbow, I felt something run right through the centre of my body.

I tried so hard not to feel anything. God knows.

Sitting right in the middle of an adjoining rock in the warm spring sun was a small brownish green turtle with orange streaks on the sides. The second we got close, the head snapped back into its shell.

He picked it up. Its legs waved in the air and he let one fall on his baby finger, the tiny curved nails gaining a comforting foothold. He laid it flat on his hand and proffered it in my direction.

"See? It's a painted turtle."

The scrunched-up head was encircled with tiny folds of skin. He grabbed my hand and slid the turtle onto my palm. The bottom of the shell, the pastron, was cold and wet. The small feet were folded neatly under the edge of its upper shell. It was adorable.

I stared at its tiny-ness, the little black eyes and pointed nose all retracted under the edge of the carapace.

"Can you put it back in the river?" I said.

"Sure." He gently placed it back on the stone and we both stared at it, waiting for something to happen. Nothing did.

I looked over at him with an inquiring look. "Shell-shocked," I said. He laughed.

When we climbed back up the bank to the patio, I could feel his eyes on me. That was a strange feeling. A bad feeling and a good feeling.

A day came when things were particularly awful, when I was at the store by myself, angry.

I had had enough. Why did I put up it all? How did I get into this mess? I didn't deserve it. I should just go home. Then I started crying right into my hands, right there behind the counter.

Well, he came in the back door to do the deliveries, and I was wiping my eyes and honking my nose in a tissue. I just hung my head. I couldn't even look at him.

That's when he came over and put an arm around me. I cried against his shoulder like a baby. He touched my cheek with his finger and gave me a soft little kiss, like don't worry, it'll be all right. His hand went up and down the length of my arm, respectful, like always, just inquiring. "Are you okay?"

I could have stopped it right there. Why didn't I?

It was too damn easy to slide my face under his again for another kiss. My hand went to his chest. *It's too late to stop anyway,* I was thinking. Actually, I couldn't think very well at all.

That's when he pulled my hand to his belly. Then lower. Then he put my fingers on his zipper and undid it.

I was a sinner. I was weak. And God saw it. That's why everything happened.

The whole scene played out on an endless loop inside my head, day after day, night after night, for weeks on end. Haunting me. Especially those shy looks. Those liquid blue eyes staying with me as I tossed and turned, remembering, reliving, trapped in a swooning spiral of bliss.

It was all so very wrong. I knew I was going straight to hell.

And I didn't care.

I never felt so special, so beautiful, in my entire life.

Chapter 27

In the newspaper business, death was handled with delicacy and officiousness and reverence. It kept things safer for the world of the living.

A certain tone must be imparted from a reporter's story, assumptions made. A respectful account was teased from the facts, the police report, the coroner's description, the mournful remembrances of the grief-stricken. A delicate hand would ensure the best possible light no matter how questionable the circumstances of departure. The subject cheated of life. Because always somewhere were a grieving mother, father, brother, sister, child, co-worker, best friend. Lover.

A parent was gently asked about their son testing the limits of a new car. And the story went that he loved life, that the car was the first purchase from a new job, to get to college. And he took it to see his girl after work, the girl he planned to marry some day.

The deer was completely unexpected when it ran out of the woods at dusk. It burst out of the shadows and when the car came roaring up and over the crest of the hill with the radio blasting away, there was a bang. And that was it.

A woman's husband loved to help his friends: he would give the shirt off his back, lend a hand with every job in the neighbourhood, never refuse a request. Sure, a little partying on weekends, but he knew better than to drink and drive.

At least that's what he said. Until the day came when he had one too many and got behind that wheel and lost everything. Including his life.

It was obligatory to consider the bereaved first, with sympathy, with an inhaled breath, outlined against the facts of the matter. The time of mourning, of poignance, of pain, was not the time for lessons learned.

Weaknesses were polished into strengths, choices moulded into the errors of an innocent, and the story that went to press consoled all those who struggled to understand why. For some, that piece in the paper would sustain them for the months, the years to come, helping them endure the worst of days and move forward to the next without falling to pieces.

It was only afterward when the funerals had ended, and the monuments had been planted, the vigils and memoriams over; the last conversations faded and the storytelling laid to rest, it was only then that onlookers could put the pieces together, sit in judgment, and ponder words to the wise, for themselves and for others.

And when Kate sat on her balcony with Alfred in her lap with a little bit of sky overlooking the yard, where she could put it all into perspective — she could cast aside the artifice. And most of the time she would say to herself, this person or that person had been playing a game of dice. That here was a victim who had marched towards the possibility of peril somehow, in some way, through their own decision-making. That there could have been an avoidance or a shift or an alternative or something, anything, that would have changed the tragic but inevitable outcome.

It was not being cruel, although the truth could be. It came from statistics, from demonstrable observation both on and off the job, from probability, from studies and experts and science.

Science was the basis of all fact, and fact was the foundation of truth.

And truth was the enemy of evil.

Chapter 28

Along with Kate, almost the entire town of Waterford attended the funeral of Julie Crawford. The Waterford Presbyterian Church, right across from the elegant Penmarvian Retirement Home on Grand River Street North, was packed.

Dressed in suitably proper attire — plain black slacks, low-heeled dress shoes, and a simple white blouse — Kate was now standing in front of the old red brick Romanesque revival building, camera slung diagonally across her chest and resting in the crook of her elbow, pen and paper in hand. She picked a spot where she was shielded from the bright sun by the church spire.

The hard concrete sidewalk was already killing her feet. She really wanted her runners. But they could wait until things were done. It would be an easy way to end a hard day.

The other media were still inside the building, writing notes, conducting interviews, taking photos of the service. Kate was done with all that. She had carefully shot the interior scenes without a flash, telephoto lens full out and the ISO bumped up to eight hundred. She had held the camera perfectly still, bracing her shoulder against a pillar, snapping panoramic shots of the attendees from the balcony over the sanctuary, carefully ensuring she wasn't blocking anyone's view. She managed to get good photos of most of the people there looking at the minister at the front of the room. And she hadn't disturbed anyone.

She was glad to be back outside where there was a heck of a lot more fresh air.

Speakers had broadcast the service to a crowd on the front lawn where even more people sat on rows of folding chairs between the sidewalk and the church. Some stood to one side.

The minister had talked about Julie's untimely death. A kind and beautiful young woman who was snatched away in the prime of life in a sudden and most tragic manner. He spoke of her commitment to family and her two young daughters, her support for her husband and her loyalty to his business and customers. He lauded her work ethic and community service. How she managed to do her job at the store, and still be a good neighbour and friend, a mother, a wife, a loyal church goer, a volunteer.

She managed to squeeze a lot into her days, Kate had thought.

He talked about her love and devotion to her parents. Her gentle soul, her happy nature. "We all have benefited from her strength, her warmth, and her compassion," the reverend intoned. "And we can all take inspiration from her faith and courage, and hope they will sustain us in the loss of this very special wonderful young woman who touched so many of us in the community. May God rest her soul."

It was all so true. Kate felt tears well up in her eyes and she wiped at them with a tissue she had folded into her pocket for that very purpose.

She was embarrassingly soft-hearted, Kate was, one of her most private weaknesses. She turned her head away and stared at the ground to hide her eyes. And when Marshall's parents, the elderly Mr. and Mrs. Crawford, stepped into the church's doorway with Emma and Sarah, then back inside again to shield them from the coffin entourage, it was all Kate could do to hold it together.

But in a minute Kate was yanked back out of her grief.

There was Chelsea Darling, right at the foot of the church walkway, in her standard uniform of short skirt and high heels.

It would have been nice if that skirt covered more of that butt. But at least it was black.

Kate shook her head.

Six men including Marshall, awkwardly carried the casket down the steps of the church and over to the hearse. Chelsea snapped her camera shutter every five seconds, it seemed, oblivious to the people behind her craning their necks.

The church began to empty out. After watching for a short time, Kate carefully circumnavigated the throng and walked the sidewalk a short distance to where it ascended onto a hill. Looking back towards the church, she was struck at the view. It was just past one o'clock and the sun was high, illuminating the panorama. The front lawn was filled with people and chairs and hugging and sadness and yet so much support. It was one of the finer things about a small town, a rural community: people reaching out to their friends and neighbours, giving solace at a time of need.

She snapped the shutter a few times, carefully framing her shot.

Finally, Marshall emerged from the church once again, standing in front of the crowd. He had retrieved the girls. He held Emma in one arm, and linked to Sarah with the other. He paused momentarily and looked up at the distant sky. Suddenly, Chelsea was there once again, and only a few feet away. The scene seemed staged perfectly to tug the hardest at one's heartstrings. She snapped her shutter wildly, then quickly departed.

Huh, Kate thought. *Chelsea's timing had been impeccable.*

Marshall spoke with friends and neighbours, thanking them for coming.

A shiny black limousine waited for him at the curb, all set to lead the procession to the cemetery. His parents were in another vehicle, ready for the children. He dropped off the girls, made his way to the limo, and the door slammed shut.

The whole sad ordeal was coming to an end. Kate breathed a sigh of relief. The throng dispersed and she walked back to the car, puffy-faced. The burial would be off-limits to everyone but close family members.

She would go straight to the office and start processing photos.

Was she being too cynical thinking that shot with Chelsea had been staged by Marshall for the benefit of *The Waterford Reporter*?

No one would do that at the funeral of their own wife.

Would they?

Chapter 29

DAYTIME BREAK AND ENTER
WATERFORD POLICE DEPARTMENT |
Posted on 2001-09-13 | Print View

(Waterford, ON.) –
 On September 10, 2001, members of the Waterford Police Department (WPD) responded to a report of a daytime break, enter and theft on Broadway Street West, Waterford.
 The culprit(s) trespassed and accessed the home by breaching the front door. Once inside, the culprit(s) stole jewelry.
 Residents of Waterford are reminded to immediately report suspicious vehicles and persons to police by calling 9-1-1.
 If anyone has information about this incident, they are asked to contact Constable Leonard Kowalchuk at the Waterford Police Department at 519-447-1000. Or to remain anonymous, call Crime Stoppers and you will be eligible for a cash award.

- 30 -

Chapter 30

Kate considered her camera her best friend, a digital Nikon D1 with a state-of-the-art 400 millimetre telephoto zoom lens and a 5.3 megapixel sensor. It had auto focus, shot three frames per second, and had the remarkable ability to get sharp pictures in low light without a flash.

Gone were the days of lugging around heavy flash assemblies with batteries and more batteries, only to produce photos with distracting shadows, necessitating tedious cropping and burning around figures by hand in the darkroom.

The D1 made it easy to bring along a camera all the time. Its vibration reduction feature was a significant advantage. No more anxiety about having perfectly steady hands when she pressed the shutter. It meant that she could stop at accident scenes and fires and take a picture with a quick in and out, before the powers-that-be could get to her and deny access. She could shoot a casual event turned into a universal moment before anyone could pause to re-arrange their faces. There was no opening of canisters, no winding rolls of film onto tiny sprockets only to hear the celluloid snap off at the first shot. Or worse, not to hear it snap off at all, then to take pictures that never actually made it onto the film. That was an unmitigated disaster. And it had happened more than once in the old days. A whole day's work for nothing.

There was no forgetting the small fact that the camera and lens had cost her three thousand dollars, a king's ransom. It meant no long distance birding trips, no unnecessary spending on reference books and birding gear, and nearly uninterrupted working for an entire year. It almost killed her.

But the camera did not disapppoint.

It never lied. It never confused. It had no motive. Its memory was flawless. It could be relied upon every minute of every day and every night for its service. And it always told an interesting story full of useful and straightforward information.

It had been worth every penny.

If only humans would aim to be more camera-like, Kate sometimes thought. *The world would be a much better place.*

Chapter 31

There were the photos from the funeral, previewed on the computer screen with her new cutting-edge photo editing software. Something called Photoshop.

Kate scanned through a few dozen shots. Some were simply the backs of peoples' heads with the church service taking place just beyond. *Now why did I take those,* she thought. *Last ditch shots in case I needed them, I suppose.* Insurance shots.

She recognized most of the people in the photos: shop owners and their families, church members, neighbours. An older couple, likely Marshall's parents, sat on the front pew of the church, to one side. Marshall, the girls, and some of Marshall's friends occupied the rest of the pew. *Odd,* Kate thought. *There's something not right about that scene.* She couldn't quite put her finger on it.

Then after a second or two — *just a minute. Where were Julie's parents?* Surely all the immediate family members would have sat together. Still, Kate couldn't locate any couple who would obviously be Julie's parents.

She scanned through a few more interior shots, then went to pictures of the crowd coming out of the church. One of the first to leave and, she suspected, one of the last to arrive at the service was a white-haired man in a baggy brown suit from the eighties, steered about in a wheelchair by a stout middle-aged woman. A bandaid on the side of his forehead.

There was an unfamiliar heavy-set man in his forties in a dress tunic with shoulder epaulets and silver buttons. He was barely visible in the angle of the shot, mostly hidden behind the people in front of him. He had curiously large heavy eyebrows.

Kate went to the next couple of shots that shifted the angle slightly, and got a better look at that man. Dark hair cut short, like a cop. But those epaulets reminded her of something. She zoomed in on the lettering and made out B.E.S. Belleview Emergency Services. A paramedic.

There were her neighbours, the Hacketts, with Sam and Conner. Stu and Moira must have taken the morning off work. What were they doing there? Maybe Stu and Marshall were friends. He had so many of them.

Finally, there was a photo that stood out from the rest, that gave one pause.

There was always one photo that stood head and shoulders above the rest. Always. It was rarely planned in advance or with much precision or even intention, but nevertheless there it was, a shot that made one's eyebrows shoot up. It was called photographer's luck.

It captured a special moment. It told a story far beyond the margins of the image. It was aesthetically balanced and drew the viewer into the scene. There was something in it that was compelling, that made you slow down and take a closer look and think oh, so that's the way it was. Yes. I see.

It was a long shot taken from the sidewalk above the church looking down at the scene. There was the church with the open doors, the congregation flowing down the steps and onto the front lawn. There was Marshall staying behind, chatting with friends, framed in the doorway. On the grass in front of the church, Mr. and Mrs. Crawford leaning over Emma and Sarah. There were rows of newly emptied chairs on the lawn. There were the men and women off to one side, dabbing at their eyes and blowing their noses.

The shadows from the chairs made a sort of box around the Crawfords and the girls, segregating them from the small groups off to the side. The girls' faces were turned up to meet the concerned gazes of their grandparents. Confused. Innocent.

There was the old man in the wheelchair, off to one side, watching the scene with great sadness.

There was the harsh late summer sun angling down like a knife blade, shading the lawn, illuminating the players in the tableau like a Greek frieze.

That was the money shot.

It was a go for the front page.

Chapter 32

What I was doing was scandalous. I had to pinch myself at night when I thought about it. Me, of all people.

Who would have thought that we could be a couple. I daydreamed about it constantly.

But you know, in some ways we were the same. We shared so many simple things. The things that mattered. I felt so free, so at ease.

He made me feel so good, so whole. Complete. He liked *me*. A lot. Not just for the way I looked. For the way I was. For myself.

He could be sensitive and charming. That's not the way he normally acted around people. Just around me. He never once used a swear word in front of me. Never. Always polite. And considerate. I really liked that.

I loved to just think about him.

He had a beautiful body.

Slim but muscled. Soft smooth skin, all over. A line of hairs leading to his private parts.

So sweet. He'd bring me little presents. A little cake. An antique necklace. A precious little silvery dragonfly with spread wings and a long thin body. He said he bought it at a thrift store.

It was beautiful. I loved wearing it. He knew I loved old things. Unlike my own man, who never asked me what I liked. Ever.

And never touched me the way I liked. Ever.

There was nothing more delicious than stealing a secret hour in the bedroom, feeling his hands on me, feeling his softness, his hardness, lying against his body, feeling its gentle warmth. Like the warmth of the Ambien. It was a piece of heaven.

We went to a photobooth one day and clowned around in front of the camera. Maybe it was silly but I was proud to wear the dragonfly necklace. I loved those pictures. I kept a bunch of them in my purse all the time. I'd pull them out and stare at them and get that same feeling,

over and over, seeing us both together like that.
I was reborn.
Surely, God could forgive me for having such happiness.
I have found the one whom my soul loves, Solomon said.

Chapter 33

Dear Editor:
  Thank you for several years of enjoyable reading in your newspaper. We have recently moved to another area, so we no longer need the coverage your publication provides. Thank you again for many years of excellent reporting. Sincerely, Sam Harrison.

Hello Sam.
Thank you for the kind words. You're very welcome.

Dear Editor:
  Your article on the sale of my beautiful historical home was plain nasty. It was negative and all your facts where wrong. When we talked I asked you to send me a copy, but you didn't. Waterford as a community is being lead down the garden path by your half-baked facts and figures. Your rabid need to be negative with the town does a lot of harm and you should be ashamed of yourself. Jacob Bingley

Hello Jacob.
It's LED down, not LEAD down, you witless turd.

  Kate chuckled. She tapped "quit." The message would lay for eternity in the ethereal miasma of draft emails and responses never sent.

Chapter 34

Some researchers and people with Asperger's Syndrome have advocated that society should shift its attitude. Asperger's was a different approach to life, rather than a disability that must be treated or cured.

In one sense, Asperger's was a way of effectively dealing with the sensory overload of the wide world, a way of categorizing phenomena in the most essential of scientific or mathematical terms, no better and no worse than any other way.

One expert wrote in defence of Asperger's: In the social world, there is no great benefit to having a precise eye for detail. But in the world of math, computing, cataloging, music, linguistics, engineering, and science, an eye for detail can be of enormous benefit.

That was precisely the way Kate felt.

Chapter 35

He was so sweet and kind. He opened his heart to me. He was mixed up in some crazy things, he said, things he regretted. But he couldn't go back. He was in too deep.

It worried me. Why was he doing those things? Why was he with those people? They would ruin his life. He could still get out if he wanted. All he had to do was try.

He just shook his head.

"But you have a choice," I said. "Follow your heart. Do the right thing. You can't live like this. Remember, God is on your side."

I offered to help. I said I would go to the police and tell them the whole story. That he was misled. That it wasn't his fault. That he wanted out.

But it was no good. He wouldn't listen.

I think that was when he started to pull away. I could feel it. The pain was agonizing.

Then the whole thing went downhill.

He got rid of him a week or two later. He found out somehow. I'm not sure how.

Then the kid showed up. Took over the deliveries, did the routes, picked up the shipments. Chores around the store.

And not too long after that: How about you and me, you know, get together, you know, like you did with … He would gaze at me lewdly as I totaled up the sales for the day, his stare following my body from head to foot. How about it? You're a young woman, I'm a young buck, we should do something. Why not? Maybe you can teach me a few things. What do you think? Grinning.

The message was, it was his turn now.

I was outraged. I ignored him, prayed he would just go away. I stared down at the rows of numbers, red-faced. Trembling.

Instead he moved closer. He put his palm on my rear end.

I whipped around and slapped his hand away, hard. He stood there with his hand in the air, grinning.

"Don't you dare touch me. You little punk. Don't you ever do that again, do you hear me? Or you'll be sorry. I know everything about you. Everything!"

He faked an injury to his hand, shaking it from the wrist like I'd hurt him. Grinning. "What's the matter?" he said. "I heard you liked that. I heard you liked Xanax, too. Well I got some. Want some?"

I began to shake with fury.

Just then the door opened and a customer walked in. I choked back my outrage, straightened my spine, and stretched the bottom of my face into a tight smile. Out of the corner of my eye I could see the kid walking out the back door, but not without raising his eyebrows questioningly and gesturing with his head.

I slammed the back door and locked it shut.

I hated him.

The kid was not to be trusted in any way. I didn't like him going near me. I didn't like him going near the cash register. I didn't want him in the store at all. I complained to my husband, not that I thought it would do any good.

"Don't worry, I'll keep an eye on him," was all he said.

"But why do you need to have him around at all? He's just trouble. Big trouble."

"Let me worry about that, okay?"

He was probably glad to see me suffer.

Chapter 36

Few things in life give a person more pleasure than the company of a good friend. To laugh at the same jokes, to talk about the same people, to dip in and out of each other's lives updating the general progress of things and watching with a sympathetic eye — that was all you could ask for from a person.

Kate was basking in that luxury at Waterford's Riverview restaurant, waiting for the arrival of Dorothy Ambush, whom Kate had known for many years, ever since she had put out her sign for *The Tecumseh Challenge*.

Dorothy Lugansky Ambush was half Russian, something Kate shared along with the blunt ironic stoicism of the Slavs. And the sarcasm, too. They had hit it off right away.

The Riverview was a medium-sized dining establishment on Grand River Street North with a wonderful view from a glassed-in balcony that jutted out over the Grand River. It was the ideal location to sip a frothy cappuccino in big, wide white china cups sprinkled with nutmeg and cinnamon, the best in the county, made by Stavros Papadopoulos, the handsome curly-haired restaurant owner with the distinctive broken nose.

Kate was sure she knew how he got it. His winning personality.

She settled into a seat at the window and observed that summer was surely departing. Nevertheless, it would not be disappointing to leave behind its suffocating heat.

Beside the river bank were hints of fall colour: small streaks of yellow in the birches and the rough mixed earth tones of ragweed, goldenrod, and Queen Anne's Lace.

Steve called out to Kate from the bar where he was polishing glasses. "How are you today? You look like you've been standing on a corner all day."

Kate plastered a fake smile on her face and waved.

Francesco, the waiter, grinned and winked, and swiftly brought over ice water and linen napkins. She caught his glance, widened her eyes in mock outrage, and shook her head. *The things I put up with from advertisers,* was the look on her face.

In the background, Kate could hear Stavros levering up the Faema.

"Cappuccino?" Francesco asked.

"Please."

Dorothy, on the other hand, would make a point of giving Stavros his due. Being sixty-six years old, she had a right to. Kate could hardly wait.

Dorothy, short and stout, scurried through the door and eyeballed the room. When she spied Kate sitting at their usual table at the back, she waved and chuckled. Steve nodded towards Kate's table and said: "You have a woman waiting for you, Dorothy. The newspaper lady."

Dorothy leaned over the bar. "I hope you have lots of that moussaka next weekend. It's my favourite. The spices are just perfect. But last time I had supper, the kitchen ran out."

"Yes Dorothy. Dear," Stavros replied, rolling his r's. "We slaughtered a big fat lamb so that we could make a very big moussaka this week, just for you."

"Good man," Dorothy said, and she shook her finger and said something about, "and make sure it's hot this time, too."

Kate winced, waiting for what was to come.

Stavros kept polishing glasses without missing a beat. "Yes madam, I will make sure I sit on it so that it's nice and warm when you get it."

Kate rolled her eyes. *Here we go.*

"Now Stavros, you behave," Dorothy said. "We're some of your best customers."

Thankfully before Stavros could say anything more, Dorothy trundled over to their table and seated herself.

"Hello Dorothy. How are you this afternoon?"

"Hello my dear, hello hello." Dorothy had dressed for the occasion. Jewellery sparkled on her hands and ear lobes. She unwrapped a silk scarf from around her neck and blew out her cheeks. Waved at the air in front of her face. Chortled with laughter. "Hot flash. Just wait till you get to be my age, kiddo."

She took off her coat, draped it over the back of the chair, and pulled in closer to the table.

Francesco placed Kate's cappuccino on the table. "For you, madam, as well?" He looked at Dorothy.

"Sure, Francesco." Then to Kate: "How goes the battle, dear?"

"Argh." Kate waved her hands in the air in a crazed gesture. "Everything gets so busy in the fall ... all at once ... and everyone ignores my deadlines all over again. Same old story."

Dorothy clucked sympathetically. "But think of the money you're making, my dear," and she leaned over and laid a comforting hand on Kate's arm. "You're a good businesswoman and you've got a successful product. You should be proud of yourself. A young female entrepreneur."

"Yeah, if only I was rich too. Then it would all actually make some sense." Kate sipped her cappuccino, and the cinnamon and bitterness of the coffee mixed on her palate like a song. The tension of the day melted away.

"Life doesn't make sense," Dorothy said. "Most of the time. Trust me, I'm an old lady. I know these things."

Francesco slipped another cappuccino on the table and she took a sip.

"Mmmm." Dorothy smacked her lips. "Catherine's on a reorganizing blitz again. Everybody's worried about their job. And so am I, although I have to say, I've got the bedding department pretty cleaned up these days. A lot of compliments from the customers. Catherine pays attention to stuff like that."

"Yeah," from Kate. "That's nice. Good for you, Dorothy." She would let her chatter on. It was so very soothing to hear the ins and outs of Dorothy's days.

Dorothy, semi-retired for about a decade, had struggles of her own. It was hard to make ends meet on a pension. She had been working part-time for a few years at a local craft store for extra money. But there was the roof. The furnace. The car. And the many, many tchotchkes that called her name. Her living room resembled a gift store. Or the main aisle of the Sally Ann.

"And the roof is leaking in the bathroom, again," Dorothy wailed. "Just when I got it fixed. I'm going to call that guy and give him an earful. I paid him good money for that. Money doesn't grow on trees, you know."

Money money money, Kate thought. *The world revolves around little rectangles of coloured paper. Is that why we're born? To chase paper?*

Francesco arrived with their meals: quiche and a Greek salad for Dorothy and smoked salmon on a Greek salad for Kate. Their lunch order never changed.

"Everything okay with you ladies?" Stavros came out from behind the bar.

"Perfect, thanks," Kate said.

"Your friend the mayor was here yesterday, having lunch in the back room. Big secret meeting. With the government."

"Really? Was it hush hush?" she asked disingenuously. You never knew what you could pry out of Stavros, given the right question at the right time.

"Who knows." He shrugged. "They looked like the secret service. Or the cops. All short hair." He brushed the side of his hand against his neck to show just how short.

"No liquor, just steaks and ginger ale. How's someone supposed to make a living around here?" He threw up his hands in despair.

"The restaurant business is a tough business," Dorothy said. "I know how hard you work. And look how well you're doing." She waved her hand around the room with its plush chairs, mahogany tables, and steel and glass accents. "You've got a wonderful place here, Stavros. It's the nicest restaurant in town."

Thanks, Dorothy, pour it on. I need it. Kate gave her a little thank-you nod and turned to Stavros.

"Any changes to your ad this month?"

"Eh? The ad? Not a single call. I don't know why I bother," Stavros said. "You should run it for free. Why don't you get rid of the front page picture and put my ad there instead."

"What?" Kate said with alarm. "I can't do that. Didn't you get a response? I saw a ton of people here last weekend."

"Dead. Like a dead dink. But call me for the next issue. I want to make some changes."

The phone rang and he was off like a shot to take a reservation.

Kate looked distressed. An ad without a response was a catastrophe.

"I was sure the restaurant was packed last weekend," she whispered to Dorothy.

"Ach, the guy's just riding your ass." Dorothy waved her hand dismissively. "Wants a free ad."

Kate rolled her eyes and relaxed a trifle. "Geez. I always take stuff like that so seriously."

"The guy's a prick," Dorothy said in a low voice. "And a bullshitter. But I like him. Don't ask me why."

"And he's got one hell of a Greek salad." She chortled and stabbed a Kalamata with her fork.

Chapter 37

Crack is worse than cocaine because it hits the system in less than ten seconds. The cocaine base is boiled and the rock is taken out, cut up, and sold.

The high lasts five or ten seconds, then decreases when you exhale.

After that first time, I never got as high again. And then I was always in a cranky mood. Tired, jittery. Never comfortable. Clenching my jaw and grinding my teeth. The more I smoked, the worse I felt. Miserable really.

Days and nights became the same scenario, played over and over. The only way to feel good again was to smoke more crack.

I really wanted to stop. *Really* wanted to. Because everything became a big mess. A big fucking mess.

Chapter 38

POLICE CHECK UNCOVERS DRUGS, WEAPONS
WATERFORD POLICE DEPARTMENT I
Posted on 2001-09-14 I Print View

(Waterford, ON.) –

At approximately 9:00 p.m. on Friday, September 14th, 2001, a vehicle on William Street attracted the attention of Waterford Police with a traffic violation.

Officers stopped the 1992 Ford Focus and saw evidence of drugs in plain view.

Police investigated and conducted a vehicle search. They uncovered 125 grams of marijuana, narcotics, housebreaking tools, weapons, and a large sum of Canadian money.

Greg Malloy, 21, of Tecumseh County was charged with driving without insurance, one count of Possession of Schedule III Narcotics for the Purpose of Trafficking, two counts of Possession of Schedule II Narcotics, one count of Possession of Schedule II Narcotics for the Purpose of Trafficking, and Possession of a Controlled Substance.

The investigation is continuing, and any witnesses or anyone with information relating to this incident are encouraged to contact Constable Leonard Kowalchuk at the Waterford Police Department at 519-447-1000 or visit CrimeStoppers.ca.

- 30 -

Chapter 39

"Hey, did you see that picture of the funeral in *The Reporter*? That girl, the one from the men's store. Marshall's wife."

"Julie Crawford." Kate asked. "She was a friend of mine."

"Oh dear, that's too bad." Dorothy put her hand over Kate's. "I'm so sorry, Kate. What a shame."

"Horrible."

"*The Reporter* showed a picture of the casket and another one with Marshall and the two little girls."

"Yeah, I saw it."

"Oh my gosh Kate," and Dorothy reached out again. "I cried when I saw that picture with those two little girls. No more mama. Poor things."

Kate knew exactly how and when that photo was taken. But she said, "Heartbreaking. Julie loved those girls a lot."

"I didn't know she was thirty-three. She looked a lot younger than that. Like a teenager. Did you read the article? About how Julie died?"

"Yeah, I read it."

"She had depression. Committed suicide."

Kate gave Dorothy a look. "That's what Marshall said. Maybe that's what he wanted everyone to think."

Dorothy paused. "I thought the police said that."

"That did not come from the police. That came from Chelsea Darling. I asked the police about that very thing. They said it was an error in *The Waterford Reporter*. Chelsea's assumption. And she put it into print. That's terrible."

"Really?" Dorothy looked confused for a moment. "Are you sure about all that?"

"Absolutely positive."

"Hmm. Well, that's strange."

"More than just strange." There was silence for that to sink in.

"Are you saying collusion?" Dorothy said. She chased a morsel of quiche with her fork.

"I think Marshall had something to do with Julie's death, and he might have wanted to throw out a red herring."

Dorothy successfully speared the quiche morsel with a jolt.

"Whoa, really? Hold on. Maybe you're accusing him because you don't like him." She gently wagged her finger at Kate. "Pre-judgement."

Kate nodded. "It's true. I think he's full of shit."

"I don't know why you hate him so much. Marsh is so good-looking." Dorothy shivered and from her lips came a little "ooh." She grinned.

Kate shook her head. "You, on the other hand, are pre-judging him because you have a crush on him."

Dorothy mouthed "nooooo" but she was still smiling. She raised a forkful of crust to her mouth.

"But that's exactly it. People give him a lot of leeway, people are completely swept off their feet, and he takes advantage. And I have yet to see him do something that didn't benefit him directly."

"Maybe," Dorothy mumbled through a mouthful of food. "But he is active in the community. You've got to give him credit for that."

"I do," Kate said. "But it's hard."

"Whenever I've been at his store, he's been charming as heck."

"Yeah, he specializes in that. But charm is only skin deep."

Dorothy chuckled. "But it sure is nice for an old lady like me."

"Dorothy, he's had affairs with other women. Including Chelsea Darling."

Dorothy's eyebrows shot to the top of her forehead.

"Eh? What do you mean? Why didn't you tell me?"

"I'm telling you now."

* * *

Kate first bumped into Chelsea a few months after she started *The Challenge* and had familiarized herself with all aspects of the competition. She had yet to meet them face to face.

She envied *The Reporter* for its overwhelming number of ads. She had heard all about Chelsea's fabulous customer base and how she went to high school with all the people in Waterford who were now her loyal customers and readers.

It was impossible for Kate, an out-of-towner, to compete. So she made her living from the rest of the county.

Chelsea was a masterful name-dropper and her chatty grammar-bereft editorials were popular, particularly with the younger crowd.

Kate was not overly impressed. Being chatty was one thing, but being a journalist was another.

She had no idea how Chelsea had managed to keep Marshall so long as a customer. But she found out the day she walked into the shop, turned to close the door, and was nearly steamrollered by a petite flouncy woman trying to leave at the same time. In the confusion, a purse smacked Kate in the behind.

For just an instant, Kate took in the bright red lipstick and the low-cut silky top, the child-like blue eyes, and the red hair.

"It's you. Just get out of my way," Kate heard the woman mutter. For some reason, she seemed to know exactly who Kate was. But Kate didn't know that woman. She didn't want to know that woman.

"Tsk," the woman said. Then she let the door fall back almost snagging Kate's foot, and traipsed away down the street.

Kate hopped into the store, barely escaping being mauled by the dangerously sharp corner of the door. She whipped around to see if Marshall had witnessed the encounter. He was leaning over, busy with a tissue around his mouth. He hadn't gotten it all. From the corner of his lip streaked a tiny bit of red lipstick.

Uh-oh, she thought.

"Who the heck was that?" she asked Marshall. He didn't answer, and looked none too happy at being interrupted. Kate saw the latest copy of *The Reporter* lying on the display counter and put two and two together.

"Anyway ... I thought I'd bring down my rate card today. Would you be interested in advertising in *The Challenge*? We have a special deal going on."

Marshall threw the tissue in the garbage and began to fidget with paperwork. Glanced up quickly, then: "Sorry, I've set my budget for the year."

Now that was distressing. The last time Kate was there, he had actually indicated some interest. Had he not meant it? Was he now saying that he had changed his mind for some reason? Had she misunderstood? She decided to push back.

"But we directly cover your customer base. And we're not expensive."

"I'm sorry, but I changed my mind. Actually, we don't really need to advertise. Everyone knows I'm here."

"But not in the county. You advertise with Chelsea Darling and *The Waterford Reporter* but they don't go out there. In fact, they barely even cover the news in Waterford. But I do with my paper," she exclaimed.

He looked up.

"That paper is a joke," she added. Kate faltered even while she forged ahead. "No one even reads it. You're wasting your money with her." She knew it was probably a mistake to openly disparage the competition, but it was too late to turn back.

He paused, and Kate thought he was reconsidering. But she was wrong. The charming Marshall had built up a head of steam that was about to be uncorked.

"Look, what I do with Chelsea Darling and *The Reporter* is none of your fucking business, okay? None whatsoever."

Her eyes popped a little. She felt her face go pink.

"The answer is no. It will always be no. Why do you keep on hounding me?"

Kate flinched.

"I've got a busy afternoon with lots to do. Okay? End of story," he said, striding towards the door of the shop and waving her through. The glass practically slammed against the back of her head.

What the hell.

After that, it was impossible to ever think of Marshall with anything other than distaste and resentment. He had rattled her confidence — what little there was of it — for months. She didn't need that. Not at all.

Years later when Kate finally met Julie, she saw that Marshall's sizable ads continued to be a regular feature in *The Reporter.* Against all odds.

* * *

"So that's what happened," Kate said. "And I still notice Chelsea in and out of Marshall's store on a regular basis."

Dorothy was eying her. "But maybe there's a perfectly good reason for that."

"Maybe. But there have been other things, too. And a weird thing about Julie's funeral. Nobody seemed to notice, but Julie's parents weren't there," Kate said. "There must have been a darn good reason. I bet they knew exactly what Marshall was like."

"Marshall Crawford is an asshole."

Kate and Dorothy jerked with a start. It was Stavros. He was standing right there. They exchanged a look. How the heck did he sneak up on them so quietly? Did he attach pillows to his shoes or what?

"Hello!" Dorothy said. "Private conversation."

Stavros continued as if he hadn't heard.

"I live on this street," he said. "Over the restaurant. I see what goes on."

"What goes on?" Kate asked.

"That girl at the coffee shop. She used to work for me as a waitress. Terrible waitress. Terrible. She lasted two months. Two months. Then she didn't show up for work. Didn't even call. The little bitch."

"Okay, Stavros, okay," Dorothy said, palm in the air staving off the rest. "What about that girl? What are you saying?"

"You know, her and Marshall." Steve jerked his index finger in and out of a closed fist. "Screwing around. At night. In the morning. The store is closed."

Kate and Dorothy, mouths gaping, exchanged looks. They tried to decide whether they were more shocked by the crude gesture, or by what Stavros was actually saying.

"How do you know?" Kate finally said. "Did you actually see them together?"

"Ha ha. Look, why would she knock on his door wearing practically no clothes. Looking like a whore."

Kate winced.

"Well, maybe they're just friends. Maybe that girl is a relative. Maybe she did some after hours shopping."

Stavros gave her a look of complete disdain. "I'm not stupid you know. And that woman, his wife, the classy one, what's her name."

"Julie."

"Julie. She found out. She showed up one night, late. Caught them."

"How do you know?"

"I heard them fighting. Like cat and dog. I was sitting on the upstairs balcony. I could hear everything. It was his fault, the whole thing. He should have been happy with that Julie. The knockers on her!" He flicked his finger and thumb against his mouth and made a kissing sound. "And two kids too. He was so stupid. And now she's dead. Suicide. Why? For what? For that asshole? What a waste."

A moment or two passed while the women mustered an effort to interpret Stavros' lavishly descriptive commentary.

It struck Kate that Stavros probably saw a lot of what went on in the downtown. His opinion might well be based on years of observation. On the other hand, he probably liked to indulge in melodrama as much as anyone.

"What do you think, Stavros? Do you think she actually did commit suicide?" she asked.

"Sure she did. She went for a walk before the store opened and never came back. I saw her."

The two women took in the statement. Then something occurred to Kate.

"Stavros. Why do you think that was the day she committed suicide? What day was that?"

"It was Monday for sure. I remember because on Monday I open the door at six thirty, early, to get the deliveries after the weekend.

"I saw Julie crossing the bridge on William Street. Look." He went to the window and pointed north. "You can see the bridge from here. She was wearing black shorts and a yellow top and running shoes. You know, exercise clothes. Tight."

Dorothy caught her glance and rolled her eyes ever so slightly. *Not surprised he remembered what she was wearing.*

" I didn't see her come back. Marshall was in the store. The light was on. It wasn't open though. No sidewalk sign. The next day she wasn't in the store all day. That's not like what she always did. She would take her breaks and eat her lunch beside the river. Always. Always always always. And then the next day she wasn't there any more, just like that. Look. I can see the back of the store from here."

He placed the side of his head almost flat against the glass window and peered the other way, south. "Come here. You can see it too."

Kate and Dorothy rose from the table and obediently looked in the direction indicated. He was right. They could plainly see the small deck at the back of Marshalls Mens Apparel.

He paused. "Some cake, ladies? I'll send Francesco over with the dessert menu."

"No thanks, Stavros, just the bill please," said Dorothy. It was ditto for Kate. Dessert was too expensive. And unnecessarily fattening when just as much energy at a much lower glycemic index and a much higher lipoprotein value could be attained from eating nuts and fruit. The latter of which was waiting for her at home in a dish on the counter, as always.

"I'm going to get to the bottom of this, one way or the other," Kate told Dorothy after Steve disappeared into his office. "Julie was a friend. She was a good person. She didn't deserve to die."

"But even Stavros said it was suicide," Dorothy said.

Kate's look of skepticism was off the charts. Dorothy registered.

"Okay, okay. We're talking about Stavros here. But how accurate can you be without proof?"

"Only Locard's Principle can determine what really happened. I want to give it a try."

Francesco was on his way with the bill. Dorothy fished out a bill from her wallet and Kate laid a credit card on the table. Francesco left to get the portable credit card machine.

"Whoa girl, you're way ahead of me. Locard's Principle. What's Locard's Principle?" "Locard's exchange principle. Two objects in contact will always transfer material to one other. It's the basis of forensic science. Science always tells the story of what happened. With everything. Who or what was where, when, and how. All it takes is a properly done investigation."

"You mean by you? What? Kate, you're not a professional. You're heading into dangerous territory. How in the world will you do an investigation? You'll get in the way of the police. They won't like you interfering. Besides, they've already buried her. What are you going to do about that?"

"I have a few ideas. And according to Kowalchuk, the police aren't conducting an investigation. So I will. Something drastic needs to be done. Urgently."

"Kate, girl, cool heads. Experienced professionals have handled this already. They know what they're doing. Surely. And who the heck is Kowalchuk?"

"Kowalchuk is my contact in the Waterford Police Department. I think they've been schmoozed by Marshall too."

Dorothy gave her a straight look. "There's all kinds of things that could have happened besides murder. You don't know all the circumstances."

Kate nodded. "Absolutely correct. And that's exactly what I intend to find out. For Julie's sake. And for the sake of those two little girls you saw in that photo."

Dorothy shook her head and put her hand on Kate's arm.

"Kate dear, be careful."

"Aren't I always?"

Chapter 40

"*It spans a space of 780 feet, and the railway track at its summit is ninety feet above the river. It is built of iron and wood-work, on the Howe truss principle. There is 140 feet distance between each of its pillars of massive stone. It was built by Mr. Farrell, from the plans of a Mr. Wallace, of Buffalo. By one of those exceptional escapes which sometimes occur to baffle the common sense of experience, the builder, Mr. Farrell, while walking on the summit, lost his footing and fell 90 feet down into the river, and, except for a few days' confinement, was unharmed.*"

*The History of the County of Tecumseh, Ontario: containing a
history of the County, its townships, towns, schools, churches, etc.
— By J.H. Weir & Co. 1884*

Chapter 41

It was an exceedingly warm day for the seventeenth of September when Kate found herself driving towards the trails near the river where she had, in the past, taken so many restorative runs in the forest.

She glanced at the towering elevated train bridge straddling the Grand River in the heart of Waterford: three massive stone piers supporting a criss-cross of heavy cast iron beams.

Stories abounded how some — on a dare or inebriated or otherwise — would walk the entire length of the river crossing, emerging from the shrubbery on the other side. Kids liked to climb the rough sides of the elevated tracks off Portland Street, and would head down the tracks as far as they could before turning around and running back from whence they came.

It wasn't hard for kids to access the bridge. All they had to do was clamber up the bank near the walking trail. Or make a small detour near the cemetery. Could have been the way Julie had climbed onto the tracks, Kate surmised.

It was close to noon. There were few shadows in any direction, and the warmth of the day was steadily climbing to a peak. On a Monday, there was little chance that she would meet up with dog walkers, strollers, runners, or anyone else.

That was the advantage of having your own business, she thought. Maybe the only one. You could do things on days when most people were away at work. All kinds of things.

She followed Willow Street and carefully watched the side of the road for an access laneway. Walnut Street appeared and almost immediately intersected with Portland. She took the narrow road its entire length, and finally up a perilously steep incline where there couldn't have been enough room to pass an oncoming vehicle. The stone passageway under the tracks passed on the left, and a small section of road led into the parking area beside the Waterford Cemetery.

She packed the camera and binoculars into a knapsack, slipped the shoulder straps over her arms and groaned. Damned heavy.

She jammed on her hat, placed large protective sunglasses over her eyeglasses, and squinted into the distance, trying to calculate the length of the walk. The sun high in the sky burned the back of her neck as she took the short distance down Portland Street. To one side, ruts cut through shrubs and trees into an elevation that carried the train tracks. She ducked into a narrow path that looked less steep, scrambled over loose gravel, and with the help of a few sumacs and weeds solidly rooted in the ground, pulled herself and the knapsack up and onto the train tracks. Dusted off her palms.

The view was enchanting, even two hundred metres away from the river. The far end of the tracks was sheltered from view by treetops tinged with colour.

According to the schedule, the next passenger train was three hours away. She was pretty sure there was only one freight train. Much later.

But nevertheless, her heart beat a little quickly. Had she ever heard a train horn blaring in the early afternoon? She could not seem to recall any such sound until perhaps mid-afternoon when the first dinner-time commuters passed through. It was a worry. If she had to, could she quickly scramble off the tracks without injuring herself?

She retrieved the binoculars and viewed the edge of the tracks, sussing out the height and the sort of footing she might need for a quick exit. It seemed sufficient. The crushed gravel between the ties and the sides of the track was heavy and jagged and dotted with shards of what looked like black rock. Anthracite coal.

She took out the camera and recorded a series of photos from up close, right over to the other side of the river, using the full range of her telephoto lens, listening for distant rumbling the whole time. Then a series of photos of the length of track ahead.

There were no shadows, just the way she had planned. Not at mid-day.

She proceeded along the wooden ties, difficult because they were spaced too close together for comfortable walking. They were heavily stained and smelled of creosote. The sun was merciless and there was no relief from a pulsing wind. Dust filled the air at regular intervals.

Carelessly tossed candy bar wrappers and fast food containers littered the edges. Apparently other people had walked the tracks too, and recently. It gave Kate only the slightest feeling of security.

She reverted to taking two ties at a time, awkward but faster. The tracks rose higher and higher and soon she could see that the railway company had installed a metal guard rail at regular intervals on both sides. A safety measure for workers, and likely for daredevils too. The rail didn't look very sturdy, nor very high. Maybe three feet.

Within minutes the tracks broke through the trees. She found herself in the wide open air about six stories above ground. When she couldn't help but look down, her stomach lurched, and she realized she was right above Willow Street.

Two-metre long safety platforms could be seen off the side at four locations, allowing her to step off the tracks if needed. That was a relief.

She inched ahead, then picked up speed, looking to the left, then the right, then ahead for any signs of trouble. Then just like that she was over water. The breeze had picked up and the dank odour of the river hit her in the face like a wet towel. She was more than ninety feet above the river. Her heart pounded in her chest.

Marshall was right — the view was breathtaking. Upstream, the Grand River flowed around a bend, limpid and green with algae. Trees, dead and living, obscured both banks. On a small grassy flat, a flag pinpointed one of the more scenic holes of the Waterford Golf and Country Club.

Looking down, the river was murky, frothing at the edges. The odd branch bobbed along in the current.

No train whistles. No rumbling. No traffic in the street behind her. Through the binoculars she could see a great blue heron poking around in the shallows.

She analyzed what lay adjacent to the bridge. To the right, the side furthest from town, was the parking lot of the elegant old Victorian Penmarvian mansion, a pricey retirement home. Even further up river, treetops massed to the edge of a precipitous drop-off to the water's edge. The spire of the Waterford Presbyterian Church stood out like a gatekeeper.

To the left, the rushing noise of a shallow waterfall came from an old Grand River Conservation Authority dam curving across the width of the watercourse. Then more foliage with just a few tiny views of backyard lawns.

Beyond and even further south, the riverbank sloped more gently up a short incline that was interrupted by a canoe launch, a couple of paths carved out to the water's edge, broken concrete, and patches of grass and weeds.

Then the William Street bridge and the town of Waterford stretched out like a toy village, the downtown bustling, and traffic stopped at the lights.

It all looked so orderly and civilized. And peaceful.

The camera emerged from the knapsack once again, and Kate steadied herself on one knee to take more photos — forward, behind, and to both sides. Down into the water and along both banks to the south where the current flowed downstream.

She looked ahead at the tracks before her. I bet it would take less than five minutes to cross the rest of that thing, she thought. If you had the nerve.

Kate knew she did not.

That was when she heard a distant train whistle. It took a second or two for it to sink in. Then the hairs on the back of her neck stood up.

Oh my God, it can't be. Oh my God.

I was sure Marshall said it was only mornings and evenings. And so did the train schedule.

Shit. Maybe it was an unscheduled freight train. How far away was it? Where was the nearest safety platform?

A break in the rail around two descending cast iron steps was five metres ahead. How far away was the bank behind her? She whipped around; the bank was visible some sixty metres away.

Before she could think twice, the rumble ascended, then there was the whine of metal against metal and she knew the train was imminent.

There was only one choice. She ran towards the roar as fast as she could.

The trestles became launching strips. She sprinted to a break in the guardrail.

The whine transmuted into a scream and she leapt into the safety platform, striking her knee against the metal, crouching down with her arms over her head, shielding the camera with her body. With a bang, the train hit the connection between the track and the bridge, and Kate's stomach lurched simultaneously.

There was a monstrous roar. The squeal and bang of the clackity-clack of the wheels filled the air around her like an inferno. A hurricane wind pushed the stink of diesel and blasted past her head.

The conductor pulled the horn, enveloping Kate in a whirlwind of misery and anguish and she wanted to scream and cry, anything, anything to stop the horn. Anything.

Peace, joy, serenity. Peace, joy, serenity.

She just couldn't focus. The rickety little platform vibrated and jerked with every bump and clack of the wheels and Kate prayed the old cast iron wouldn't jar loose.

Your bag of tricks. Immediately. Concentrate.

She listed all the prime numbers to one hundred. She recited the Periodic Table from the left. Group One, the alkali metals: hydrogen, lithium, sodium, potassium, rubidium, caesium, francium. Group Two, the alkaline earth metals: beryllium, magnesium, calcium, strontrium, barium, radium. The new ones she could never remember: darmstadtium, roentgenium, coperni ….

And just when it seemed that the roar and the screeching and the dust and the blaring of the horn would never end, suddenly it did, and a numb emptiness dropped like a load of bricks. The train was gone with a grimy cloud of offence and pollution, just as speedily as it had arrived.

Kate stayed perfectly still for just a second and waited for the trembling to stop. Her ears rang and throbbed and she knew she was covered in dirt and debris.

She could hear the waterfall gushing downstream.

She stood up, brushed herself off, and looking into the far distance, caught the faint glimpse of the tail end of a caboose.

Oh my God. I'm going to get myself killed. What the heck am I doing here?

Sliding the camera into the knapsack, she clambered back onto the track and ran its length, stumbling a little over Willow Street. She met the embankment where she had seen a little path. She descended the rutted stone track sideways using stems and weeds to stabilize her footing until finally, untidily, she slid to ground level.

Her clothing was soaked in sweat and layered with dirt and dust.

She walked the short length of Portland Street back to her car, uphill as it were, in the scorching heat. Her knee hurt like hell. Nevertheless it felt wonderful to have solid ground beneath her feet once again.

If someone had seen her on the bridge crossing Willow Street, she speculated, there might be police waiting to meet her.

Apparently no one had. There were no cops. She was lucky.

She took a deep breath.

The pictures will tell the story.

She drove back home, spent. The safe feeling of being back in her own familiar vehicle was overwhelming. And when she got home and washed all the dirt out of her hair and off her skin, the feeling of cleanliness and renewal was a comfort.

It had been a long and arduous afternoon.

Hopefully, a useful one.

Chapter 42

The long shots of train tracks were unnerving, even in the photos.

Kate was holding an ice pack to her knee in an attempt to lower the swelling. She hadn't dared look at the colour of the bruise.

The tracks hovered in mid-air, it seemed, nine stories above the river.

The view was magnificent, all the more so for its dangerous vantage point. Especially if the viewer was the reckless type, Kate thought. A teenager or a crazy thrill-seeker.

Sure, there was a guide rail along the sides, and the small emergency decks gave the impression of security. But the view of the tracks compared to the bank on the other side, and the water below, sent a chill down one's spine.

It must have been terrifying for Julie.

It certainly was not the choice for a walk with family on a nice summer day. The risk would have been extremely daunting.

What on earth would have driven her to go there?

Kate scanned the shots of the river and magnified the photos segment by segment. About forty metres down river from the bridge on the east bank, a trail of crushed vegetation to the water's edge spoke of the rescue attempt by emergency services. There was not much to look at: multiple overlapping footprints from heavy boots in small sections of mud beside the water. A couple of skid marks and tire ruts in the bank showed where someone had slid a gurney to an ambulance.

That must have been where they picked up Julie's body.

Across the water at the bridge just below Penmarvian, Kate could see another area, almost vertical, where the bank was scarred.

Now that's interesting. I wonder what went on there?

She enlarged the image but could not see much more than crushed weeds and bruised ground. A small clump of tansy to one side. Above, the bank was almost a sheer drop.

I'd love to pay a visit to that part of the riverbank. But how?

She shut down the computer and sat on the backyard deck with her ice pack, Alfred at her feet. A cup of chilled orange pekoe sat to one side while she stared at nothing and thought about nothing.

Miles Davis on the trumpet soothingly flowed from the CD player inside.

A part of her brain ticked away all by itself, piecing things together, looking at this then at that, imperceptibly filing away possibilities.

Slowly, a picture was being drawn.

Chapter 43

In Korean, "tae kwon" is translated as kicking and punching, and "do" means the path to enlightenment.

Taekwondo, whose roots go back to fourth century A.D. Chinese Buddhism, is not simply a matter of physical conditioning, and kicking and punching in self defence. It is mental training and philosophical study. It is a way of life, a means of achieving a peaceful spiritual existence based on harmony between the self and nature.

The martial art offers a philosophy by which the student can rid themselves of the ego and live as one with the universe, aligning with the forces of nature, and solving life's problems with serene contemplation.

— Choi Ung Lee, The Art and Mastery of Taekwondo

* * *

The evening was perfect for a leisurely run before sunset — plus thirteen, a little wind, overcast, no glare. Kate would have to hurry before night fell.

She donned a pair of shorts, thick athletic socks, a quick dry shirt, sports bra, jacket. Her running shoes were equipped with orthotic inserts for over-pronation.

After precisely twenty minutes of stretching and Pilates, she drove to the Preservation Park trailhead which joined the paths along the Grand River with adjacent fields and forest. No one was there. She breathed a sigh of relief.

Kate performed a few passive Taekwondo extensions, gradually extending her muscles until their limitations could be felt. She stretched her ankles, her hamstrings, her hips, her waist, her shoulders, her neck.

She held each stretch for thirty seconds. She gingerly stretched her sore knee. She was hoping some exercise would help it regain proper mobility.

She performed some side extensions, jumping jacks, straddle splits — increasing her blood flow and preparing her body for movement. Then she set off along a worn path through a weedy field alongside a series of retention ponds, home to a fascinating array of insects, plants, and animals. She had photographed and studied many of them for her private journals.

When she passed through the opening in the first clump of trees, the air grew silent and still, then just like that, the world was transformed.

Within seconds the noise of the road was a faint memory and all she could hear was her own breath in and out, running shoes softly sinking into the woodchip path, arms swishing against the sides of the nylon running jacket.

A straight narrow path took her through pine trees. Then, there it was, the first bit of challenge on the trail, the inclined clay mound that led to the boardwalk, a slippery bit of business in the mud of dusk. She took it at a slow sideways clamber, and the long winding boardwalk was hers.

It was her favourite part of the trail system, the boardwalk built by a stream of volunteers a few summers ago, transversing the maple, birch, and cedar wetlands for about half a kilometre.

The gloom had deepened considerably within the forest proper and she strained her eyes to ensure nothing had fallen on the wooden boards that might cause a trip and a fall. Suddenly she noticed that yes indeed, a plump dark object could be seen ahead, slowly progressing forward. Immediately, she knew what it was and her pace slackened. She jogged on the spot while the animal did its best to scurry along.

It was a porcupine. She had seen it many a time on her forest runs, blunt nosed, slow, clumsy, dragging its heavy burden of white-tipped quills like a monk's cowl. Kate gave a small, three-note whistle to let the animal know it was her and to hopefully somewhat reduce its panic. It relaxed and slowed its frantic pace, glancing over a shoulder before slipping over the edge of the boardwalk and onto the forest floor.

Kate gave it a couple of minutes of breathing room before resuming her pace. She wanted to see it safely up a tree or under a pile of branches. And sure enough, there it was in the crook of a tree branch not far off the ground, already gnawing on a pine cone. It didn't even glance in her direction as she continued along, and that was fine with her. The porcupine didn't consider her important. That's the way it should be, she noted with satisfaction.

The boardwalk ended at the other side of the forest and Kate burst into the open where the path tracked up a short hill and onto the level floor of a wide walking trail that followed the edge of the woods for another kilometre. It was the least enjoyable section of the run, exposed to wind at all times. When the sun dropped below the horizon behind her, Kate carried on, descending into the gloom of the forest once again and barely able to make out the trail unwinding before her like the thread off a spool. She picked up the pace and after about ten minutes of negotiating turns and skipping over roots, she broke into the open air again, at a set of abandoned farmers fields, austere and somber in the rapidly advancing nightfall. A full moon rose in the sky.

One day in May, she had spent a few hours tracking down the bleating of a recently born fawn and along a little deer trail in this section, there it lay on the ground, legs fully tucked under, half hidden in the shade of ferns, bawling for its mother like a goat. Without touching the sweet-smelling creature, she leaned over and shushed it, settling it down with sheltering motions, and it curled up and fell asleep. Kate still remembered the relief that had washed over her.

Then she was back in the forest again, a short distance through gnarled cedars and their treacherous twisted old roots, then straight rows of evenly-spaced pines, yet another boardwalk, and soon it was the final stretch through a patch of shrubs. There it was: the last length of maple swamp and the final rise to the trailhead, backlit like a welcoming beacon.

Then she saw them.

A group of three men, all in deep shadow, jackets hanging carelessly open, heads together, leaning over something at chin height. A flash of light, then one of the men blew out smoke. Something was passed around, bigger than a cigarette. A pipe.

They completely blocked the route out of the forest.

She made a complete stop and as soon as she did, the night's chill began to leach into her sweaty clothes. She shivered. The forest behind her melted into pitch black and a cold lump of fear dropped into the pit of her stomach.

She quickly reviewed the topography of the area in her mind, searching for an alternate way out. Slowly and silently, she backed up, turned around, and retraced the last part of her route, stumbling and cursing under her breath more than once as she gingerly felt her way over roots and branches. In the dense section of cedars where it was inky black, she hunched over and took one step at a time, arms out for branches and tree trunks, fending off the smaller pieces. More than once an errant branch whipped her face and she swore out loud, knowing a sharp red line would be etched on her skin. Her bare legs pricked and itched from the tiny unseen thorns of cedar boughs.

After what seemed like an eternity, she was finally out of the cedars and stepping through swampy mud, gingerly tracking the edge of a small clearing. The full moon had risen high in the stars, pouring a silvery sheen on the landscape. A stroke of luck. Finally, she saw a tiny deer path, and one step at a time, she followed the twisty little trail, carefully feeling her way around hillocks and downed trees. Then miraculously she could hear traffic and she knew the road was not far off. She pushed aside fallen branches, ducked under boughs, and clambered over logs. Dewberry spikes tore at her exposed legs and the backs of her hands.

Finally, moonlight glistened on asphalt. She mounted the shoulder of the roadway and stamped her feet on the hard surface to shake off as much mud as possible. She rubbed the circulation back into chilled, scraped, scratched-up legs, wincing and scowling.

The rest of the way was a sprint to the parking lot to finally see her lonely car and no other vehicle. She was overcome by both relief and fear that someone could yet show up in the parking lot.

The Audi started on the first turn, another stroke of luck. Kate cranked up the heat and sat for a few minutes, rubbing her legs back and forth, trying to warm up. As soon as the shivering slowed, she reversed the car out of the parking spot, and onto the road.

She wasn't sure if she would ever feel safe running in the forest again.

Chapter 44

It was still warm a few days later when Kate made a point of visiting the clay and sand shelf on the east side of the Grand River where a handful of fishers in hip waders were tossing lines for smallmouth bass just above the dam. They stood in water about waist high. On the bank, a man wearing a camouflage cap and T-shirt was tying up a lure. Kate approached.

"Hello."

The man raised his head, surprised. "Hi there."

"I was wondering ... can you tell me how deep the river is on the other side?"

The man looked like he wasn't sure what he just heard, then glanced over his shoulder to where Kate was pointing. "Well ... I'd say that's about as deep as it normally gets this time of the year," he said, nodding at the two men up to their thighs in the water. "The water's down some after those heavy rains. It's not too bad."

"And the river bottom. Is it safe to walk along it towards the train bridge?"

The man pursed his lips. "Yeah, pretty safe, when I was there yesterday. Why? Gonna try your luck?" He smiled a little.

"I just want to cross the river wearing these ..." and she pulled out a pair of hip waders, men's size medium, from a plastic bag. His eyes widened ever so slightly.

"Anything I should know before I give it a shot?" she asked.

"Well gee, let me think," he said, scratching his head. "Okay. Just be careful with each step. Make sure your footing is secure every time," he said. "Wait, why don't you use this?" he said, handing her a tall sturdy walking stick. "Feel your way across and you'll be okay. Just leave it here when you go."

Kate grabbed the stick. It felt good in her hand. "Thanks," she said. "Much appreciated."

The man nodded and resumed fly tying, glancing back curiously at her over his shoulder every now and then.

Kate pulled the heavy rubber hipwaders over her shoes, her sore knee, her jeans, and hoisted the straps over her shoulders. Then she donned a knapsack and a baseball cap. Her camera was in a plastic bag in the knapsack which she wore backwards, on her chest, strapped high, where it could be hugged by an arm if necessary. The equipment could not get wet or it would be ruined.

"Step off that part," the man indicated, "and walk over to just above where those guys are. That's a pretty safe section." It was at least a hundred metres away. Not an insignificant distance to cross.

"Here goes nothing," she muttered to herself.

The first step landed in two feet of water plus a couple inches of oozing sludge. The water was warm and moving slowly, the current pushing against her boots with soft pressure.

Her knee, now bound in a tensor bandage, was still not in the best of shape, and the real pain didn't show up for a few days. But at least the knee was usable.

There was plenty of room between her knapsack and the water and she relaxed, stretching out with the stick. It went into the riverbed, and with the opposite foot, she took a small step.

The stick went into the water again. Two more steps. The water was green but not too turgid to mask the view of rocks and cement chunks lodged in the sludge. The stick, and more steps. Soon she was in the middle of the river. Kate paused on a sturdier patch of elevated riverbed, a mixture of gravel and pebbles. She turned and looked back at the man on the riverbank, and he gave her a thumbs up. She returned the gesture, moved forward, and soon met the opposite bank.

Moving directly against the current, Kate carefully felt her way along with the pole and the soles of her boots. A weed-tangled bicycle wheel was avoided. Plastic bags snagged on a branch. Stones and rocks. Sand and sludge. She searched for her landmark.

A short and gratefully uneventful time later and there it was. The clump of tansies.

She firmly lodged the stick between rocks and leaned it against the bank. One boot dug into the riverbed, the other braced against a rock. She leaned forward and peered at the ground angling up a few feet from her nose, and did a grid search.

There were the abrasions in the dirt, the broken weeds. But Kate did not rely on her vision alone. From a zippered pocket in the knapsack came a magnifying glass and another grid search of the ground. About eighteen inches up the bank she noticed what looked like a flood line.

Hmm. Unzipping the knapsack, she removed a sterile knife and scraped a sample of slimy dirt from below the flood line into a small plastic bag. The procedure was duplicated with soil above the flood line, except that Kate slightly tore the plastic just above the seal for extra identification. She checked that the bags were zipped securely closed before returning them to the knapsack.

Off to one side there was something glinting in the sun. She stood on her toes and leaned forward. And gasped. Muttered to herself. Shook her head.

She felt inside her knapsack and out came the camera. She snapped photos of the object in situ, time stamped. Double checked the photos in the camera display. Good.

The camera was returned to the knapsack, the compartment zipped up once again, and Kate re-crossed river, stick in hand. The fishermen were gone. There was no one there to ask her any nosy questions, she thought. *Thank goodness.*

She propped up the stick against a nearby tree, to hopefully be retrieved by the helpful fisherman on his next outing.

When she returned home to her computer and studied the photo of the mud-encrusted item in detail, the hairs stood up on the back of her neck. It was incontrovertible.

It was a silver earring in the shape of a heart.

And where the two sides met at the top, a tiny diamond.

Julie. How on earth did you end up there?

Chapter 45

Diatoms are single-celled microscopic algae that are dispersed throughout the watery environment and specific by type to light, pH, nutrient availability, and salinity. They have individualized hard glass-like silica cell walls that are resistant to decay and thus diagnostic over long periods of time, handy for species identification and forensic comparison.

The microscopic nature of diatoms assures their forensic potential as trace evidence. It is highly unlikely that a suspect would take into account the transfer of diatoms at a crime scene, thus enhancing their capacity to be recovered as evidence.

The presence of diatoms in a recovered body should be considered suspicious.

If a person is still alive when entering the water, and inhales water through the lungs and drowns, diatoms will enter through the lungs and be transported through the bloodstream to the brain, kidneys, and bone marrow. If a person is dead prior to entering the water, the circulation of diatoms to the organs is prevented.

When a body is recovered from water, and it is unclear whether the body entered the water ante-mortem or post-mortem, the presence of diatoms in the body tissues is diagnostic.

In drowning-related death cases, a correlation should be made between the diatoms extracted from bone marrow, liver, and lung samples and samples obtained in situ from the drowning medium.

Diatom analysis should be considered positive when the number of diatoms is above the established standard: 20 diatoms per 100 mililitres of pellet obtained from 10 grams of lung sample; and 50 diatoms from other organs.

— Forensic Biology Level II, by Aarav P. Banerjee, Division of Biology, State Forensic Science Laboratory, Ministry of Home Affairs, Government of Jharkhand, India

* * *

Kate let Alfred into the backyard, returned to the kitchen, and carefully unpacked the plastic bags from her knapsack. She held them up to the light then headed upstairs to the spare bedroom — a research library and a makeshift lab with a table and a lamp, a microscope, and a stool. The four walls of the room were lined with books on ornithology, biology, chemistry, botany, forensics, anatomy, medicine, agriculture, physiology, criminology, meteorology, climatology, history, law.

The compound microscope had a post with a camera attached, and connected to it was a computer screen. The area was lit by a fluorescent light in natural outdoor tones. Kate had devised the setup herself, after some rudimentary research on the internet.

She slid the protective plastic cover off the microscope. She donned latex gloves, and using a tiny sterile spoon, removed one millilitre of slimy soil from the bag without the torn plastic, dropping the sample into a glass tube stenciled with measurement lines. The tube was topped off with sterile water, then placed in a centrifuge and hand-cranked for a minute or two.

The supernatant was decanted, leaving any diatoms sticking to the bottom of the tube. A sample was placed on a slide, a few drops of distilled water were added as a medium, a slip cover placed over top with tweezers, and the slide set on the stage of the microscope.

On a sheet of paper she wrote "Bag 1 - Below Flood Line."

A bottom lightbulb was switched on, and the eyepiece revolved to one hundred times. Kate carefully lowered the eyepiece and did a quick scan through the lens. *Aha,* she whispered to herself. She switched to the four hundred times eyepiece, and resolved the focus.

Yes.

She left the stool, switched on the camera, and a blurry image appeared on the computer screen. It looked promising. The eyepiece was carefully focused until the shadows sharpened up. An array of shapes appeared — rods, circles, threads, and modified rectangles and triangles, and she searched for a representative sample. The mouse clicked and the screen was photographed.

She scanned the entire view and on the pad she wrote: Bacteria 3 clumps diplococci, 10 squiggly, 18 rods. Fungii 4 strands. Nemotodes

0. Protozoa 1 flagellete, 1 ciliate. Algae diatoms: round 34, elongated 5, worm with pinched ends 2, rectangular 3, double rectangular 3, short thread 5, sarcophagus shaped 38, oval 7, fat short earthworm shaped, shreddie-shaped 14.

She individually photographed all the diatoms she could find.

The contents of Bag 2 - Above Flood Line were sampled the same way. Bacteria 14 clumps diplococci, squiggly 3. Fungii 1 strand. Nematodes 0. Protozoa 2 flagellates. Algae Diatoms: elongated worm 72, worm with pinched ends 108, oval shaped with centre point 49.

Not very many different species of diatoms, Kate thought, *considering there were more than 100,000 in the world.* Pollen 2, silica and minerals 35, Springtail 1, Other 2. Pollen 0.

Three types of diatoms dominated the sample from the floodwater-soaked area of the riverbank. She photographed those as well.

She leaned back on the stool, arms crossed, and gazed blankly out the window.

She pulled *Freshwater Algae of North America* off the shelf and scanned the hundreds of diagrams.

Yes, there it is.

A very straight worm shape with pinched ends. *Fragilaria ulna.* And this one. She pointed at it with her index finger. A very straight worm shape, pinched ends, and an enlarged middle. *Fragilaria capucina.* Flipped through a few more pages. And this one too. Oval shaped with slightly pointed ends, and striations radiating slightly from a central axis. *Navicula minima.*

The collection of photographs was slid into two envelopes, one marked Bag 1 - Above Flood Line, the other Bag 2 - Below Flood Line.

Now. The weather patterns over the last month.

She knew just where to look: a government of Canada website that was occasionally perused to anticipate what types of winds might be blowing migrating birds in or out of the area, based on historical trends.

The Ministry of the Environment Daily Data Report for the City of Cambridge for the first twenty days of August 2001 was compared to the ten previous years. Two hundred and seven millimeters of precipitation compared to sixty-four. About three times average. A significant difference.

No wonder the Grand River had run so high up its banks, she thought. And no doubt, the Cambridge sewage treatment plant had overflowed as it sometimes did, releasing superfluous raw sewage and bacteria into the river. Which accounted for the excessive number of diatoms of only three select species.

She recalled the smell of all that excess the night at the parkette during the council meeting break.

Huh.

Things were starting to make sense.

Chapter 46

The next morning Kate woke early. She needed to get out of there. Let her mind work on things in the background.

She donned her birding gear, ate an apple while packing a lunch, and loaded the car. As she locked the house door with Alfred and his leash in one hand, she looked over to the road. The sun had spread a cold yellow light through the gnarled towering trees that lined High Street. The tinny sounds of breakfast-making and morning newscasts emanated from homes.

She would be leaving all of it behind. She sighed with pleasure.

Soon she was speeding through downtown Waterford, leaving the messy tangle of her life in her rear-view mirror. Her car mounted the King Edward Street hill to the main county road, then a few minutes later, rolled down the ramp to the highway. It was Highway 403, an arm of Highway 401, the six-lane highway that transported millions of vehicles a day from one end of the province to the other.

Alfred lay in his dog kennel on her back seat, sighing and emitting noxious gases at regular intervals.

She was headed to a small, mostly undiscovered nature sanctuary situated about half way between Long Point and Rondeau, opposite the cliff edge of Lake Erie.

Just before the highway signs announced the first exits for London, the Audi circled down a ramp and headed southbound through Elgin County, a mostly agricultural area still showing a few precious plots of pristine Carolinian woods and wetlands hugging the Catfish and Kettle creeks.

Solitude Nature Reserve was a treed parcel of land on the shoulder of Dexter Line that often escaped the notice of the birding community. It was close to the far more popular birding destination of Hawk Cliff with its parade of migrating raptors and unctuous raptor counters, and thus was mostly ignored. That was only one of the things Kate loved about it.

The Audi finally slid into the rough lot that prefaced the reserve. There was no sign of other visitors. A single set of tire ruts was faded and worn.

She let Alfred out of the car and around the first camping area for some fresh air, bladder relieving, and leg stretching. Then it was back into his kennel in the car.

"I'll be back in a few minutes," Kate told him. She would give him a good long walk before they left. The windows were left open a couple of inches but in any case, it wouldn't be a hot day.

She slung the binoculars diagonally over her chest on the way to the pond. She was on the hunt for odonata. It was a good time of the year to see some of the flashier, more exotic species of dragonflies with names evocative of the quiet, sheltered corners of still waters. Shadow darners. Pondhawks. Black saddlebags. Red saddlebags. Twelve-spotted skimmers. In the early fall, they all migrated south too, closely followed by ravenous migrating birds.

Her favourite part was near the beginning of the stonedust trail where a damp marsh blended with a tangle of low shrubs and fallen trees. In the dense thicket of buckthorn bushes and wild grapevines, small shapes slipped between the shadows and the sun, quick and nervous, emitting tiny sweet chirps. They were almost certainly tiny warblers wearing the drab colours of fall.

When she began to sort them all out, an insect helicoptered into view, facing her head-on. Kate froze in position and analyzed the colouration. It was a large, heavy dragonfly, bejeweled in blue and green, wings semi-transparent and edged with gold. It was just as curious about her as she was about it. It backed up, moved forward, then circled. When she turned to follow it with her eyes, it darted away then zoomed around to meet her in front. It zipped in close, then when she made an admiring chirrup, moved closer still, seemingly to tease. It hovered right in front of her face for a few seconds and she took in the huge ochre compound eyes and the bull's-eye marking the centre of his forehead, the signature identifier of a green darner.

Dragonflies had excellent vision and surely he was mirroring Kate's examination in multiples, seeing in colours that mere humans could not even begin to imagine. What did he think of the funny glass windows suspended in front of her eyes on the thin metal frame, she wondered. *What a curious thing,* he must be thinking. Since his two compound eyes gave him a viewing range of about 360 degrees, at the same time he was probably eyeing the bluets touching down on the waist-high Queen Anne's Lace nearby, and in the air behind him, other darners and pennants.

If only humans had that kind of vision.

But then again, Kate reminded herself, *we have tools for that. Like mirrors. And scopes. And cameras. And computer software.*

Within seconds, he had rattled off in an arcing flight that was almost faster than light, more concerned with repelling a rival than with the hypnotic gaze of a silly human being.

Kate could only marvel, knowing she would never see him again. His trip south was one way, covering about ten miles a day. It would be his winter-hatched offspring that would greet her the next May.

In the meantime, something flickered in her brain.

Wait a minute. The dragonfly necklace.

Now I remember where I saw it before. Moira. Moira had been wearing it. A couple of years ago. I'm certain of it.

And something else.

There was something she had neglected to check in the photos.

And it had to do with compound vision.

Chapter 47

Harvestfest, Waterford's biggest annual tourist draw, was the third Saturday in September and Kate's assignment was right downtown.

She had already decided that she wanted the petting zoo, taking place from two to four o'clock, for the front page of *The Challenge*. For one of the inside pages, there would be secondary photos of the colourful Harvestfest parade.

She placed her pre-packed camera bag in the car and set off to find a parking spot.

Downtown Grand River Street North was fenced off at both ends, and jammed with families, couples, squealing kids, smiling seniors, dogs on leashes, baby buggies, and the odd wheelchair. A more than slightly out-of-tune rock band bawled cover tunes on a flat-bed tractor trailer parked on the east side of the main street. Along the west side were lined up booths, displays, and food trucks.

Shop owners threw up their hands in resignation knowing their wares were no competition for the weekend's attractions, and lolled about on the sidewalk, exchanging pleasantries with passers-by.

The petting zoo was not far away in the municipal parking lot on Broadway Street West, also fenced off from traffic. It was roped off for a small carnival: bumper cars, a dunk tank raising money for the Waterford-Tecumseh Kiwanis Club, a bean bag toss, face painting, an old-fashioned merry-go-round, cotton candy.

The petting zoo was surrounded by a low rustic fence and anchored with bales of hay. The denizens — an arthritic goat, a miniature pony, dusty clucking chickens, a floppy-eared rabbit, and an obese woolly sheep — munched on treats and endured the sticky palms of dozens of impertinent children. They poked and prodded and wailed when the goat ate their ice cream or the wasps got tangled in their cotton candy, and Kate thought it was all just about perfect fodder for a good photo.

She had a funny feeling though, and held onto the Nikon hanging over her shoulder with a vice-like grip.

A blond, tousle-haired toddler in a red jumpsuit and a flowery yellow hat had just sat down on the pony. Kate headed for the parents and began her spiel.

"Hi, I'm Kate from *The Tecumseh Challenge.* Can I photograph your little girl for the ..."

Abruptly, someone stepped right in front of her, shoving her off balance.

What the ....

Kate was staring at the back of the head of an auburn-haired woman dressed in a tight miniskirt, heels, and big round sunglasses. The auburn hair had very dark roots, she noted.

Oh God. Chelsea Darling had not only walked right into her, but had managed to hip-check her camera at the same time. But the camera hadn't budged, thanks to Kate's steel grip, and Chelsea was rubbing her hip.

Hah, nice try, Godzilla. Better luck next time.

"Hello there, hello there! What an adorable little baby you have. How would you two like to be in *The Waterford Reporter?"*

Chelsea called out instructions on how people should look, ordered everyone around with suffocating authority, and snapped away with her camera, employing a flash that was completely useless in the stark September sunshine. A group had gathered to watch. There was lots of loud high-pitched, cloying commentary and fawning praise.

Kate edged her way out of the throng and stood back, scanning the petting zoo for another possibility.

There. She saw it.

A little boy, dressed in bright blue with a lime green oversized baseball cap, clutched the lop-eared bunny. The bunny was brown, Kate noticed, which wasn't great. But it would do. Mom wasn't dressed in black, thank goodness. Pink and blue. Fantastic. Wouldn't destroy her camera's white balance.

"Don't squeeze so hard," Mom admonished. "Here, Tyler, let me show you how to hold him." She rearranged his arms around the rabbit while Kate moved forward.

"Now that's an important lesson," Kate said with a grin.

"No kidding," the mom said, looking up with a smile. "Don't kill the pet bunny. Bunny wants to live another day."

Kate laughed. "How about if I take your picture for the next edition of *The Tecumseh Challenge*. Exactly in that position. With you moving the arms of your little boy around the bunny. It looks adorable."

The woman smiled. "Sure," she said. "My husband's going to love it."

"I'll mail you a copy of the paper," Kate said. "Just give me a minute and I'll take down your mailing address." She scribbled it down on the paper she had folded in her pocket beforehand.

She took a test shot, quickly set the camera settings to bright sunshine, and called out: "Smile, big smiles. Think how happy you'll be when this weekend is over with."

The woman laughed. "Moooom …" the little boy complained. She gave him a hug and there were smiles again.

Kate pressed the shutter more than a dozen times, focusing at various spots including the boy's face, the mom's face, and the clothing slightly below their faces.

You never knew exactly what the camera would read for the shot. It might overexpose for their faces. It might darken down to get colours. It would compensate for whatever conditions the settings dictated. A cloud moving over the sun, or a slight change in focus could change the parameters considerably.

And — it would impossible to predict which expression would reproduce the best. Their smiles ranged from broad to a slight curling of the lips and back to grins again, tempered by a bit of conversation. It all radically altered their faces and the shutter clunked away, taking it all in.

Something was bound to work out. Afterwards, she would study the shots in her office, and pick the best one.

She previewed the frames, saw a couple that seemed okay, and wrapped things up. "Thank you!" she called out and waved goodbye. They returned the gesture.

On Grand River Street North, the festival was still in high gear. But now, just beyond the edge of the pylons, floats for the Harvestfest parade were making their way down the hill, around the corner to

William Street, and across the river to the marshaling area at Syl Apps Arena. When the parade kicked off at four o'clock, the river crossing would be choked with floats and parade goers, effectively bisecting the town.

Kate frowned. The route had remained unchanged from last year. Once again, the downtown would be completely cut off from through traffic, a potentially fraught situation for emergency vehicles.

Why hadn't the police flagged it as unwise? They never seemed to pay attention to these things.

Last year, police had also halted traffic at the top end of town for four or five hours and diverted drivers to a lengthy and tedious river crossing some distance to the north in Glen Morris, adding half an hour onto people's drives.

It was certainly an inconvenience, but also a longstanding tradition that the town seemed to revel in. Imposing their small-town values on the busy lives of big-city commuters. As a former big city denizen, Kate got the message.

It was also a very stupid way to do things. The unnecessary aggravation was only one factor. What about the more important issue — safety?

How many editorials did she need to write about the municipality not providing an emergency through-route during festivals and parades. Some day they would pay the price, she had warned.

Kate tried to not think about all that, along with the crowds, the noise, the dust, and the heat, as she bided her time with everyone else, behind scattered rows of lawn chairs and an excited uproar awaiting the ramshackle floats and their hit-and-mostly-miss decorations.

It was not how she preferred to spend her time. After all, it was also a big fall raptor migration weekend. But there was very little choice. Too many local businesses were sponsoring floats and waiting to see which one would make the papers this year. Hopefully in *The Challenge* it would be one of her better advertisers, Kate thought. A little something extra for supporting the paper. It was the least she could do.

Kate was also keeping an eye on what was taking place on the other side of Grand River Street North.

Chelsea Darling was tottering in her high heels, red hair going all to hell in the blustery breeze as she pointed and encouraged in a falsetto about a dozen small children to stand together on the sidewalk. She backed onto the road, oblivious to traffic. She was shooting a straight lineup with as many bodies as possible.

Line 'em up and shoot.

Typical *Reporter* pap, Kate mused. It was the same for every edition. Reader butt-kissing junk.

And the parade had begun. Tractors of all types — antique, modern, middle-aged. Farmers were proud of them all. Hoppers, wagons, balers, tottering sprayers. Massive automated harvesters that barely fit the width of the roadway. Classic cars. Floats from the Lions Club, the Optimists, and the Kiwanis. Fall-themed decorated pickup trucks, carts, and wagons representing various downtown businesses.

Forward moved the usual stream of irreverent parade inclusions including a cart full of miniature clumsy clowns, a pink scarecrow, and a farmer with a jack-o-lantern head. Then a boom truck from the hydro department, a backhoe from the county's road department, and the police supervisor's vehicle complete with flashing cherries, high intensity four-ways, and Waterford Police Chief Bill Pound himself in the driver's seat. They all rounded the corner and ascended the Grand River Street North hill to the fairgrounds in the north end of town.

Kate could never understand why the police had to ride in the parade. It seemed like a terrible waste of expensive resources; community relations taken one step too far. What if there was an emergency, she had often thought. How the heck would that officer get out of the parade, or — and here she thought about her editorial again — get from one end of town to the other with the parade blocking the bridge right in the centre of town?

The vehicles continued to creep north up the Grand River Street North hill.

But suddenly, when the first side street was met, the police car came to halt. Chief Pound, red-faced and anxious, leapt out the driver's door, stood at the barricade and gestured to the crowd beyond, sitting in their chairs plugging the entrance to the street. There were confused looks, incredulous glances, then finally, as one, they rose and all the lawn chairs, the bags, the drinks and food, the coolers and sun shades, the kids' scooters and the leashed dogs, were cleared to one side. It took some measure of time, but finally the road was open. Pound jumped back into the car, and sped down the side street, lights still flashing.

Huh. Told you so.

In the meantime, she took advantage of the halted traffic to shoot the road from a side angle, capturing a colourful lineup of vehicles, floats, and equipment.

She scanned through the shots. There, that should do it. But she would stick around just in case something fabulous came up. Sometimes it did.

About fifteen minutes later when the last flatbed truck, antique car, and candy-tossing clown had disappeared up the hill, Sammy Scarecrow, the Harvestfest mascot, finally made a grand appearance in an antique fire truck. The crowd showed its appreciation with a roar; screaming kids, clapping adults, and whistles and cheers all round.

Cue Chelsea.

Sure enough, Chelsea ran right up to the truck's driver, proffering some animated gesticulating and a lot of red hair tossing, and had a short exchange with the old geezer who was only too happy to put the old vehicle into park. Sammy Scarecrow climbed down from his seat.

Kate groaned. Only Chelsea would have the nerve to put an actual stop to the Harvestfest parade to take a picture for the paper.

Chelsea yelled directions and pointed, and Sammy grabbed a toddler off the sidewalk and held her in his arm while standing in front of the fire truck. The toddler looked a bit shell-shocked.

Chelsea's flash went off like a machine gun blast.

"Guaranteed that shot's going to look like crap," Kate muttered. *She's shooting right into the sun. I can hardly wait to see the page one photo of next week's Reporter,* she thought. *No wait a minute, maybe I can.*

She shook her head and walked back to her car parked way back on a side street, sensible rubber-soled shoes gripping the sidewalk that lined the Grand River Street North hill. She felt good wearing those shoes.

She tried to feel sorry for Chelsea in her heels, but it was impossible.

Chapter 48

Back at the office, she dumped the shots off the camera card into preview mode and processed the most promising one. It went straight into a desktop file marked with the date of the next edition, then a sub-file labelled "final pics and cuts." She dug out the scrap of paper where she had written the names of the little boy and his mom, added their address to her mailing list, and typed up a quick cut line with their names. Added that to the same folder.

There, all done.

Kate sat back. She would have a quick meal, and there would still be enough time for a walk with Alfred.

She whistled. Alfred came running and nudged her leg with his head. She scratched him behind the ears and found the leash. They stood on the side porch for a minute while Kate fumbled for her key.

Darn, left it on the hook. She dropped the leash, left Alfred by himself on the porch, and returned to the kitchen. He would be fine for a minute or two.

The key wasn't there.

"Oh for gosh sakes," she muttered. *Maybe in the pocket of my shorts.*

When Kate finally opened the side door again to the porch, Alfred was nowhere to be seen. Sam's pink skateboard sat in the middle of her driveway. She put it against her neighbour's house behind the overflowing garbage cans, and lined it up beside the black longboard. They both fell sideways, and Kate lined them up again.

I hope they can find them here. Or maybe I hope they can't find them here.

"Alfred!" She called. Nothing. "Alfred!"

So much for reliability.

She walked out to the end of the driveway. There he was, buried nose-first in a thick tangle of morning glories climbing up the side of the house, working away at something. It couldn't be good.

"Alfred! What are you doing? Come here."

No reaction. Alfred was absorbed with something far more compelling than obedience.

"What the heck," she muttered, and pulled apart the vines to see what was going on.

"Alfred! What have you got here?" A running shoe completely covered in stinking muck. Alfred dragged it out to the driveway and looked up expectantly. Can I play with it?

"No, absolutely not. Alfred. Cripes, what a stench." Kate gingerly held one corner. "No wonder you found it." She extracted its match from behind some nearby lilies and held out both to compare. They were a pair.

Abruptly, there was the sound of a latch, followed by a few clicks. The Hackett's front door opened with a squeak. A tall heavy broad-shouldered short-haired woman stepped out and fumbled with her purse. Then she caught Kate's gaze with an undecipherable look.

"Hello, Moira."

"Yeah, hi."

"I found these beside the driveway. Don't they belong to one of the boys?"

Moira craned her neck for a look. Then: "Maybe." A pause. Then: "You know, I really didn't like your editorial last month."

"Which editorial?" Kate said warily.

Everyone always assumed Kate knew the exact thing they were pissed off about, and that she had written it specifically for that purpose. However, Kate wrote a lot of editorials. And pissed off a lot of different people in a lot of very different ways. How was she to know exactly which way she had pissed off Moira now?

"You know. The one on the Waterford Police Department. The 'best before' date thing."

"Oh. Right." She mentally reviewed what she had written, highlighted some of the more contentious parts, dug down, and prepared her usual defensive strategy, readying appropriate rebuttals in advance of the charge.

"Well, that's ridiculous," Moira continued. "Police departments do not have 'best before' dates. They're always improving their training and their procedures. Did you know that? Did you even ask the WPD before you wrote that?"

Kate raised an eyebrow. "I don't have to ask permission from the WPD before I write something," she said.

"Well, maybe you should cuz what you said was just bullshit. A lot of people in town like things exactly the way they are. There's no reason to bring in the OPP. They're from the city. Us country people don't like city people barging in and telling us what to do."

Kate remained silent. As someone who sometimes mentioned her Toronto roots, she knew that would apply to her too.

"My job depends on the WPD staying in Waterford. Do you understand that? You know I work dispatch at the department, don't you? I need that job. I need it to support my family."

There was a lull, convincing Kate to set aside her strategy in favour of steering clear of Moira's imminent profanity-laden temper tantrum, and taking the opportunity to bring up another topic that needed airing.

"Moira, while I have you here and just to change the subject a bit if I may, can I ask you to please ask your kids and their friends to stop parking in my driveway? It's disruptive and noisy. There are times when I need to get away in a hurry and when there's a vehicle blocking the way, I can't get out."

Moira glared. "Well, all you have to do is come to our door and ask."

That was irrational. Kate's blood pressure notched up. "Moira, I don't want to have to ask permission from the neighbours to use my own driveway. That's unacceptable. I live here. I work here. I need to be able to come and go when I need to."

"Oh for God's sake," Moira exclaimed. "Why do you have to make such a big deal about it? They're just kids. It's only for a minute or two."

"Moira, do you understand what I'm saying? I'm asking you people to not park in my driveway. At all. Ever. For any amount of time. I don't want to have to go to the police."

"Yeah, right. Well, you go ahead and go to the police," Moira said. "Doesn't worry me. I know everyone there anyway."

Kate was so angry, words evaded her. She reminded herself about who and what she was dealing with, and just to ignore the digs of a bully. At the same time, she realized from which branch of the family tree Sam and Conner had sourced their neanderthal-era tendencies.

She said: "Listen. I'm trying to get along with my neighbours. You're not. It's a two-way street. People have to cooperate."

"Whatever," Moira said. Kate glared, frustrated.

"Anyway, I just wanted to give you my opinion on your little newspaper. You don't know all the people in town. I've lived here a lot longer than you. You don't know what goes on around here."

"Yes. Well, thank you for your viewpoint."

Before Moira could retort, Kate held up the shoes. *Get it over with, and get out,* she told herself. The best strategy in a pinch.

"Look," Kate said. "Do you know who these belong to? I found them beside my house. They look like men's running shoes. Maybe they belong to Sam or Conner," she reiterated.

"What the hell were they doing beside your house?"

"How should I know? They don't belong to me. I'm asking you."

Obviously. Oh you horrible illogical woman.

Kate scratched the mud off the side of one shoe. "Red Nikes. It says Presto on the tongue. See?" she flipped them over. The soles of the shoes had a trendy pattern of rectangles, curves and waves, something that indicated the runners had probably cost a fortune.

The Hackett's front door opened and Conner poked out his blonder than blond head. "Mom, when's dinner?" Then, "Hey, those are my shoes! I was looking for them everywhere!"

"Take them," Kate said, passing them over. "Please. Be my guest." He grabbed them and the screen door slammed shut. "You're quite welcome," Kate said to the closed door.

Moira darted back inside her house. "Give me those," Kate heard her yelling. "They're garbage."

"You asshole," Kate heard Conner yell. "You wrecked my shoes!"

"I did not!" It was Sam. "They were already in the garbage!"

"You're lying! They weren't in the garbage. They were on the driveway next door. Why can't you keep your fucking hands off my fucking stuff!"

"I didn't touch your fucking stuff!"

"You always do, you moron!"

"Shut up! That's enough!" Moira shouted. "Shut the fuck up! Both of you! Now which one of you little bastards went through my jewellery box?"

Oh my God, what an insane asylum.

"C'mon, Alfred, let's get the heck out of here," Kate told Alfred, picking up his leash. He got to his feet and happily wagged his tail. Finally. You humans talk way too long. Waaay too long. And about stupid things, too, not surprisingly.

They headed to the sidewalk and off they went, Alfred's ears perking up, indicating he was already over any disappointment about having his stinky toys removed.

There was something about those shoes. Something familiar.

Kate sniffed her hand. What a God-awful smell.

When they got back, there they were once again, sitting on top of the Hackett's overflowing garbage bins at the side of the house, along with a Mickey Mouse T-shirt and a pair of jeans.

Hopefully, they would be out with the trash next week, Kate prayed.

In the meantime, they were stinking up the entire side yard.

Chapter 49

It was later that evening that Kate found herself randomly scanning through her photos once again, following up on her hunch from Solitude Nature Reserve.

It was the way that dragonfly had viewed the world. A 360-degree range. Multiple angles. Multiple viewpoints.

She thought about her photos of the railway bridge. She had tried to achieve a 360-degree range too, but one factor had been overlooked.

Point of view. A 360-degree view not *from* the bridge, but *of* the bridge.

The trek up the embankment and the nerve-racking procession down the railway tracks played through her mind.

The scene off the side of the bridge.

Was that Julie's last view before she toppled off the side?

Kate looked at a long view of the train bridge. It was impossible to know exactly where Julie had stood. You needed to have been right there. And the only other person who was right there, was the perpetrator. There were no other eye witnesses.

Or were there?

The three sisters of evidence. Forensics. Confession. An eye witness.

In the photos, the sun blazed so intensely that the sky appeared white, sending most of the greenery into black shade, something to which she had not paid much attention. She played with the shadow elimination feature of Photoshop, bringing out the background details and the colours of the ground. There was something greyish in the far distance behind all the trees, something the colour of dusty cement. She brought in that section of the photo for a close-up view.

Indeed that was it, the cement of a parking lot. Right beside a stately three-storey high yellow brick Victorian building with a turret overlooking the Grand River.

Penmarvian. Originally a modest building erected by Waterford founder Hiram Capron, then a refurbished nineteenth century mansion, a paean to Victorian-area industrial success by textile millionaire John Penman, one of Waterford's greatest industrialists and philanthropists. Now an elegant retirement home for a dozen well-to-do seniors.

She stood at the tall window that overlooked her driveway and faced the Hackett's yellow brick wall, a hunch manifesting at the periphery of her consciousness.

She would need to pay a visit.

Chapter 50

"There wasn't very many cops in those days and every now and then they'd send one up from Belleview. John Cruickshank was a policeman in Waterford and in the 1930s he'd patrol the whole town day and night, making sure people didn't act out of line. A lot of stuff was solved on the spot. He was on duty all the time and didn't have to go out much at night. There was no bad violence like there is now. They didn't have much trouble with drunks because they just got drunk and fell asleep somewhere. They didn't do any damage."

— Art Lishman, retired police officer,
Waterford Museum and Historical Society

It was morning, and Kate made her way downstairs to let Alfred out in the backyard, then straight to the office to check emails on the computer. The September twenty-eighth edition of *The Tecumseh Challenge* was soon due at the printer's.

While she scanned through the new email messages, the sound of garbage trucks droned and banged incessantly in the background, and she shuddered. Why were they taking so long today? Then she remembered they were handing out new raccoon-proof four-foot-tall wheeled green bins. She didn't actually need one, but perhaps she could find a good use for it.

She glanced out the window. There were two trucks making the rounds, and finally she saw her new bin standing at the end of her driveway. She grabbed her jacket, retrieved her blue and grey bins, then wheeled the new arrival to the end of the side yard beside the cedars. It wasn't the best place, but it would do for now.

She ate her even-days breakfast of oat bran, almond milk, and honey, supplemented with vitamins.

A low glycemic index. Yes, the honey was mostly fructose and glucose. But it also provided precious traces of enzymes, amino acids, vitamins B and C, minerals, and antioxidants, all of which were not efficiently supplied by any other food in that particular combination.

She first clicked on emails from addresses that looked familiar in a good way. Aha. Two ads. Exactly what she needed. Her spirits lifted. The ads needed to be designed and proofed, but they would bring her over the edge of loss and into the territory of profitability. She could breathe this month.

An email with a crime report from the Waterford police department flashed on screen. Kate copied and pasted the story into a waiting text file. Then started to read.

FROM/DE: Waterford Police Department
DATE: September 24, 2001

ROBBERY AT RESTAURANT |
WATERFORD POLICE DEPARTMENT |
Posted on 2001-09-24 | Print View

(Waterford, ON.) –

On Saturday September 22, 2001, Waterford Police investigated a report of a Robbery at a fast food outlet in Waterford. An unknown amount of money was removed by suspects. There were no injuries, and police believe the suspects used a vehicle to leave the scene.

"If anyone has information about this incident, they are asked to contact Constable Leonard Kowalchuk at the Waterford Detachment at 519-447-1000. Or to remain anonymous, call Crime Crime Stoppers and you will be eligible for a cash award.

- 30 -

Cripes, there wasn't much in the way of information. How did they expect reporters to write a story based on that miniscule set of facts?

She would try to get through to Kowalchuk. He occasionally offered snippets that helped round out the story. And in light of their friendly encounter the other night, he might be even more receptive.

She picked up the phone and got him right away.

Where did the robbery take place?

It was the fried chicken store in the south end of town.

"Do you have the time or any other details?" Kate asked. "Description of the suspects? That sort of thing?"

"Sorry, there's nothing more I can give you here," he said. He was being annoyingly closed-mouthed. And actually, more so than usual. *What the hell.*

"There aren't too many basic facts," Kate said.

"I know," Kowalchuk said.

There had been other times when the Waterford Police released as little information as possible, but in Kate's experience, it was either because the incident was so inconsequential that in reality there simply wasn't much information, or else the incident involved minors who could not be identified or linked to the incident in any way because of the requirements of the Young Offenders Act. Or if it was a major crime like a murder, perhaps there was a genuine shortage of suitable public facts.

The robbery seemed to neither qualify as relatively minor nor a Young Offenders Act situation, in her opinion.

There must be something else going on. But what?

"If you release a few more relevant details they might help people remember if they saw something at a certain time," she pushed. "Like what about the number of suspects and their descriptions. Or a description of the getaway vehicle."

"Sorry," he said, "we can't reveal details. We want viable witnesses to come to us with the correct information."

"I know. If you release too much information, it could taint evidence, making it inadmissible," she said, taking the other tack. This way, that way. She was trying from every direction.

"Right. We might not be able to get a conviction. You're with the media. You know all about that," he said. There was an uncomfortable silence while Kate waited to hear more, even a couple words more.

Nothing.

There was no point in hammering at it any more. Her time and patience had run out. She said thanks, goodbye, and clicked off the phone.

Yes, there was police procedure, she thought impatiently. But if the police didn't release enough information in the first place, there would never even be a trial. The media certainly understood the concept of jeopardizing evidence. But releasing even just a general time of day wouldn't prevent a fair trial. And it might help jog a few memories.

It took a bit of effort for Kate to bury her displeasure. But just before she was ready to go to print, something occurred to her. Maybe she could get some facts on her own.

She would give the Southern Fried Chicken people a call. It was not what she normally did. It could get her absolutely nowhere. It could rub the police the wrong way. It could alienate a potential advertiser who might not want the details of their bad luck publicized.

On the other hand, the store had never advertised with *The Challenge* in the past, so perhaps she really didn't have much to lose. It could be worth the effort. And the cops? She would take her chances.

She searched Southern Fried Chicken on the web to locate the owner's name. As luck would have it, there it was, on the website of the Waterford Business Association: Chuck Ferretti, owner and operator, Southern Fried Chicken, Dundas Street, Waterford.

Just as she rang the phone number of the store, something caught Kate's notice.

She glanced at her wall calendar.

Wasn't the robbery the same day as the Harvestfest parade?

Chapter 51

"**S**outhern Fried Chicken, how can I help you?"

It was eleven o'clock in the morning, a time when most restaurateurs were hard at it in the kitchen, prepping raw vegetables, organizing the supplies for the day, and pre-cooking anything and everything. Kate knew. She'd been in a few restaurant kitchens in her lifetime, summer jobs, then more recently, scribbling ad copy for restaurant owners too damn busy to email or come to the phone.

"Hello, is this Chuck Ferretti?"

"Yeah," the man said. "How can I help you?"

"Chuck, this is Kate Messenger from *The Tecumseh Challenge.* I'm calling about the robbery on September 22nd."

There was a small silence, but he didn't hang up. "What would you like to know?" Cautious, but nevertheless, giving her a chance. Maybe he was familiar with the paper.

"First of all, can you tell me what happened?"

Another silence. "Look, I don't know how much I should talk about this. But I can tell you, I wasn't very happy about the whole thing."

Her nose for news twitched.

"Why weren't you happy, if you don't mind me asking?"

"I don't know." He heaved a sigh. "Look. I'm getting ready for a big order right now. But I'll tell you that I wasn't happy with the way the police handled the whole thing."

"Really? What do you mean? Didn't the police ask you the right questions?"

"Hah," Chuck snorted. "I really wish that was the problem. The problem was, the bloody police weren't even there. For two hours. After calling 911. Then their stupid cruiser sat in front of the store for another hour before anyone even came in."

"Holy cow," Kate said. "What in the world was going on?"

"That's what I'd like to know," Chuck said. "Especially when one of the guys had me tied me up in the back room with a gun pointed at me. You know, one of those old-fashioned ones. Like out of a western. I could see Smith & Wesson engraved on the barrel, it was so close to my head."

"No!"

"The second guy had a knife."

"No!"

"They cleaned out my entire cash register and took off. Not the first time I've been robbed, but the first time with a gun."

"Oh my God," Kate said. "Were you okay? Did they hurt you?"

"Yeah, I'm okay. But at the time I was scared out of my mind," Chuck said. "I was working alone. I didn't know if those guys were coming back. I have a family. I wanted to see my kids again."

"Oh my God, absolutely," Kate said. "Did you lose much money?"

"Enough," he said. "A few thousand bucks. But look, I don't want that going into the paper. I don't want people to know how much I have in the till."

"Sure enough," Kate said. "Tell me though, how did you get hold of the phone to dial 911?"

"I didn't," Chuck said. "A walk-in customer heard me yelling in the back room. He said he saw their van speeding down King Edward Street on the way to the highway."

"Oh my goodness. Then after that it took police two hours to get there? Why?"

"You tell me," Chuck said. "That's the thing. That's what I'd really like to know. As a matter of fact, why don't you go and ask the police yourself? Maybe you'll have better luck than me. Because actually, now they won't talk to me any more. Geez, they probably could have caught the guys red-handed if they had moved their asses and got in here right away," he said. "In fact, that's what I told them."

Kate suspected there was a link between that and the police not returning his calls any more.

"What time were you robbed?"

"About three thirty. Just when business died down."

"Right before the Harvestfest Parade started."

"Exactly," Chuck said. "Exactly. Look, I gotta go, I gotta go now. If you need to call back, I'll be here after two."

Kate clicked off the phone. *Oh my goodness,* she thought. *The parade route* had *completely blocked off all of Waterford's emergency routes. Maybe the police should have paid more attention to my editorial.*

Then — it hit her like a ton of bricks — maybe, in fact, *the bad guys had thought: what a great idea.* The perfect time for a robbery, while the police were stuck somewhere in the downtown and couldn't get through the parade congestion.

Holy cow, I bet the police were blaming the whole thing on me. Oh my God.

She felt a trifle chagrined. But then again, how could she be at fault? If she hadn't thought of it, probably someone else would have, eventually. At least she had sent out a warning. It wasn't her fault if the police had ignored it.

Kate recalled the afternoon of the robbery. Chief Bill Pound was supervising the afternoon of the Harvestfest parade. She had seen him dash down the side street off Grand River Street North in his cruiser. not too long after five. She was pretty sure of that.

Maybe she would give him a call even though she knew exactly how far that would get her. But at least it would give them fair notice that questions needed to be answered.

Sure enough, no one at the police station would confirm the staff on duty that day — due to privacy slash personnel slash security-of-the-municipality blah blah blah. And Pound would not return any of her calls or emails. Not surprising at all.

She could say she tried to get a comment from police. That needed to be in the article somewhere.

In the meantime, the existing facts would be assembled for a front page story just in time to go to print for that month's edition of *The Tecumseh Challenge.*

"Hah," she said aloud.

What an amazing scoop.

Chapter 52

"Thieves get away after brazen hold-up," Kate had typed.
"A witness maintains that two men robbed the Southern Fried Chicken store in Waterford on Saturday, Sept. 22 and police are looking for the culprits.

"The robbery took place mid-afternoon. The source said two male suspects, one armed with a handgun and the other with a knife, escaped in a vehicle after the incident and headed north on King Edward Street.

"It took police more than two hours to arrive at the scene of the robbery, the witness maintained.

"Chuck Ferretti, store owner, condemned the delayed police response and said he had feared for his life. In an interview, he told *The Challenge* that he felt the suspects might have been nabbed if police had arrived at the scene of the crime more quickly.

"Ferretti said that the thieves cleaned out the till but declined to mention the amount stolen. He also said it was not the first time he had been targeted by robbers.

"He was slightly roughed up by the thieves but said that thankfully, he was left more or less uninjured.

"The incident took place at the same time as the Harvestfest parade in downtown Waterford. The parade travels through the centre of town and cuts off access between the north and south ends.

"Police did not return telephone or email inquiries from *The Challenge* about the incident by press time.

"The investigation is continuing, and any witnesses or anyone with information about this incident is encouraged to contact Constable Leonard Kowalchuk at the Waterford Police Department at 519-447-1000."

The next day on the website of *The Belleview Kernal:*

"Waterford Police responded to a robbery at the Southern Fried Chicken store on King Edward Street, Waterford during the afternoon of Oct. 6.

"Two armed suspects removed the day's proceeds from the till and fled. There were no injuries, and police believe the suspects used a vehicle to leave the scene, heading north on King Edward Street.

"Any witnesses or people with information are asked to contact Constable Leonard Kowalchuk at the Waterford Police Department at 519-447-1000. Or to remain anonymous, call Crime Stoppers to be eligible for a cash award."

www.belleviewdailyjournal.ca/2001/09/25/letters-to-the-editor-southern-fried-chicken

Reader's comments »
If you already have an account on this newspaper, you can login to the newspaper to add your comments. By adding a comment on the site, you accept our Terms and Conditions and our Netiquette Rules.

15 comments
Leave a message
Newest

Belleviewbound • 35 minutes ago

Let's be clear. The police showed up way after the bad guys got away. WAY after. It was already in The Challenge.

Muggingforthecamera • 2 hours ago

I own a store and I am considering hiring my own security guards. Maybe I will take my two HUGE sons with me for back-up. The police are too busy handing out seat belt violations and the like.
Reply › Share ›

Sunset Hill • 3 hours ago

Come on we know why no cops - Timmies' donuts just came out of oven.
Reply › Share ›

VictoriaBeckham • 3 hours ago

Its only money and your life is not worth risking or the trauma to your family, you are justified to think that. If you were a police officer, you'd think the same.
Reply › Share ›

Hockeyguy • 4 hours ago

Take Smith and Wesson with you for back up. They're about as good a backup you'll get around here.
Reply › Share ›

ContraryKate • 5 hours ago

The next time carry a .45 with you. Shoot the thief. Call the police. Bet the police will respond in a heartbeat, but to charge you.
Reply › Share ›

RockinRobin • 5 hours ago

If you had fired a bullet into the ground the cops would have been there in a nanosecond to arrest you. Oh, Canada.
Reply › Share ›

Plumberlarry • 5 hours ago

But reported crime is down? Oh right, because the cops can't be bothered to take the report.
Reply › Share ›

Ianaminute • 6 hours ago

Police are overpaid lazy donut-eating crybabies. Oh I have a high risk job. Well too bad, that's what you get paid for, to put your life on the line and even though no one got hurt this time, how about next time. Someone else can get hurt or even killed because they don't want to do their job. You bunch of pathetic hypocrites.
Reply › Share ›

Samspade • 7 hours ago
I had a coffee shop and a fight broke out inside. I called the police.

They said they were too busy answering calls. I said OK and hung up. Five minutes later I called back, said I shot them, and not to worry. They arrived promptly, arrested the fighters, and said to me, you said you shot them. I said yeah, and you said you were too busy to come. End of story.
Reply › Share ›

Painoftruth • 6 hours ago

When you're lying in a coffin, it's too late for the congratulatory handshake for protecting somebody's property.
Reply › Share ›

Bradpitt • 8 hours ago

Maybe it's time to replace police services in Canada with private security companies that follow orders and have a vested interest in upholding the law as well as protecting people and property. Police apathy is becoming absolutely ridiculous.
Reply › Share ›

Weightlifterwalter • 8 hours ago

Today we have 2 classes of police. The first are the ones who are big fellas who at one time were in good shape and eager to do a good job but had too many donuts. They are badly out of shape. Too much exposure to the dregs of humanity that inhabit many neighborhoods in this city has left them jaded. Then you have the newer fellas that are too small to have ever really qualified to be a cop and they spend every free minute at the gym but in the end they are still guys with a bad case of "little man syndrome" and basically cowards with guns. This is really sad and honestly I used to be a huge supporter of police but there is really nothing to support these days. The end result is that cops really can't be bothered to do their job any longer and the good people of the city suffer for it.
Reply › Share ›

Whynotme • 8 hours ago

And we pay taxes for what again?
Reply › Share ›

steve972 • 9 hours ago

  Had the same thing happen with one of our tractor trailers that had GPS. We arrived in the morning and found our truck was missing. Used the GPS log to see where the truck had been moved to. We were able to see that it had been driven from our yard to a local business stopped there for 20 min then continued on to a rural property and then the truck was returned and parked three blocks from our yard. We contacted the local business when they opened and told them our stolen truck had been in their yard, they went out to find three pieces of construction equip (worth over 250k) were missing. We called police and gave them all this info along with a roadmap to the rural property. When we contacted them three days later to see what was happening they acted surprised to hear from us as "we got our truck back." Turns out they never went to the rural property for over a week. By that time the equipment had most likely been loaded in a container and was on its way out of the country never to be seen again. Made us wonder why we even bothered reporting it.
Reply › Share ›

  On CPKP's News at Noon broadcast, Pete reported the robbery almost verbatim from the press release.
  "Peter, Peter," Kate murmured.
  That week in *The Waterford Deplorer:*

On Saturday October 6th Waterford Police were called to investigate a report of a robbery at Waterford's Southern Fried Chicken, a fast food outlet on King Edward Street. An unknown amount of money was removed by suspects who witnesses said were armed with a gun and a knife.

  In an interview with *The Reporter*, police said they responded quickly, ensured that the victims had no injuries, and secured the scene. They said they believed the suspects used a vehicle for their getaway and drove away down King Edward Street.

  If anyone has information about this incident, they are asked to contact Constable Leonard Kowalchuk at the Waterford Detachment at 519-447-1000. Or to remain anonymous, call Crime Stoppers and you will be eligible for a cash award.

"How do you know it was *down* King Edward Street," Kate muttered to herself. *Maybe it was up.*

She crumpled up the paper into a missile ball and lobbed it directly into the recycling bin.

Chapter 53

The sun was blazing through the south-facing window of her upstairs study.

Kate was sitting at her lab desk once again, studying diatoms. They were yellowish and ovoid-shaped, continually searching for bits of food as they steered through the brackish liquid medium. She watched them bump along, occasionally sweeping tiny microorganisms into mouth openings, sideswiped by long filaments of bacteria and round little rotifers that bounced off objects and bombed through the viewfinder like meteors.

Suddenly, a spikey long-legged water flea swept into view, poking one diatom in particular, following it, prodding its hard silica shell. The diatom was assailed wherever it went, stabbed and pummeled. It was having a hard time, that diatom.

Finally, it halted on the spot and began to expand, tossing the water flea out of its path, becoming bigger and bigger until it burst through the slide cover and escaped into the air, revolving in the sunlight and absorbing it until becoming part of the sun itself, then a brilliant glass orb that finally just drifted lazily into the corner of the ceiling and vibrated.

Kate stared, mouth gaping, hands gripping the armrests of her chair.

The orb gazed at her, benevolent, omniscient. It called her name. Kate was frozen in place, although she wanted to flee and hide, to not hear the orb or see it. Then she felt her body warmed through and through and she relaxed.

Kate, it called. *It's okay.* The orb dissolved into the face of someone she knew, with beautiful large sad eyes and dark curly hair. It was Julie.

Help me, Kate.

Kate wanted to say, Julie, I'm trying, I really am, but she was robbed of the power of speech.

Julie just smiled, a tender, loving, forgiving smile.

Don't give up, Kate, she said. Keep on looking. I left everything there for you.

She was shimmering a little, wavering.

It will be all right, she said. *Don't forget me Kate. Don't forget.*

Then just like that, Julie faded away and the light in the room grew brighter and brighter until it was almost blinding.

Kate's eyes popped open and the rays of morning light sliced under the blinds which for some reason she had forgotten to fully draw shut the night before. It shone directly into her eyes. She shielded her face from the light.

"Oh Julie, I really wish I could help you," she said aloud, and lay there under the sheet. Her eyes pricked with the wetness of tears.

She turned to look at the clock. Just before seven a.m. She slowly sat up and hung her feet over the edge of the bed. Buried her face in her hands. When she rose from her warm bed, the shock of the cold wooden floor cleared her mind only a little.

Something slammed shut beside her house.

She lifted the end of the window blind. A battered blue van with a bright red GMC logo idled in her driveway. Fuzzy dice hung from the rear view mirror,.

Oh my God, she said to herself. *Things never change around here.*

The driver, an emaciated young guy in ripped jeans and a ragged T-shirt too thin for the weather, stood at the Hackett's door, conversing with one of the boys.

Then Kate watched the van reverse out of her driveway, gravel spraying everywhere, and roar away down the street. Conner dashed out of the house, jumped into his souped-up pickup truck, and followed his acquaintance at top speed.

Off to no good, of course.

And in a hurry to do it.

She shook her head and went downstairs to let Alfred out the back door.

Chapter 54

"Constable Kowalchuk," Kate emailed. "I have some photos that you need to see. They have to do with Julie Crawford. You said if I had any useful information to let you know. Are you in the office today? Can I come in with my camera card?"

"Kate, I'll be at the detachment two to three."

Even though she had a ton of work piling up on her desk, Kate wanted to get those photos over to the Waterford police as soon as possible. She cancelled her list of tasks for the afternoon and arrived early at the former old post office building that served as the leaky, mouse-infested home of the Waterford Police Department.

She knew it was leaky and mouse-infested because the WPD had so often complained to council about it. They wanted a modern improved building closer to the town's many new subdivisions that were being built. Of course, it would be expensive. A new OPP building would come with provincial funding. A new WPD building would not. Another elephant in the council chambers that no one wanted to discuss, especially with Kate.

"Okay, what are these pictures you have?" Kowalchuk was sitting at a table in the building's dingy conference room, arms crossed, legs apart.

"They're on an SD card," she said. "Can I show you? I brought my own laptop in case you guys didn't want to insert a foreign card into your system."

"Sure," he said.

Kate searched for the nearest wall plug and set up her computer. Kowalchuk pulled up his chair. Kate tapped away at her keyboard. The smell of a guy working all day in a hot, sweaty uniform pricked her nose. She ignored it.

She clicked on a folder titled "Julie." Clicked on Riverbank-detail Sept 18 2001.jpg. It opened up to show a patch of earth holding a silver heart-shaped earring. The earring had a tiny diamond on the top.

"That's Julie's earring," she said.

A pause. "How do you know it's Julie's earring?"

She opened up another image. Her photo of Julie and baby Emma from a few years previous. She zoomed in on Julie's ear. "Here's the earring. I took this in 1996. Those were Julie's favourite earrings. An anniversary present."

Another pause. "Where did you find this earring?"

Kate opened up another image. It was a photo of the bank from about ten feet away. "Here's an expanded version of the spot. The Grand River near the bridge."

"What were you doing there?"

She opened up a photo called Riverbank2 Sept 17 2001.jpg.

"I took this photo from the train bridge after the police investigation. Remember I asked you where they pulled the body out? Look. The ground's been disturbed in two locations. The camera shows it. See?" She pointed to the two sections of the riverbank.

"The bigger one looks like the area where the firefighters went into the water to pull her out. And the EMS. All roughed up and trampled," she pointed. "But there's this smaller area..." Moved the tip of her finger "... closer to the bridge. That's where I found the earring. See those tansies? That's the landmark. I went into the water with my hip waders and took a look."

"Hip waders." Kowalchuk said. "Uh huh." Kate looked at him for a moment.

"I didn't touch the earring," she said. "It should still be there. I didn't want to disturb the scene."

She closed the photos, quit Photoshop, ejected the camera card.

"Here," she said, handing him the little SD memory card. "You can have this. It's a copy of the original."

Kowalchuk was still silent. He didn't touch the card.

"What do you think?" she said, trying to encourage comment.

His eyes re-focused.

"It's hard to say."

"What do mean? It could be another crime scene, don't you think?"

"Well, I don't know for sure," he said. "I'm not sure if it's worth getting the tech team over there for a look."

Kate sat back in her chair and stared at him incredulously. "Who else could the earring belong to?"

"Maybe someone else."

"Do you really think that's possible?"

"Anything is possible."

She stared at him, hard.

For the life of her, Kate couldn't decipher what was going on. Then all of a sudden, she got it.

"Right. You're not interested. Or rather the WPD isn't interested." She rose to her feet and began to gather her things. "I guess you won't be wanting this after all," she said, holding up the SD card. "Sorry to take your time." She packed up her computer case.

Kowalchuk stood up. "You know you're interfering in an investigation. You know you can be charged for that. You can't do that."

Kate whirled around. "You said there was no investigation. You said it was a suicide. You said, don't hesitate to get in touch if I had solid information."

"I said it wasn't an active case. That didn't mean we're not investigating it."

Kate pressed her lips together and shook her head. "That's a contradiction. You know it and I know it and I know what you meant at the time and that's what I went by." She zipped up her computer case and prepared to leave the room.

"It wasn't an active case at the point when I talked to you. It doesn't mean it can't be reopened any time."

"So what's wrong with right now? This is solid forensic evidence."

"In your opinion."

"Not just my opinion," she said. "If you don't act, this evidence could disappear. That could be a serious mistake. This could be a homicide. By not investigating, you could be letting a killer walk free."

"I think the Waterford Police should be the judge of that."

She was standing at the door with her hand on the knob. She faced him directly. "I hope you honestly believe that what you're doing is the right thing."

Kowalchuk's face was a blank.

"And by the way. You might want to find Marshall and ask him why he had a pile of photos of Julie all the same in his top drawer, ready to give out to the press. The one that I got. The one we all got the day her death was announced. Or maybe that's not worth investigating either. I personally thought that it was very, very strange."

Still no response.

"I'll be honest with you," he finally said. "The chief wasn't very happy about that story you wrote about the fried chicken robbery. You caused a shit storm over here. There was no need for you to write what you did."

Kate's expression changed, but she let him continue.

"And he didn't like your editorial either. I thought a face-to-face conversation would be better than phone or email."

"So you let me come here to ambush me instead of listening to what I had to say. Why are we even talking about that fried chicken robbery or my editorials? Isn't Julie's death more important?"

"Of course. And I genuinely wanted to see your photographs. But I also wanted to impress upon you that there were details about the Southern Fried Chicken store robbery that we were hoping to keep out of public knowledge."

"Like what? Why?"

"Information about the robbery. To not jeopardize our witness accounts."

Kate stared at him. "Come on. How do you expect people to call in information about the robbery if you don't let them know what they should be looking for and when?"

He shrugged. "There are ways."

"That doesn't make sense."

"There was one more thing. The tenor of your story. I think you went too far. Exaggerated. You made us look bad. Without knowing all the facts."

Right, Kate thought. *The real reason. And nothing to do with not knowing all the facts.* She pressed her lips together.

"Look. I don't know why I have to say this because I'm sure you know this already. You guys looked bad because you made yourselves look bad. I just happened to write about it. Like a real newspaper reporter should."

"The other media didn't run that story."

"They didn't have all the facts that I had at the time. Plus they're not real journalists."

"They didn't want the story."

"Of course not. They wouldn't know what to do with it."

He sighed impatiently. "Okay. Here's what it is. The chief doesn't think it's too late for a retraction. At least in the next issue. What do you have to say?"

Kate stared. "Are you kidding? That's ridiculous. Do you really think I'm going to conduct damage control on your behalf? You guys got yourselves into this and you need to get yourselves out of it. On your own."

He paused. "We're hoping to get some cooperation from you. Cooperation goes two ways. For a lot of things," he added for emphasis.

"Oh, okay. So now you're saying I'm cut off from any more press releases from the police department unless I publish a retraction."

No response. Then: "You should have asked for clarification before you went to print."

"I did ask," Kate said. "I asked you for more information. You said you couldn't release any. And Pound wouldn't return any of my calls or emails."

Another silence.

"Right. Go ahead and freeze me out. But it's not going to prevent me from reporting the news. Or writing my editorials."

He twitched.

"This is terrible. You people don't give a damn about Julie Crawford."

"That's not true."

The argument was getting loud. Things were going nowhere.

She heard footsteps in the hallway.

Kate shook her head, pressed her lips together once again, and shoved open the door.

Kowalchuk escorted her to the security gate and let her through, inscrutable as a stone.

The receptionist watched her curiously as she swept through the doorway and outside into damp afternoon air.

Kate found herself seated in the car with the engine running. She finally turned the key and the engine cut out. She brooded.

"What the hell," she finally muttered, and restarted the car. "What the hell did I do. Nothing. Nothing except report the news and tell the truth. *That's* what I did."

"Smokers are horrible birders, anyway," she said aloud as the car headed up Grand River Street North and took her home, seemingly on its own.

"They stink. To high heaven."

Chapter 55

Waterford Policing.

The topic listed under committee delegations gave no hint of the content of the presentation. But most of the room was only too aware of the issues at stake. The audience was packed to the rafters.

Kate sat beside Pete at the press table and opened a new screen on the computer. He sat on his phone texting, over and over.

Kate heard murmurs from the audience: Did you read that story in *The Challenge?*

Then: Oh, I think she made it up.

How could she?

Well, I didn't see any police cars there.

You idiot, they don't hang around for a week. They leave after a few hours.

She just wants to make the police look bad.

Why would she want to do that?

Sell more papers, dummy.

Mayor Bywater stared with fierce concentration at the agenda, sorted his papers with a series of unintelligible mumbles, and glanced sideways at Clerk Janice Stapleton sitting beside him. On the other side sat the Chief Executive Officer, Fred Bouchard. Janice nodded, setting things in motion.

"It looks like all have arrived who are determined to be here," said Mayor Bywater. "We will endeavour to make it worth their while." Chuckles circumnavigated the room. Clerk Stapleton shook her head and rolled her eyes, prompting a second round of chuckles.

Mayor Bywater was in typical form for the evening.

"And now we open this meeting of the Corporate Services Committee with the first item under delegations. Could we have the first delegation approach the podium, please. Actually the only delegation, isn't that right, Madam Clerk? Thank you."

Kate glanced across the aisle where the rest of the media was sitting. Kirk Steele and Chelsea Darling riffled through the pages of the agenda, desperately reading up on items at the last minute. Pete Steckler sat on her right, thumbing yet another text message into his phone.

Kate was the only media who had read the agenda ahead of time. As usual.

The audience seemed to be made up of the families and friends of police officers, Kate noted. And they were all noisy. Moira Hackett and a group of her friends sat in the front row.

Dorothy said that Moira had worked police dispatch since she was a teenager. Her dad had got her the job.

Constable Kowalchuk sat on a chair on one side of the room in his civvies, a briefcase on the floor.

The gavel came down. "Order," the mayor called out. "Order." The racket died down to a murmur.

The clerk flipped on the overhead projector. Inspector William Pound, double-chinned, sweaty-faced, Chief of the Waterford Police Department for seventeen years, blood pressure hitting new heights, desperate to leave behind a legacy of success and not failure, slid his glasses up his nose and began to read from his notes.

"Your worship Mayor Bywater and council members, the Waterford Police Department was founded in 1857 by a special order of council. It has served the town for 144 years."

There was brief applause, which died off before Bywater could locate the gavel. He felt around on his desk and finally outed the wooden hammer from under a sheaf of paperwork.

A staccato of typing spat out from the media's computers and people swiveled around in their seats with questioning looks that were duly ignored by the said media.

"We have a long and storied history of fighting crime and protecting the citizens in this community. From walking the beat in 1902 in downtown Waterford ..." and here a sepia-toned image of a uniformed officer wearing a custodian helmet and wielding a baton, lit the screen, "... to regular traffic stops on Belleview Road in the 1970s ..." Appearing on the screen was a photo of a boxy black and white sedan pulling a Buick Century off to the side of the road, "to correctional services in modern times …" an officer locking up a cell.

The six men and two women ringed around the council table tilted back in their chairs and took in the images as they flowed across the screen.

"Presently we have twenty-three active members plus two part-time and two full-time administrative personnel. An additional two full-time and three part-time on dispatch, assisting the fire department and ambulance service as well." Pound showed a group photo of the men and women in uniform in front of a wall of plaques and framed photos. In the corner of the photo was written "Christmas 2000."

"We have one police chief, one staff sergeant, and four platoons of four constables and five other officers including two criminal investigators, an officer in charge of support services, one dedicated to Crime Stoppers and high school public relations, and one to community service. Each shift has two officers in two separate vehicles assigned to patrol Waterford, plus a supervisor.

"We provide twenty-four hour access to the Waterford Police station and a night-time buzzer from 9 p.m. to 9 a.m. Dispatch and a supervisor answer the door.

"Last year's WPD budget was 2.174 million dollars and the five year estimate in total would be 8.7 million dollars, which includes all your costs. All known up front." He glanced up with a meaningful look. "That includes 2 per cent annual inflation, wage increases, and benefits."

"The force and dispatch services have been housed at the police station on Mechanic Street since 1985 when we took over the former Canada Post building as a cost-shaving measure. We like to be careful with the municipality's dollars," he said with a meaningful glance. He showed a staid flat-roofed cement block building reminiscent of so many 1960s government buildings across Ontario, with a Canadian flag flying in a tiny front yard and a squared-off fenced parking lot in the rear.

"Waterford has 30 per cent of the county's population, the greatest population density in Tecumseh County, and the most crime per square mile. The WPD is highly experienced with the town's issues and residents. We also have some experience in the rural area outside of Waterford where we have occasionally assisted the OPP and conducted other services."

Kate's eyes swept the room to locate the OPP's Pearcy and Kapoor. They sat poker-faced on the other side of the chambers, as far away from the WPD delegation as was humanly possible.

"The Waterford Police Department has mandatory day and night foot patrols in built-up areas. There are eighteen-month assignments of officers to specific zones. The WPD has lean senior management, no deputy chief, and support provided by an administrative secretary which reduces the need to have a deputy chief. Dispatch takes place out of the Waterford police station with personnel familiar with local roads. Our communication system uses tower-to-tower repeaters. Public complaints are adjudicated by the police chief. Neighbouring police forces supply specialized services such as tactical and rescue units, emergency response, canine units, and explosives disposal at some extra charge to the county, but only as needed.

"We have a good relationship with the press ..."

Kate raised her eyebrows.

"... and more plans to increase exposure and accessibility."

Good luck with that.

"The men and women of the Waterford Police Department have provided the residents of this community with outstanding safety, security, crime suppression, public service, and volunteerism. When officers negotiate their wages and benefits, they have to look their employers in the face and be accountable."

A photo of a smiling police officer directing traffic and another of two police cars at the scene of an accident filled the screen.

"Two-thirds of our members stay with the force for their entire careers. We work, shop, and raise our families in the community. We are your friends and neighbours. Most of us say hello to a police officer every day and don't even know it.

"They are examples to the community and hold themselves to a high standard. Our members each provide on average over fifty volunteer hours a year for events such as the Children's Bike Rodeo, Christmas Baskets, Halloween Tips for School Kids, Harvestfest, a kiosk at the Tecumseh Fall Fair, and our annual Auction of Confiscated Goods.

"Our members have their ear to the ground and are personally familiar with the town of Waterford. We know the bad guys. We know the landscape. We have an active network of informers and citizens who help us fight crime. We know which areas to keep a watchful eye on.

"Waterford has one of the lowest crime records in the province. Our statistics rank favourably with those of bigger police forces when it comes to ticketing, response times, and crime fighting per capita."

Kate's ears pricked up. *Really? Where's the proof?*

There was a pause as Pound fumbled with his papers and slid out a bound booklet. Opened it to the first page.

Right. Here's where things get complicated.

"For example, in some respects we have even better statistics than larger forces and that includes the Ontario Provincial Police." It was the first time he even mentioned the name of the competition.

"Please turn your booklet to page 23," he said.

After that, the rest of the presentation was a mind-boggling array of charts, graphs, and numbers illustrating the efficacy of the Waterford Police Department in Tecumseh County, the number of crimes they uncovered, the percentage solved, the number of hours the force spent on the job, the cost of policing per citizen. After ten minutes, the audience began to yawn, sigh, rub their eyes, and stretch. Kate's brain hurt. The members of council looked like they were barely treading water.

No doubt that was the desired effect.

The problem with statistics, Kate said to herself, *is that they can be very easily manipulated. And when the people gathering the statistics are the ones using them to prove something, things get very iffy.*

It always surprised her that council even bothered asking their police forces to supply statistics. What real meaning could a monthly report of the numbers possibly have? Incidents always went unreported, and officers were notoriously reticent when it came to filling out paperwork. If an incident went unsolved, it could simply be removed from the list of cases, thus pumping up the percentage of cases that *were* solved. As for accident numbers, Kate frequently saw collisions that were never written up at all by the police.

Finally, things wrapped up.

"Your worship and council. The reason I am here is because the WPD wants Waterford to have the best, most efficient, most knowledgeable policing possible. The OPP don't offer better policing. They offer big city policing. They don't have the personal approach to policing that we provide. They don't know Waterford's streets and alleyways. They don't know Waterford's residents and children. The OPP are more expensive, not more effective.

"I ask you to not consider the proposal from the OPP. It's a waste of your time. It's a waste of our citizens' time. And it's an insult to the fine men and women of the Waterford Police Department who are already providing top notch service at excellent taxpayer value. Thank you."

Moira Hackett and her gang of cohorts clapped enthusiastically. "You can say that again," a woman shouted from the audience.

"We don't want the OPP!" came from the other side.

Moira brought her fingers to the corners of her mouth and whistled. There was some shouting.

Kate and Pete exchanged looks.

Oh God. Drama.

Kate craned her neck. One of the shouters looked like she might be the wife of an officer. The other person, a middle-aged guy, could be anybody. Chelsea stood up, marched to the front of the audience and snapped a photo, centering on Moira's row and temporarily blinding everyone else.

The mayor banged his gavel. "There will be absolutely no comments from the audience," he announced. "And no whistling either. Please!"

The mayor thanked Pound for the presentation.

"There is no staff report. We will now break for a brief recess," he announced. "And clear our heads," someone muttered. Everyone stood up. Pound returned to his chair. Bywater went over to the audience and began greeting people and shaking hands, eternally prepping for the next election.

A group gathered at the back of the room, their murmuring continuing until they finally went out the back door and into the parking lot. Pete followed the crowd, most likely hoping to get some tape. Through the doorway, Kate could see Chelsea and Kirk appear at his elbow as if by magic.

Kate turned off the laptop, grabbed her purse, and made her way to the washroom. She had already noted the audience reaction and that was all that was needed for *The Challenge's* story. She passed by Kowalchuk who was in close discussion with Pound, and steadfastly ignored him. He returned the favour.

After a quarter hour, the room reconvened minus some of the audience. Not knowing how council meetings actually proceeded, people always left too early to hear the discussions, Kate noted. The really good stuff.

There were two hours of reports on matters of policy, finance, relations with adjacent municipalities, and administration, then discussions ended.

"Other business," the mayor called out. He lowered his voice to a serious tone. "Before the CAO gives his information, I just want to clear up one thing." He paused for effect.

"We do not want to insult the WPD by considering other options, but we have to consider the best interest of the municipality."

Kate saw Pound wince.

"First of all, the Ontario Provincial Police approached us, not the other way around," Bywater said in reasonable tones. "Secondly, it is the duty of council to always be considering the options, to always look at costs, at the big picture. That is our job. We are responsible to the taxpayers."

Pound was obviously trying to hide his disappointment. He had been shrewdly playing to the audience, counting on their influence with council.

Kate wondered why Pound felt he needed to do that. Maybe he felt he had an insufficient argument. Or maybe he was an unskilled administrator and didn't have the smarts to put together a good case. Maybe a bit of both.

"Okay, now the CAO has something to say. Go ahead, Mr. Bouchard."

"Your worship," Bouchard said. "I just received notice today that the OPP has made a formal request for a decision at our next council meeting in October so that they can meet their internal budget deadlines. Your choice tonight is to approve the request or deny the request, and respond accordingly."

The mayor said nothing for a second or two. Then: "Yes, I see what you mean. But there is a third option, is there not? To give a notice of motion and discuss the request at a committee of the whole to receive final input from members of the public, then vote on the request at council. That will give more opportunities for the public to comment on the request that we just received today, isn't that right Clerk Stapleton?"

"Er, yes Mr. Mayor, we could do that. Then respond to the letter."

The mayor swung around to face council, avoiding eye contact with Bouchard who knew he had been reprimanded ever so slightly.

"How does council wish to proceed on this matter. Councillor Popowich.

"I so move the notice of motion."

The hand of Mount Pleasant's councillor, Mary Chang, popped up. "Seconded."

The mayor turned to the clerk. "Perhaps the clerk could word a resolution for us."

Stapleton hurriedly scribbled on a sheet of paper, crossed out a few words, then tapped away at her keyboard.

Councillors sat back in their chairs. Cleghorne's hand shot up and she rose to the floor.

"Councillor Cleghorne."

"Your worship," she said slowly. A sigh rolled through the room.

"I believe we don't need a notice of motion. I would like to move that we deny the request from the Ontario Provincial Police."

"Seconded." From Waterford Councillor Al Biggar.

The mayor opened his mouth to say something, but too late.

She continued. "You can see from the number of people in the room," and she gazed uncertainly towards the partially depleted audience, "or I should say *had* in the room, that the majority of people weren't in favour of considering the OPP. They are too expensive and we don't need ..."

Councillor George "Point of Order" Popowich torpedoed off his chair.

"Mr. Mayor," he said. "Point of order!"

Pete quietly groaned.

"Councillor Cleghorne is discussing the issue already, and we have yet to hear, never mind vote on the staff report. Plus we already have a motion, Mr. Mayor, on the floor."

"I was merely describing what the audience had to say on the matter," Cleghorne continued. "And from what I've heard, and from what I've heard about the number of phone calls other councillors have been receiving including you Councillor Popowich, they are in the majority. Why, should we …"

Popowich jumped up again. The mayor banged his gavel simultaneously. "Mr. Mayor," he began. "Councillor Cleghorne is attributing comments to me that I never made. That is uncalled —"

"Call the vote!" Councillor Fred Terryberry hollered. "It's getting late. I've got cows to milk in the morning."

Kate and Pete could barely control their laughter.

Bywater conferred with the clerk. "The clerk will now read out the resolution."

"Whereas the Ontario Provincial Police presently oversee the County of Tecumseh. And whereas the Ontario Provincial Police has approached the Council of the County of Tecumseh with a proposal to extend its oversight to the town of Waterford. And whereas the Ontario Provincial Police gave a formal presentation on its offer to police both the Town of Waterford and Tecumseh County and has now formally asked the Council of the County of Tecumseh to vote at its next meeting. Therefore the Council of Tecumseh County proposes a notice of motion to debate at an upcoming meeting of the Committee of the Whole with a staff report and comments from the public, and a vote at its council meeting on Tuesday, October 29, 2001."

"All in favour of the motion," said Bywater.

"Wait," said Cleghorne. There was a loud exhalation of breath around the council table.

"What is it now, Councillor Cleghorne," said the mayor.

"Shouldn't we first get a staff report before we vote on the matter?"

A universal groan circled throughout the room. Councillor Popowich laid his head sideways on the desk. Councillor Mary Chang hid a grimace. Terryberry threw up his hands so hard he nearly fell backwards off his chair.

Kirk and Chelsea, in the middle of a long murmuring conversation, looked up in confusion, completely unaware of what had taken place.

"Councillor Cleghorne," said the mayor, "that is exactly what we are doing. A motion to that effect is on the table now. Could you please pay attention to the discussion. Please."

"For the love of God," Pete said under his breath. Kate smothered a guffaw.

"Well, in that case, I move that we delay voting on the issue for another cycle. Mr. Mayor, we shouldn't rush into things especially when a decision…" she faltered. "… of this magnitude is being considered. And…"

Popowich sprang to his feet. He raised his hand. "Mr. Mayor, if I could."

The mayor nodded.

"Mr. Mayor, we are giving staff and the public plenty of time to respond. By October 29th we will have enough information before us to make a decision. We shouldn't be delaying the issue at this point. Both police forces have to set their budgets in the upcoming weeks, and our staff has to prepare budget documents for our own budget deliberations in a short time."

Cleghorne's hand shot up. "Mr. Mayor."

"All right. Councillor Cleghorne."

"Mr. Mayor, if I could. I wasn't finished with my comments if you don't mind."

The mayor threw his hands up in the air. "Then continue Councillor Cleghorne. Please. Be my guest." Shaking his head, he turned to the CAO on his other side and said something unintelligible.

Another sigh went through the room.

"Mr. Mayor, as I was saying, we won't have enough information to reach a decision by October 29th. And in any case, I'm sure staff won't have enough time for a report for our next Committee of the Whole meeting."

The mayor looked inquiringly over at the staff cohort. "Gord? Maybe our Director of Corporate Services can respond to that."

Kate madly typed in the to and fro between the councillors, and caught up while Gord Sutherland, Director of Corporate Services, jumped to the podium and explained that yes, a report could be drawn up in the next forty-eight hours if necessary.

Of course. Isn't that what we pay these guys for? The question is, why is that even a question?

The droning in front of the podium continued.

"Okay, we will now call the vote," finally announced Bywater. "All in favour."

Cleghorne's hand shot up again. "Mr. Mayor."

More sighing and this time, open laughter around the podium. "Now what, Councillor Cleghorne," the mayor asked. It didn't faze her one bit.

"Mr. Mayor, can we please have the clerk read out the motion again? In case it's not clear what we're voting on?"

Pete tossed a pen into the air and hung his head between his hands. Kate contorted with laughter.

The mayor paused, then nodded at the clerk.

"And can we have a recorded vote?"

More groaning around the table.

I have to give the mayor credit, he did not roll his eyes once, thought Kate. The clerk went through the motion and grabbed a pen to record the vote.

"All in favour."

Five hands were raised.

"Against."

Two hands went up. Cleghorne and Biggar.

"The motion is carried."

"The motion is carried five to two," Stapleton announced.

There was an audible exhalation of breath in the chambers. Kate had been typing continually since Cleghorne rose from her chair. Constable Kowalchuk and Chief Pound got up from their seats at the same time, gathered their briefcases and coats, and glanced at one another. Kowalchuk shook his head slightly.

They exited the chambers with all four reporters in tow.

Kate and the others took down the standard statement she expected from Pound about being *disappointed, stated our case, optimistic the WPD will remain a fixture of the county,* etc.

"Are you confident about your proposal?" Kate asked Pound. She kept the resentment out of her voice. She already knew what kind of response she would get.

"Do you think the WPD has a good chance of continuing its

contract?"

"We will be in attendance at the next meeting as well," he said. It didn't answer the question whatsoever. "I'm proud of our record and our history. We have always provided top notch service, despite what some people seem to think."

Kate recorded the comment, thinking, *he's talking about me, of course.*

"Will you be able to maintain that service?" she added just for the heck of it.

Kowalchuk standing back from the scrum, jerked a little.

"Why the hell not?" Pound answered, his voice rising. "We always have." He turned his back to her, his jacket brushing her notepad, jarring it slightly. "Next question," he said loudly to the rest of the reporters.

Kate held on to her notepad and continued writing until she was done, pretending not to notice. Pete widened his eyes a little and shook his head.

Chelsea and Kirk had noticed the snub and sensing an opportunity, jumped in, pestering Pound with question after question. Pete held his microphone under the chief's chin. And when Pete began his line of questions, they hung around and took notes from his interview, too.

Kate returned to the press table just as the mayor tapped his gavel at the front of the room. She could feel Kowalchuk staring a hole in the back of her head.

"Adjourned," the mayor called out.

Kate had already sketched out the bare bones of her story. That night she would plug in a few quotes, slap the story into her file for the front page, and be ready to print for that month's edition.

"WPD RIPS INTO THE OPP," wrote *The Belleview Daily Kernal of Truth* the next day.

"GUNS A BLAZIN'," wrote *The Waterford Disorder* that week.

Kate tossed them both into the corner of her office.

Utterly ridiculous.

Her story would be headlined: "OUR SERVICE BEATS THE OPP, SAYS THE WPD." The subhead was: "BUT DOES IT? COUNCIL VOTES NEXT WEEK."

Chapter 56

K ate picked up the phone and punched Dorothy's key on the speed dial.

"Good morning, girlie."

It was Dorothy on the other end, up since dawn and just getting in from her garden.

Did she know anyone at Penmarvian?

"Of course. Listen, lady, I know just about everyone in town. Don't forget I've been living here since Rome was built."

Did Dorothy know any of the veterans living there? She thought someone at the retirement home might have information about Julie's murder. And with the excuse of needing a veteran's photo for the paper, she could get in the door and find out. The photo would be used for the front page of the Remembrance Day edition, and it needed to have an ornate interesting background, which Penmarvian could supply in spades.

Kate described all the events of recent days, her encounter with the dragonfly, and her lightbulb moment.

"You've been a busy lady lately, haven't you?"

A short list stood out with Dorothy. What about if Kate came along the next time Dorothy went there for her Knitting Workshop for Seniors? Wait. In fact, there was one that very night. Did she have time?

Kate glanced briefly at her wall calendar. Blank. Yup, she was good to go.

They made arrangements to meet at Penmarvian at six.

It was five thirty and Kate was standing in the somewhat musty mahogany paneled foyer of Penmarvian, explaining to Mrs. Krackow, the supervisor, that she was waiting for Dorothy, but by the way, were there any veterans handy that might provide her with a good photo for her Remembrance Day issue? And did they live in a suite where the light was coming in from the side with the river? *The most likely person to have been a witness to Julie's murder.*

Kate hoped Dorothy wouldn't get there early too. The less fuss over what she needed to do, the better.

Mrs. Krackow turned to the hallway behind her. "Haaaahnah!"

There were quick heavy steps, then a plump middle-aged woman with hair the colour of straw and hair roots the colour of the earth, stepped into the foyer.

"Hahnah. Is Mr. Ferguson still up?" Mrs. Krackow had heavy accent. Polish, Kate guessed.

"Henry? No, Henry has gone to bed early. The poor dear was feeling a bit under the weather. Dyspepsia."

Kate's face fell.

"Oh dear. And his room faces east, right?" Mrs. Krackow asked.

Hannah nodded.

"Well, maybe we can provide another room facing east. Hahnah this is Kate Messenger from *The Tecumseh Challenge*. She was hoping to do an interview with a veteran for Remembrance Day. Can you think of someone else who might be suitable?"

Hannah pinched her chin. "Well, I have to say that Mr. MacKenzie is a veteran. And I think he's in the lounge. But he's not the easiest interview, unfortunately. He has a touch of aphasia. Can't talk."

Kate was momentarily stymied. How would she find out what she needed to know? Would it even be worth all the trouble? But she was in too deep to retreat. She squared her shoulders. Fate would be allowed to run its course.

"Maybe I can do this a bit differently. Does he have any interesting pictures from the war?"

Hannah thought for a second. "Now that's a good idea. He's got a whole album as a matter of fact. And he does love talking about those old photos of his when he can talk. Let me see what I can do. Maybe it will get his pipes going again."

She departed and Kate heard murmuring in an adjacent room. Hannah returned. She nodded and smiled.

"I'm going to bring down his picture album, dear, and he'll show you some of his photos. He seemed anxious to say something, as a matter of fact. What a good sign. If you can't get all the information you need, contact me later and I'll fill you in."

Kate heard the regular muffled creak of steps being ascended then descended, and at the same time, Mrs. Krackow directed her into the next room, an old-fashioned sitting room with over-stuffed high backed chairs, a bookshelf stacked with board games and hardcover books, and a small television on a side table. A tall gaunt old man with a shawl over his lap sat in a wheelchair angled to a window with a view over the rear parking lot. He looked up with red-rimmed watery eyes when Mrs. Krackow introduced Kate.

Hannah entered with the photo album and opened it on his lap. A buzzer sounded within the building and she hurriedly left.

"He has cataracts, but his close-up vision is not bad," Mrs. Krackow said. "I'll leave you two at it." She departed.

"Thank you," Kate called out. She was discouraged but it wasn't the end of the world. At least there would be a good photo coming out of it for a future edition of *The Challenge.*

Kate stood back with her camera, framing the shot. The sun was low in the sky on the other side of the building, leaving much of Mr. MacKenzie's face in shadow. It was a somber view of an unsmiling elderly man, sad and hollow. She pressed the shutter several times, then went to the knee that wasn't sore to shift her angle from below, giving the man more dignity.

The camera returned to the its case, Kate drew up a chair next to his, and sat with her pad of paper and a pen.

"How are you today, sir," she said, her eyes full of sympathy. He so reminded her of her own disabled father.

She placed her hand over the back of his cold one on the arm of the chair. The warmth of Kate's hand penetrated his paper-thin skin. He seemed to relax, and the corners of his eyes crinkled.

She leaned over the album and stared at the arrangement of black and white photos glued to the page with black corner holders. A faintly mouldy odour emanated from the album. She pointed at the image of an athletic-looking man in a uniform, chest thrust forward, visored hat angled rakishly, golden circles of foxing bleeding from one side of the photograph.

"What a handsome man. Is that you, Mr. MacKenzie?"

Mr. MacKenzie cracked a tiny smile and grunted.

"Mr. MacKenzie, can you tell me anything about yourself? How do you like living here? It sure is a beautiful place."

A cross between an "umm" and a "yes" came out of his mouth. This wasn't going to be easy. Then something occurred to her.

"Mr. MacKenzie, would you like to write something for me? Here, take this pad and this pen. It's easy to write with. It's a marker. Write something for me. Anything. Here you go."

He peered at her a bit confused, then comprehension dawned and he slowly reached out and stared at the pad. Then he began to scratch something down.

Kate rose from the chair, crossed the floor, and read the spines of the books propped on the bookcase. Agatha Christie. Charles Dickens. Poems by Mary Oliver and Rumi. The Bible. All the things that gave comfort to a person in the later stages of life.

She turned to look out the window. The view was a wall of orange and yellow trees that crowded against the bank of the river. Leaning forward, she looked more intently and could just pick out the crimson feathers of a cardinal as it streaked from one set of leaves to another. calling out a ringing "puweet puweet puweet phiew phiew phiew." Kate stood and watched as it bid farewell to the setting sun.

Mr. MacKenzie was still struggling with the marker but he seemed to be progressing. Kate looked over his shoulder.

"The woman…" she read aloud, then hesitated. It seemed to have absolutely nothing to do with Remembrance Day. "The woman … deh … What does that say, Mr. MacKenzie?" She pointed at the word.

Mr. MacKenzie's mouth opened but only garbled guttural noises emerged. He looked up at Kate, crestfallen.

"Can you tell me what you are trying to say?"

He stared up at her with a look that was despondent and frustrated at once. Finally, he shoved his head forward and grunted again. Loud. He looked up at her. He made the universal throat-cutting gesture. "She Day," he said. "Day. Dayd. She dayd."

Dayd? Dead. *Oh my goodness.*

Kate stifled her amazement. She crouched down so she could look him face to face. "Mr. MacKenzie, what do you mean? Someone died? A woman died? Is that what you're saying?"

He nodded his head and lifted a finger at the window in the direction of the train bridge.

"Rain," he said. "Drain. Train."

"The train? The bridge? How? How, Mr. MacKenzie?"

He stared at her and instead of trying to speak he brought forward his arms and made a pushing gesture, nodding his head with every jerk as if saying: this, this.

Kate stared at him in wonder.

And just at that moment, she heard a buzzer sounding at the front of the building. She grabbed the notepad. She didn't want anyone to know what had taken place.

Mrs. Krackow's shoes clacked down the hallway. A door opened and a familiar voice called out: "Hello there. Hello, hello! I'm here for the knitting class. Why, hello Mrs. Krackow. Is my friend Kate here?"

"Are we all done now?" Hannah was in the doorway. "Did you get your picture, dear?" She slid the photo album off Mr. MacKenzie's lap and laid it on the side table. "It'll soon be time for bed. I'll get you ready for the night."

She smiled at the old gentleman and adjusted the shawl over his lap. She bustled out into the hallway to get a wheelchair.

Kate slowly packed up her camera. She opened her mouth to say something to Mr. MacKenzie, but it was too late.

"Aha, there you are!" It was Dorothy. "Mrs. Krackow said you got here early." She nodded her head at Mr. MacKenzie.

"Hello there, sir. How are you today?" There was no response but Dorothy was undeterred. "Isn't it a lovely evening? Will you be joining us for our knitting lesson?" she asked, turning to Kate. "Maybe we can give our group some free publicity. After all, I have an in with the editor of the local paper." She winked.

Kate obligingly stayed for part of the knitting demonstration and chatted with a few of the residents, elderly grandmothers already half-way through their Christmas projects for the year. A white-haired woman in a red blouse was finishing off a blue, green, and yellow Fair Isle sweater and Kate could not resist photographing it.

Plans were made with Dorothy to meet up for lunch that week, then Kate waved good night to the group. "Thank you," someone called out, "for attending. And the publicity. We really appreciate it."

Kate left that night with what should have been a warm glow. But instead it was the anxious feeling of an opportunity lost.

Chapter 57

Kate was lying in the bathtub, the water caressing her body as she floated.

It was the end of a long day, and she was glad it was over.

The water was warm, soothing, calming. She ducked her head under. The water was emerald green, and it covered her like a blanket.

She waved her arms up and down at her sides to make an angel, up and down. Her arms grew longer and waved all around and in circles, forwards and backwards, and she somehow picked up speed through the water, bumping into strange objects that made their way around her. She felt her head butt into an immoveable object, a barrier, and her clothes snagged.

Then all of a sudden there was a lurch, and she was grabbed out of the water and hauled into the open air.

She opened her eyes and tried to scream but there was nothing except gurgles and wheezing and an agonized intake of breath. Her top came up over her arms, then twisted around her throat, tighter and tighter and she reached out, then clawed and scratched and grabbed at the thing around her neck that was turning and yanking and choking her without pity. Her feet kicked out aimlessly without connecting. *No,* she screamed in her mind, *no, no. Please. I'm begging you. Please.*

Then there was nothing.

She was a sea creature, a limped octopus or an anemone, the water around her once again, caressing, turning, rolling her body, cleansing her inside and out.

It's okay, she heard the water say. *You are mine, you are part of me, and I am part of you. Take in the light. Take in the current.*

She could breathe the water in and out and that's what she did, stretching out once again. Floating, floating, floating.

Then her foot caught on something and her body hit a solid object once again, soft and hard at the same time, and her progress was halted.

She opened her eyes and the world was brown and green and she felt sad.

Another lurch.

Kate sat up straight in bed, gulping for air, coughing, choking, tears streaming from her eyes, heart pounding.

The sea green all around was transmuted into the white walls of her bedroom.

She pressed her palms against the mattress and consciously made the effort to control her breathing and her panic, counting to a hundred, slowly inhaling the air, sweet and pure. She rubbed her neck, the pain ebbed away, and there was nothing constricting her throat any more, nothing at all.

Wheat wheat wheat wheat. Chuck chuck chuck chuck chuck.

A cardinal. It reminded her.

She rose, dressed quickly, let Alfred out in the backyard, and jumped into the Audi.

The parking lot at the back of Penmarvian was empty at that time of the morning. She pulled into a spot, grabbed her Nikon, and quietly closed the car door. The back of the building faced east, and she walked back and forth until she could see part of the train bridge. Snapped a photo.

She walked the asphalt perimeter all around Penmarvian, not knowing what she was even looking for.

When she circled back around to her car, she was surprised to see a wheelchair at the edge of the parking lot with a person sitting in it. It was Mr. MacKenzie, all bundled up, the wool blanket across his lap.

Then, behind her, she heard the heavy roar and rattle of a diesel engine. An ambulance pulled up to the side of the building.

The old man turned his head, then fixed his watery gaze upon Kate.

She did not want to startle him. She knelt down on one knee, her good knee.

"Hello again, Mr. MacKenzie. It's Kate, from last night. Kate from the newspaper, *The Tecumseh Challenge.*"

A moment passed, then he nodded.

"Mr. MacKenzie. Do you sit out here every morning?" He nodded.

"Can you tell me anything more about that day you saw the woman? The woman who died?" She made the same gesture that he had that night, a neck-slicing motion.

He stared for a minute. He made a writing motion against his other hand. Kate went to her car, got out a pen and notepad, and returned.

He wrote: I saw them.

Okay.

"Them? Who? A man? Was he young or old?"

He shrugged.

"Did you see him driving anything?"

He shook his head.

"Can you tell me what time it was?"

He wrote "7".

"Can you tell me what day it was?"

He wrote "Monday".

"Was it raining that day?"

"No."

"Can you tell me anything else?

He paused. He wrote: "Bad man." Looking at her directly, he made a pushing motion once again.

"Thank you, sir, you have been very helpful." She took the pad from him, tore out the page where he had shakily written the meagre description and handed it back.

"Can I get you a coffee or a tea or a donut? At Tim Hortons?"

The slightest of smiles tweaked his lips. He shook his head.

Kate put her hand over the back of his. "Mr. MacKenzie, if you remember anything else, anything at all, write it down and call me. Here's my number." She wrote her name and phone number on the front of the pad. "Or tell Dorothy. The knitting lady. She's my friend. You take care, now. Enjoy the morning."

He nodded but Kate felt he probably hadn't understood most of what she said. She sighed.

She rose and as she turned to head back to the Audi, there was someone watching her from the cab of the ambulance. The door opened and out stepped a large man in dark pants and a white shirt with a Belleview EMS patch on the shoulder. Eyebrows that resembled hickory tussock caterpillars.

"Hello there," he called out.

"Good morning," Kate said.

"I couldn't help but notice you were talking to one of my patients, Hugh MacKenzie."

"Yes," Kate said slowly. "I'm Kate Messenger. I write for *The Tecumseh Challenge*. Mr. MacKenzie is part of our Remembrance Day feature," she felt compelled to explain.

"Jay Blackfoot. I'm doing a patient transfer here." As he extended a handshake, she said she was following up on their interview.

"You know he has aphasia," he said.

"Yes," she said. "His photographs are part of our Remembrance Day edition. I'm contacting the nurse here for some background information."

He nodded. "I couldn't help but overhear your conversation. You were asking him about that woman who jumped off the bridge."

"Yes, I did," she admitted.

"Okay," he said. "I'm not trying to be nosy," he said, "but I was wondering why you were asking that."

Kate wasn't sure if she should tell him, but finally she did.

"He said a couple of things the other night. I wasn't sure what he meant. He could have been imagining things. I thought I'd talk to him again." Then: "Why are you asking?"

Blackfoot paused. "I was at the recovery scene. Where we found Julie's body."

Kate stared.

"I guess the reason I'm having this conversation with you now, is maybe the same reason you had a conversation with Hugh. I heard some things. Saw some things."

"You did? About Julie?"

"Yeah."

"Like what? Can you tell me?"

"Look, I read your little paper. I think it's pretty good. I know who you are. I think I can trust you. There were contusions on Julie's body that I thought were unusual. It's just that the police didn't think the same way."

"Really."

"Yeah. It upset me, the way it was done. It was basically swept under the carpet. I felt so bad, I even went to the funeral to pay my respects."

All of a sudden it hit Kate. The uniformed man with the heavy eyebrows.

"I saw you there," she said, pointing with her index finger. "I was taking pictures for the paper."

"Yeah, there were a lot of people there. I knew most of them. I'm from Waterford."

"So you know Marshall," Kate said, thinking about the day of the funeral.

"I've known Marshall for many years. We play in the same hockey league."

She took a deep breath. "What do you think about the whole thing? Do you think Marshall could have killed his wife?"

He paused. "I don't know. I like Marshall. But I think it's something that should have been investigated. Julie had bruises behind her ears. And petechiae. Broken blood vessels in the eyes. Those things don't come from falling off a bridge."

"Where do they come from?"

A beat. "Strangulation."

Kate's eyes widened. "Oh my God. Why wasn't there an autopsy? Surely the police would have seen the same thing."

"That's what I wondered too. It seemed inexplicable."

They both stood lost in thought.

"By the way," Kate said, "can you tell me what she was wearing when they found the body?"

"Yellow top, black shorts. Both spandex."

Just like Stavros said.

"Look, Julie was a friend of mine. Is there any way that a proper investigation could still take place?"

Blackfoot shrugged. "It would take exhumation. The coroner needs legal authority. Something would have to come from a Justice of the Peace. If the police won't swear out an affidavit, maybe the crown attorney might. I don't know. Maybe I could have a chat with her."

Kate paused. "There's something I didn't tell you. I have evidence. Good forensic evidence. A while ago, I showed a Waterford police officer a photo of a possible crime scene along the river bank. With

Julie's favourite earring. He chose to ignore it. I didn't. I couldn't."

Blackfoot's eyes widened.

"Kate. Here's my contact information. Could you email me those photos as soon as possible?"

Kate took the business card. "Yes, I will." She looked up. "Jay, is there any chance justice can still be done?"

Blackfoot nodded.

"Maybe. We've got to try."

A weight Kate didn't even know she was carrying lifted a little off her shoulders.

Chapter 58

The staff report arrived in Kate's inbox the afternoon of the Committee of the Whole meeting. She eagerly clicked on the link and went straight to the recommendation: The OPP's proposal was favoured. In a nutshell, it simply offered more resources for the municipality's buck.

Oh man, the WPD sure won't like that.

She roughed out a story in advance. The one issue with the OPP, though, was long-term costs. The report noted that at some point, Tecumseh County would be obligated to match the salaries of Toronto police officers that set the bar for all police forces province-wide. Toronto police officers had a super strong union. Salaries could only go up and up.

The council chambers were packed that evening. At one side of the room, the Hamilton television station manned a camera sitting on a tripod, escalating the level of excitement.

Bang. Mayor Bywater left the gavel sitting on the block within reach of an easy grab. It promised to be an exciting night.

"I now call this meeting of the Committee of the Whole to order. We have many letters from the public, a few delegations, and correspondence. I will ask the clerk if there are any additions to the agenda. Clerk Stapleton, can you please give the latest update on that."

"Yes, Your Worship. The Waterford Police Department would like to give a final presentation."

"On ..."

"On the OPP's policing offer. The WPD have some additional information and questions."

"Additional information. That's okay. But questions. Is that proper?" He glanced inquiringly at the Gordon Sutherland, the Director of Corporate Services. Sutherland got to his feet.

"Your Worship, if I may clarify, the WPD wants to know what criteria the county will use when it comes to vote on its final decision about the two police forces. And if the county needs more information, the WPD wants more time to prepare the numbers."

Sounds like a stalling tactic to me, Kate thought.

The mayor looked around the council table. "Does anyone object or concur? Maybe we need a motion for that."

Councillor Cleghorne got to her feet. "Mr. Mayor, I don't have a motion prepared specifically for that ... purpose ..." she faltered. "But I will move that we hear the presentation from the Waterford District Police."

"Second the motion." It was Biggar, from Waterford, with his hand up. "In my opinion, the more information the better," he added.

"Fine, thank you Councillor Biggar. All in favour?" Most hands went up around the table.

"Approved. I would like to point out that we have a report on this matter from Gordon Sutherland up for debate under 'discussion.' Now. Would you like to approach the podium, sir?" The mayor nodded at Chief Bill Pound who was rapidly shuffling through a pile of papers in his briefcase. Beside him sat SS Grimaldi, and Kowalchuk. Kate avoided looking in his direction.

On the other side of the room sat Superintendent Don Pearcy and Inspector Roger Kapoor, both inscrutable.

Pound stood at the podium and straightened pages against the lectern. Then came the reading glasses.

"Your Worship and councillors, members of the audience and the press."

He gave a perfunctory nod towards the press tables at the back of the room. *Hah,* Kate thought. *He must be desperate.*

"You may be aware that the Waterford District Police gave a fully costed presentation of its policing strategy at last month's Corporate Services Committee meeting. However, for the sake of those who couldn't attend, here are the highlights once again."

The audience exhaled with a sigh. They were in for a rough ride.

All the numbers and statistics were reviewed. Personnel, hours, shifts, crimes uncovered, crimes solved, cost of policing per citizen.

Kate had heard it all the first time. She stopped typing and went to the internet to look at bird videos, wondering if the OPP would be afforded the same opportunity to re-do their presentation. She knew the answer would be no.

Maybe Bywater was giving the WPD an advantage on purpose. Maybe because he wanted to be able to say, "look, we gave them every opportunity, even more than the other guys ..."

Finally, Pound came to the crux of the matter.

"Mr. Mayor, I've seen the report and we are prepared to offer a five-year plan, compared to the three-year plan offered by the OPP, with no increases, subject to any unforeseeable situations. And if the OPP change any part of their offer at this point, we would like to be notified right away so we can provide a counter plan."

Right. They wanted to reserve the right to give a slightly lower offer with advance knowledge of the OPP's numbers. And after a year they would come back with slightly higher numbers to cover the ground they lost before, and new ground for the year ahead, because of "unforeseeable circumstances." With none of the resources that the OPP had to offer. *How does that make sense,* Kate pondered.

The same thought must have occurred to Councillor Chang. She raised an index finger.

"Mr. Mayor, I believe we would be giving the WPD an unfair advantage if we allowed them to bid with knowledge of the other party's figures."

The mayor nodded. "Any other comments? Councillor Biggar."

He stood up. "Mr. Mayor, I don't consider that to be an advantage. That would just be consideration and courtesy for a police force that's served this area so well, for so many years."

There were grunts of agreement from the audience. The mayor banged his gavel.

Chang's hand shot up. "Your Worship, we have to call a spade a spade. If these were two companies bidding on the same contract, we would legally jeopardize ourselves by giving one party pecuniary knowledge and not the other. That sort of thing ends up in lawsuits and court."

Kate nodded.

"All right," said the mayor. "Now how would council like to deal with the request from the WPD?"

There was a lull.

"I move that the presentation be received without further action." Chang.

"Hands in favour." Three of six. Then the mayor put up his hand, breaking the tie.

Now that was interesting, Kate thought. She began to type.

"The motion is passed. Received. Next on the agenda. A staff report titled CS 01 dash 47 Comparison of Policing Bids. There is the recommendation before you. Mr. Sutherland, you have the podium."

Gord Sutherland strode to the lectern holding a few sheets of paper. He fiddled with a desktop computer and a chart appeared on a screen behind the mayor and the clerk. The mayor left his chair and sat in the audience to get a better view. The other councillors sat back in their chairs, heads tilted up.

A comparison between the two forces was made across the chart under various headings: staffing, patrol units, hours, salaries, benefits, equipment costs, administrative costs, communications, special teams, complaints mechanism, public relations.

Kate had already gone through the details, and the conclusion was obvious: it was the OPP, hands down. The lights went up and she waited for council discussion to begin. Cleghorne, of course, was first to leap to her feet.

"Mr. Mayor, the report from our director of corporate services was very informative but I would like to suggest that there are more things involved ..."

Frantic typing ensued from the reporters in the room.

"... than just dollars and cents. Like the personal care we get from these men and women who live in our area and know people, and know how to do things efficiently and ... properly."

"You mean like the Southern Fried Chicken robbery?" Councillor Terryberry said without raising his hand to speak.

"Ha ha," someone hooted from the audience.

Pete glanced at Kate with raised eyebrows. She widened her eyes, smiled behind her fist, and shook her head. Laughter and muted discussion broke out between audience members.

The mayor had been prescient about the gavel. Bang! Bang!

"Please, councillor, through the chair. I won't have councillors engaging in cross talk with one another. You know the rules."

"As I was saying before I was interrupted ..." she glared at Terryberry who had a mischievous twinkle in his eye, " ... our WPD know local families and where the bad guys live and don't waste time on other things."

A hand shot up. "Mr. Mayor." It was Popowich. "Mr. Mayor, where is this going? Mr. Mayor, I don't think Councillor Cleghorne should be commenting on the way officers do their jobs. She's predicting that some officers are going to be worse than others doing the same job and that is intrinsically unfair." He was a little red-faced.

Oh goody, Kate thought. *Fireworks.* She exchanged a significant look with Pete who was madly taking notes. Kirk was deep into a one-sided discussion with Chelsea, laying out the issues and assuming she knew nothing, which was very likely the case. Afterwards, they would both scramble to get the story straight with the clerk.

"It's unhelpful to the discussion and I think that we should be careful where we go with this," Popowich continued. "We need to deal with facts and figures, not with speculation and personal opinion."

"Councillor Popowich," Cleghorne retorted. "I will have you know that my personal opinion *is* based on facts and figures. Not speculation. I resent that. Are you calling me an exaggerator? Or a liar? Mr. Mayor," she turned to face Bywater, "I would like an apology."

Popowich sat bolt upright. "Mr. Mayor, I was not calling anybody any names whatsoever. Councillor Cleghorne is taking this to a ridiculous extreme. She is again confusing the issue. We need to avoid being distracted at this point. It's important for council and for the community. And I think Councillor Cleghorne should take that seriously."

A loud murmuring swept the room.

"Now please councillors," Bywater began. "We must make sure the discussion sticks to the issue at hand. It's very important that we look at things somewhat ... let me just say ... dispassionately." He gave another couple of raps for the heck of it and nodded at the table. "Councillor Biggar."

The short stocky man got to his feet. "Mayor Bywater, we can't ignore what's in front of us. Changing over to another police force would mean changing history. And I'm not sure I'm in favour of that.

My family …"

"… has been in Waterford for over a hundred years," stage-whispered Pete.

"… has been in Waterford for over a hundred years and things have run pretty smoothly with the Waterford Police Department."

Oh, come on. How would anyone know that for sure? Kate wanted to ask.

"Why should we want such a huge change?" Biggar threw up his hands. "I think it's unwarranted. And so do the majority of my constituents, from all the phone calls and emails I'm getting." Clapping ensued from the audience.

The gavel sounded with a force louder than usual. "Please. Please. We must have order from the audience. Please. We cannot have comments or cheers from the audience. Or we will have people removed. Regrettably. Councillor Pickett."

He slowly rose to his feet. "Now I must say after having spent the better part of my life in the navy …"

Kate rolled her eyes. Pete gave a little mock slap at his forehead.

"… that I've learned a thing or two. And that is, when there are heavy seas ahead, we must man all stations on deck. And make sure the life boats are ready. On the other hand, if there are light seas and no swells, then remedial action is not required. So we should show our loyalty to our crew here, get on board, and keep on steering the ship in the right direction. If necessary." He sat down.

There was a silence in the room.

"What the hell was that?" Pete muttered.

The mayor looked confused. There was a low buzz from the audience.

Bywater shut his eyes, gave an almost imperceptible head-clearing shake, and scanned the council horseshoe once again.

Biggar had his hand up. The mayor nodded. "Let's not forget that Toronto police officers make a shitload of money." The audience guffawed. Down went the hammer. "There will be no profanity at this table," the mayor said in a mild tone of voice.

It was just a show for the audience. Everyone knew the mayor didn't mean it. He cursed all the time when there was no audience there to catch him.

"I withdraw that word, Mr. Mayor. But it's a very important point, Your Worship," Biggar continued, "that we're looking at paying our officers Toronto wages for small town work. And I for one don't think we can afford it. Nor do I think it's necessary. We don't have all the problems big cities have. Why do we need all that specialized service?"

A hand went up. "Councillor Terryberry." Surprise in his tone.

Terryberry remained seated. He laid his hands flat on the desk.

"The most important thing has already been said. 'We can't ignore what's in front of us.' And that's this report." He waved the agenda in the air.

Four sets of reporters' ears strained to hear his words. It was rare for him to speak so seriously.

"What's in front of us are more resources and more skills from the OPP than from the WPD when you compare apples to apples. And that's the bottom line. The question is do we want to make a decision based on dollars and cents, or on some tomfoolery. Now I've lived in the county all my life, and so did my father and grandfather before me. And we've seen changes. Some of them we didn't like. But even though we're just farmers, we understand that change is going to happen whether we like it or not. And we've seen that things generally change for the better. And that's what we're seeing here. And that's all I'm going to say on the matter."

He sat back in his chair, crossed his arms over his belly, and that was that.

Councillor Cleghorne took to her feet. She briefly glanced at the mayor who nodded.

"Well, I for one don't think that all change is good, Councillor Terryberry," she said. "We have to look after our people and that includes the ones here in Waterford, our police officers. They're good men and women and we need people like that. How do we know what kind of people the OPP are going to bring in? They're strangers. They don't know our county the way the WPD does."

"Hear, hear," someone called out from the audience. The gavel rapped again. "Please," said Bywater. "No comments from the audience. Otherwise there will be ejections. I've said it before and I'll say it again."

Councillor Popowich jumped up. "Your Worship, we're just going around in circles here and getting more and more confused and opinionated." Cleghorne glared. "There is some urgency with this. We need to come to a conclusion, a proper conclusion, so that staff can start setting budgets for the next year." All three directors at the side table nodded.

"Director Sutherland has produced a very satisfactory report for us, and I have trust in the analytical abilities of staff. That is what they are trained for. That is what we pay them for. I will move that we wrap up discussion at this point, study the details, and gather comments from the public before a final discussion. And unless there's new information coming forward, we should be prepared to vote on the issue at our next council meeting."

He took his seat and downed the contents of his coffee cup.

Chang's hand went up. "Seconded."

Four hands went up around the table. Then the mayor's. "All in favour. Against. Motion passed."

There was a presentation from the WPWA, the Waterford Police Wives Association. Two women came to the podium and spoke. Kate winced at their glaring biases.

Then it was the CAC. Citizens Against Crime. A group from local families of the OPP. Slightly more reasonable and disputing the assumptions made by WPWA.

Finally: "Motion to adjourn."

People were slowly rising from their chairs and filing out the back door. Pearcy and Kapoor went to the front of the room and briefly conferred with the mayor. "Oh really?" Kate heard. "Yes, well, at our next meeting. That will be a very, very good thing. Yes, thank you indeed." As one, the WPD delegation turned around to listen but it was too late. Pearcy and Kapoor made their way down the side of the room and out the door. The WPD men looked at each other quizzically, shrugged, and gathered up briefcases.

Chelsea and Kirk trailed councillors Cleghorne and Biggar into the front hallway.

"So," Kate said, snapping shut the lid of her laptop. "How goes it?" Pete looked a little pale and sleepless.

"Actually, terrible," he said.

Kate swiveled around. "What do you mean?"

"I should have taken your advice."

"What advice?"

"About Tiffany. I saw her coming out the back door of Marshalls Mens Apparel three nights in a row. Three in the morning. Conveniently just down the street from her apartment." He grimaced.

"No ..."

"Yeah. Her and the guy who owns the store. He's like forty-five. She's twenty-two. Gross."

Kate was at a loss for words. Then: "Wow, Pete. I'm sorry to hear that."

"You're not the only one. It's over, let me tell you. I don't know why I got mixed up with her in the first place. I'm totally sick of living in downtown Waterford anyway. It's a cesspool. I'm moving."

She paused. It sounded like he needed a bit of comfort. *Okay,* she thought, *I'll listen to whatever he wants to say. But only for a few minutes.* She was that age too, once. "Want to go for a coffee?"

He gathered up his tape recorder. "Sure, just let me tape this interview with Pound before he leaves the parking lot. I'll meet you at Timmie's in half an hour.

"Okay."

Chapter 59

W hen she pulled out of the municipal parking lot and reached Grand River Street North, then Burwell Street, Kate felt her car veer right instead of left almost of its own accord. In only a few minutes she found herself parked at Southern Fried Chicken. It was just before nine o'clock and the store was winding down for the night.

The screen door snapped shut behind her and she faced a dark-haired man in his forties wiping down the front counter and hauling wrapped bins of food into the walk-in cooler.

"Chuck?" Kate said.

"Yeah." He looked at her curiously.

"I'm Kate. From *The Tecumseh Challenge*. I just wanted to come by and thank you for giving me that information about the robbery. I thought I'd drop by and introduce myself."

"Sure," Chuck said. "Thanks. You're the only reporter who seemed to care about what happened."

They shook hands. "Hey, maybe I'll subscribe to your little paper. Send me something by email okay?" He dug out a business card for her.

"Sure, thanks. By the way, are you okay?" Kate asked. "It must be hard to work your shift when you're by yourself. I'd be pretty nervous."

"I am," he said. "I still haven't gotten over it. You know, I can still see the barrel of that gun. It gives me real nightmares."

"I don't blame you one bit. "

"I read all those comments people were making on *The Journal* website. They were right. The Waterford Police are a complete disgrace. I even went to a lawyer," he said. "They said there wasn't much I could do."

Kate nodded. "Too bad. Well, I just wanted to drop by to see how you were doing. Thanks for the subscription and for this." She held up the business card. "I'll be in touch."

She turned around to leave. And just then, Chuck said, "Hey, there's one more thing."

"What's that?"

"It's the craziest thing," he said. "I've got a little story for you. But I don't want this to go in the paper."

"Okay, off the record."

"Okay. Well. I swear I recognized one of the guys from the robbery. He came by the other day to pick up an order."

That stopped Kate right in her tracks.

"You have got to be kidding."

"No, I wish I was. It was completely bizarre. But I really think it was the same guy. Something about his eyes. During the robbery he had a scarf over his face, you know? But I could see his eyes. Grey like velvet, and crazy. And very, very skinny. I swear it was the same guy."

"Holy shit."

"Yeah, I know. I got the creeps when he was standing there. It was weird. My body seemed to know right away something was wrong. Then my brain kicked in. It was hard to look at him and give back the change. But you know, when I did, he had a funny expression on his face too. Nervous-like. Maybe he could tell I noticed something."

"Did you happen to see what he was driving?"

"You know, I did. I peeked around the shade when he couldn't see me looking. He got into a dark blue GMC van with a tan strip along the bottom. The driver's side. There was another guy there too. Blond.."

That hit Kate in the gut.

"That van didn't happen to have a pair of big fuzzy dice hanging off the rear-view mirror, did it?"

Chuck stared at her. "How the heck did you know that?"

"Geez," Kate said. "That's unbelievable. I've seen that van around town." She declined to be more specific. But she knew exactly where around town she had seen that van. And it hadn't been far from home.

Chuck just looked at her incredulously.

"Do you think we should report this to the police?" he finally said.

"The Waterford Police? They won't have anything to do with me anymore. And you know something? I'm not so sure that they would do anything about it, anyway."

"Yeah," Chuck said thoughtfully. "Maybe I'll bypass the police and go to the county's Police Services Board. But you know something else? I got the guy's name on the order. As a matter of fact, I kept it. I still have it here."

He left to unpin something from a bulletin board in the back, then brought it to the counter.

"Look," he said, pointing.

A long strip of paper listed all the various permutations of chicken baskets, chicken wings, chicken fingers, chicken legs, dark meat, white meat, side orders, condiments, drinks. Checked off were two orders of wings with hot sauce and fries on the side, plus two pops. And at the top of the order was a name scrawled in capital letters. It was easily readable.

Kate drew a breath.

Pound.

Chapter 60

Kate was nursing her decaffeinated tea and had transformed a press release or two into useful articles before Pete finally pushed open the door of the Tim Hortons coffee shop.

That girl with the long dark hair at Marshall's store, Kate thought. *That must have been Tiffany. Pete's Tiffany.*

There was something she wanted to ask him.

The laptop slid back into its case. Pete set his cup onto the table top and slumped into the chair. Kate eyed him over the top of her mug.

"Get the interview?"

"Yeah. Pound's mad as hell that council didn't give him what he wanted."

"What he was asking for was kind of ridiculous. Desperate measures if you ask me."

"I asked him what he would do if he found himself out of a job and he nearly took my head off."

"Ha ha. That took a lot of nerve. Now he's going to cut you off like he cut me off."

"What do you mean?"

"The WPD cut me from the press release circulation."

"Huh? Why?"

"Long story. They disagreed with my reporting style."

"You mean your story on the Southern Fried Chicken robbery."

"Yeah."

"And your editorial on the WPD policing bid."

"Yeah. How did you know?"

"Not surprised. That's what it's like around here. Hey — did you know Bill Pound's kid — I think his name was Charlie, something like that — was charged with theft and drug possession in Cambridge last year? That's where I worked before I got here. Anyway, Pound phoned the radio station and tried to quash the report. Said his kid didn't do it. Someone else did. And the drugs belonged to someone else, too."

"Really."

"Yeah. Utter bullshit. The kid was convicted. Served two months."

"Wow."

Kate decided to change the topic.

"So Tiffany had a dark side."

"Holy crap," Pete said. "I kind of wondered from the beginning, you know? Always disappearing. I could never find her. All those tats on her arms. A little street looking."

"Yeah. Didn't you say you liked that? Or was that just at first."

"Yeah, that's the truth. I mean, what guy wouldn't?" Kate winced. "Anyway, I didn't like the drugs."

Kate's eyes widened.

"I didn't tell you about that. She never really told me all of everything she was doing, but I could tell. Once I walked into the bathroom and she was sitting on the can with a crack pipe. Huffing away. And the people she hung out with. Booze and drugs, drugs and booze, that's all I saw, all the time."

Kate shook her head. "That's bad. That would have been nothing but trouble."

Pete nodded his head in agreement.

"How long do you think she was having an affair with Marshall?"

"Who knows. Who cares."

"Poor Julie, I wonder if she knew about Tiffany. You know it was Marshall's wife Julie Crawford who died, right? They found her body in the river in August, remember?"

"What?" Pete looked startled. "No, I didn't know. Are you're kidding? That was Marshall's wife?"

Kate stared at him, astounded. "Of course. Oh my God, Pete, you're in the news business. Didn't you realize who it was?"

He chugged half his coffee and clapped the cup down on the table. "I was kind of busy at the time. With Tiffany. Remember? I'd just met her." He waggled his eyebrows up and down.

"Oh my God," Kate slapped her forehead. "Why is everything about sex?"

"Because everything *is* about sex."

Kate rolled her eyes. "But I'm sure you did a news item on Julie."

"Maybe. I can't remember everyone. So many names, so many newscasts. Besides, it's different when you're new to the area. I don't know all the people around here. I didn't make the connection."

"Look Pete, Julie died some time at the end of August. They found her body in the river on Wednesday, August 22nd. The police let everyone call it a suicide. Personally, I never believed it."

Pete sipped his coffee again and digested the information.

There was a question Kate had already formulated in her mind.

"Were you with Tiffany the weekend before or the days before or on August 22nd?" she asked. "In the morning? You said you could never get hold of her in the mornings."

"The third weekend in August?" Pete scrunched up his eyes with a faraway look. "I had the weekend shift for sure. I get the last two weekends every month. I'm the new guy. I definitely wasn't around town. I was in studio. And the Monday and Tuesday? Not sure."

"What I'm saying is, do you think Tiffany was with Marshall when Julie died?"

"Hmm." He looked thoughtful. "Maybe. Maybe Julie found him with Tiffany and couldn't take it, so she jumped off the bridge."

Kate glared at him. "Pete. You're just as bad as those ridiculous WPD guys. That's sexist. That's a myth. That's from the Victorian era. Women don't jump off a bridge any more when they discover their husbands having an affair. C'mon."

"Oh. Yeah, you're probably right. They take revenge."

"Oh, come on. That's only in the movies.

"Okay. So what *do* they do?"

"How should I know?"

"You're a woman."

"Oh, for God's sake. Pete, these days, women probably just move out. Or they get a lawyer. Or maybe they just put up with it and get bitter and angry. There's only so many things a person can do."

"Yeah, I think they get bitter and angry first, then they get a lawyer, then they get even. Or they get even first, you know what I mean? They get revenge."

Kate rolled her eyes.

"Pete, your mind lives in the gutter. Do you think everyone behaves as badly as possible?"

He grinned. "Only when they can get away with it."

She shook her head. She hoped he wasn't right.

But it was something to ponder later, when she had time to think. Maybe strong emotions, strong reactions, and not being forced to account for them, *were* the cause of people acting badly.

But maybe people acted badly when they believed they had no other choice, too. Or when they couldn't think straight. Or if they didn't have the intellectual capacity to see the solution. Or if they didn't realize that other people had the identical problems, too, and how did *they* solve them?

As Kate drove home, she realized her brain was stuck in an intellectual rat's nest.

Marshall *could* have been occupied when Julie was being murdered. But perhaps not. But if Marshall didn't do it, who did? Who had a motive?

She needed more facts, more information to sort it all out. But where was she to find it? Who would know? Who knew more details about how the Crawfords lived their lives?

It was a puzzle, and getting more and more confusing all the time. She really could not think straight any more at all.

She clicked on the CD player with Alfred asleep at her feet.

It was Suzanne Ciani on the Buchla, normally a godsend. The infinite array of pitches and textures, the purity of its sine waves were perfect for clearing her mind and sharpening her thoughts. It made her feel so good, too. Full and satisfied, like she just had the best meal in the world.

But for some reason, it didn't help.

Nothing did. Not that evening.

That night she fell into an uneasy slumber.

Chapter 61

"**Y**our woman friend is waiting for you." Stavros waved Kate towards their table in front of the big picture window.

It was mid-afternoon and the lunch crowd had cleared out. Kate glanced at the view. The river was churning and grey, full of fall debris. A dozen Canada geese paddled in the eddies, filtering the waters for tasty bits.

"Hello there, dear," Dorothy said. Paying tribute to the fall season, she had worn a scarlet, orange, and chocolate brown outfit with a matching scarf and an oak leaf brooch. Très chic.

"We haven't talked for a while, kiddo. How ya doin'?" She sipped her cappuccino. "I've got a shitload of leaves in the backyard. Again! Those bastards next door. Won't do a damn thing with those branches hanging over my backyard. Did I tell you?"

She had. More than once. But Kate let her continue. Finally, there was a break.

"Dorothy, I need to tell you a few things about Julie." Her voice dropped to a whisper at the end. Stavros did not look up from his glass polishing at the bar.

"Like what?" Dorothy's lowered her voice to the same level.

Francesco showed up with water, napkins, and cutlery. "Good afternoon, ladies. The usual?"

They nodded. He spun around on his heel and headed to the kitchen. They heard the swinging door squeak back and forth and voices calling out. It was safe.

"There's good news and bad news. Which do you want first?"

"The bad news, of course."

"I got black-listed by the Waterford Police Department. I got hauled in by Kowalchuk. I showed them some photos, but they refused to investigate Julie's death as a murder."

Dorothy shook her head. "I told you you would get in trouble."

"It was unavoidable."

"Yes, but they probably wondered whether it was even a murder in the first place."

"You don't understand. The photos I brought in to show Kowalchuk were good forensic evidence. And he just brushed them aside."

"Really? What forensic evidence? Kate. You didn't tell me. Fill me in."

"Another crime scene on the bank of the Grand River. With Julie's earring. Pictures of everything."

Dorothy gaped. "And you found everything on your own? Holy cow. You know what? I believe it. I know you, girl. You're a little Sherlock Holmes in heels."

"You know I don't wear heels, Dorothy."

Dorothy chuckled. "Okay, a Sherlock in flats. Now what's the good news?"

"The good news is that I met someone who feels the same way I do about Julie. And he has connections with the coroner. And the crown attorney."

Dorothy gave a little whistle. "Who's that?"

"His name is Jay Blackfoot. He's an ambulance worker. He knows Mr. Mackenzie."

"Hugh Mackenzie from the Penmarvian? What does he have to do with anything? And by the way, I have something to give you." She shuffled around in her purse.

"He witnessed an incident involving Julie about the time she was killed."

"Wow." Dorothy's jaw went slack. "Well, thanks for finally bringing me up to date," she said a trifle sarcastically. "Geesh."

"I know, Dorothy. I'm sorry. You know me. I'm always working under a deadline. Never enough time to call."

Francesco approached their table with Dorothy's Greek salad and quiche, and smoked salmon on a Greek salad for Kate.

"Thanks, Francesco." Kate turned to Dorothy. "The whole thing with the Waterford police happened because they didn't like the way I reported the Southern Fried Chicken robbery. They said I made them look bad."

Dorothy chuckled. "You did. I was going to phone you. But they probably deserved it."

"They did."

She shook her head. "Bunch of incompetents. Have been for as long as I can remember."

"Really?"

"Yes. I heard lots of stories."

They both dug into their food.

"And how are your meals today, ladies? Can I get you anything? Like this? Or are you both getting laid already? Heh heh."

They both jumped. It was Stavros, of course. He was standing at the side of his table with his pelvic area thrust out.

"Oh my God," Kate exclaimed. Stavros, grinning, pretended he didn't hear.

"Hello, my good man," Dorothy said, taking the high road and ignoring the entire unfortunate display. "How's business these days?"

He leaned over a chair back. "Terrible. I'm going out of business tomorrow. This is my last day."

Kate's head shot up. "Really? You're kidding."

Dorothy shook her head. "He is. Aren't you, Stavros?"

"No kidding," he asserted.

"Oh yes, you are. I saw a delivery truck come by when I was in the parking lot. You wouldn't be getting a delivery if you were closing your doors."

"Heh heh." He changed tack. "You neighbours with the Hacketts?" He nodded at Kate. "You know, Conner and Sam."

"Yeah." Kate said. "Why?"

"That Conner is a jerk. I had him in the kitchen five weeks and yesterday he quit. The worst dishwasher I ever had."

"What? Do you mean my neighbour Conner Hackett? The kid?"

"Yeah, the kid. The tall blond one."

"He works for you? Are you serious?" *Cripes, sooner or later everyone in town works for Stavros*, Kate thought. *I just can't figure out why.*

"No more. He quit, I just told you. The worst guy I ever had."

"Well, I'm not surprised. Those people are probably the worst neighbours I ever had."

"They live right beside you? I thought they did."

"Unfortunately, yes."

"That Conner is an asshole. Now I know why Marshall fired that loser."

Kate's head elevated another notch.

"Marshall? What does Marshall have to do with it?"

"Conner worked for Marshall before he worked for me."

Dorothy nodded in agreement.

"What? Doing what? How come I didn't know this before? I didn't know the Hacketts' kid worked for Marshall."

"For about a year. He's sort of a relative." A pause while Dorothy speared a chunk of quiche. "Moira and Marshall are related."

Kate's jaw dropped. "Oh c'mon. What? You're kidding. More stuff you didn't tell me." She gave Dorothy a look.

"I didn't think it was relevant," Dorothy protested.

"It's relevant."

"It could be, I suppose, now that I think about it." Dorothy tried to look innocent.

Another look.

"Marshall is Moira's brother," Stavros said.

Kate nodded. "Really. What did Conner do at Marshall's?"

"Deliveries, chores, things around the store. His brother, the younger one, works there now."

"Wow. You mean Sam? Something *else* I didn't know."

"We've got to come here more often and discuss things," Dorothy said. "It's your own fault. You're too busy. You need some time off for real life."

Don't I know it.

"Yeah, Sam, that's his name," Stavros continued. "Another little prick. Sam and Conner both hang around here, downtown, since a long time. Since high school. They work for anyone. As long as they get the money. You know?" He rubbed his two fingertips against his thumb.

"So Marshall fires that asshole Conner in July. And he comes down the street to my store and asks me for a job as a dishwasher. Begged me. I felt sorry for the guy. Just shows you. You feel sorry for the guy and that's the way he acts. Like a jerk. Running out the back, morning, noon, and night. Here I am paying him and he's gone for an hour.

The kitchen told me. Where the fuck was he going? It was always an emergency. He said his mother, his father, his brother. Bullshit. He had a girlfriend. He would go be with his girlfriend, then come back like nothing happened."

"That's terrible," Kate said. "Doesn't surprise me."

"Who was his girlfriend?" Dorothy asked. She always needed to know these things. It might come in handy some day. Kate admired her foresight.

Stavros sat down. It was a sure sign he had something momentous to impart. He picked at his teeth with a wooden olive spear. "I heard it was your friend," he nodded at Kate. "Your Julie."

"What? Julie and Conner? You have got to be kidding. Couldn't be. Impossible."

"Shocking," Dorothy murmured.

Chewing at the toothpick, he tilted his head and his expression read, "why not?"

"People are people," he said. "They have sex with anybody. They do stupid things. They can't help it."

Kate contemplated this in silence. It was entirely possible.

It was a complete mystery to Kate why people behaved so illogically for such long periods of time. On the other hand, maybe there were mitigating factors that had caused Julie to behave so imprudently. Obviously, she had desired the relationship. Perhaps it had boosted her confidence and given her reassurance. Perhaps it was a case of forbidden fruit, all the more attractive.

She thought about Pete's comment. Maybe there were a other factors, too. Sordid ones.

"I'll bet Moira wasn't too happy about that," Dorothy piped up, delicately dabbing at her lips with a napkin.

"Ah, now that's a mother for you," Stavros said, throwing his hands in the air. "A disgrace. Always making excuses for him. Always covering his ass. Why? That kid should take responsibility for himself. She does everything for him. He lost his licence. She drives him to work every single morning. Every single day."

Kate stared at Stavros. "*Every* day?" she asked.

"Didn't I just say? Are you deaf, woman?"

"When did he lose his licence?"

"Uh? I don't know. Some time in the summer. Impaired."

"Tsk, tsk," said Dorothy. "Starting young. Not good."

"He's a bad one," Stavros said. "His brother, the young kid — even worse."

He got to his feet, straightened his suit, and picked lint off his lapel.

"Will that be all ladies? Another cappuccino? Or the bill."

"Bill, please. I'll get it, Kate."

"Thanks Dorothy. I'll get the next one." Dorothy fumbled in her purse for her wallet.

"Oh. Before I forget. This is for you." She held out a folded piece of paper. "From Hugh Mackenzie."

Kate opened it up while Dorothy waited expectantly. A few seconds ticked by.

"Well … what does it say?"

Kate passed it back to her.

In shaky handwriting were scrawled some words.

The man had red shoes.

Chapter 62

I was sick to my stomach when Sam told me.
Conner twenty-one years old for God's sake.
Her nephew.

I couldn't get that picture out of my mind. Her touching him. How dare she. She disgusted me. People were talking. All the whispering going on.

I saw her that morning.

I wanted to show her that I knew about her behaviour.

I wanted to confront her. I wanted to punish her.

And when I saw what she was wearing around her neck, that was the last straw.

Chapter 63

Lt never would have happened if Kate hadn't decided to clean out the eavestroughs that day.

Old houses were prone to having old trees. Big old trees with lots … and lots … and lots of leaves.

It was Sunday and there had been a biting wind the night before. Kate surveyed the bare maple next door, the near naked oak on the front lawn, and the thinned-out redbud leaning against the front porch. The old elm had done a number over the back deck, and when Kate checked the downspouts, they were completely plugged.

That initiated a propping up of the extension ladder to inspect all the troughs around the house, and the commencement of a thorough clean out. Manually and with a hose.

When she finally finished, her energy was almost depleted. But she looked at the running pile of leaves encircling her house and decided she had just enough strength left to rake up the piles, and haul them all over to the composter.

The Swedish composter was a marvel, Kate agreed, but its two compartments quickly filled to the brim. When she pushed down hard on the locking mechanism to close the lid, she was left with a leaf pile the size of a couple of barrels.

Now what?

All of a sudden she remembered. The green bin. The one she never used because she had her Jora. The supersized green bin delivered by Tecumseh County with its new green recycling program, the bin left still untouched beside the old cedars at the end of the side yard.

There it was, still in the same spot where she had left it. She tilted it back onto its set of wheels; it was easy to roll.

Hmm. It would actually be easier to bring the bin down on its side so she could push all the leaves in.

As she laid it down on the ground, she heard a couple of objects tumble inside and thought, *oh for Pete's sake, what the heck.* Flipped open the lid. And there they were. The same two stinky red running shoes she had seen weeks before sitting on the Hackett's garbage cans.

Wha...? What were those doing in there? Don't tell me those buggers next door tossed their garbage into my container again. And for gosh sake, they've completely stunk up my brand new green bin.

Cripes. Probably on purpose.

Just what she needed. Why were they always so idiotic? She would have to air out the whole bin over winter and hopefully, if she was lucky, that disgusting smell would go away.

She was so cursed living beside that horrible family.

She dumped the running shoes onto the ground and began filling up the bin with the leaves. Stuffed them all in. Closed the lid. Brought it back upright. Wheeled it to the road.

And it was while walking back up the driveway thinking about well, about nothing really, just about how tired she was, and how rotten her neighbours were, and how incredible it was that they always found new ways to ruin her life on a continual basis — that everything — all the feelings she had and the suspicions and all the unanswered questions — the whole thing — came together, just like that.

And she almost fell over in her tracks.

Of course. It all made sense.

It had all been right there, right in front of her eyes. And her ears. And her nose.

And now she just needed to prove it.

Chapter 64

Everyone's Goal is Mine More Coal
— Bus stop wall painting, Coaldale Pennsylvania, 1963

The largest and most concentrated anthracite deposit in the world is found in the Coal Region of northeastern Pennsylvania, a region 100 miles long and 30 miles wide, holding 20 billion tonnes of anthracite. This hard-burning smokeless coal fueled America's Industrial Revolution and heated the homes of eastern Canada, more so than Nova Scotia coal whose transportation made the product too expensive. Pennsylvania anthracite coal fueled the industries of southern Ontario and Quebec for nearly eighty years.

— George P.W. Lukacz, Professor of Geology,
The History of Powering Canada

Kate paper-bagged the shoes and brought them upstairs to her lab.

The shoes were a men's size ten. Not the biggest.

She pulled out the insoles. Footprints were clearly etched into the soft fabric-laminated rubber but there seemed to be more than one set.

She painted one of the soles with raw beet juice and pressed the shoe onto a sheet of paper. The shoe print had a distinctive lineup of rectangles on the outside half, separated by a slightly curved centre channel, then a wave-patterned inside half with a solid half-inch border.

She set a screen trap into her laundry sink drainhole, and carefully washed down one of the shoes. Onto a small plastic sheet went the contents of the screen trap. Kate poked through it with a sterile knife, spreading the muck to the sides. There were bits of gooey algae, sand particulates, stuff that might have been rotting leaves.

She took scrapings off the bottom and dissolved them in distilled water. Another sample from the screentrap. Looked into the microscope.

Fragilaria ulna. Fragilaria capucina. Navicula minima.

She wondered which diatom specifically was responsible for the smell, if any. It was impossible to tell.

Clearly, someone had worn these shoes while crossing the Grand River during the sewage overflow. But exactly who?

She repacked the shoes into separate paper bags, taped them shut, and set them aside.

Lost in thought, she stared out the lab window overlooking her driveway and the Hackett's house. Her view was that of the two skateboards, the pink one and the long black one, leaning against the outside brick wall where she herself had placed them. They hadn't moved since.

It was blessedly quiet. Next door, no one appeared to be home. She quickly went outside, looked both ways, then walked over to the boards, grabbing them one at a time and carefully moving them indoors. She took them upstairs to her lab room.

Each board was swept for an examination with a raking light. Both boards displayed a variety of prints. Both boards showed a shoe with a distinctive line up of rectangles on the outside half, separated by slightly curved centre channel, then a wave-patterned inside half with a solid half-inch border.

The same shoes on each board.

That shouldn't surprise her. She had heard with her own ears how the Hackett boys continually used each other's stuff. And that undoubtedly had included skateboards.

With a hard cotton sterile swab, she dragged the surfaces of both skateboards, dissolved the samples into separate test tubes of sterile water and turned on the microscope.

Nothing. Nothing unusual. Just the standard particles that she expected to see on skateboards. Sand, aggregate, grass, tiny weed seeds, large bits of dried-out plant material.

No diatoms. None whatsoever.

She was crestfallen. Had she been barking up the wrong tree? The red shoes. The stench of the river. The Hacketts. *Where was the connection?*

She sighed. She had better get those skateboards back next door before the Hacketts showed up. She peered out the window. Was there anyone home yet? Didn't look like it.

She speedily returned the skateboards to their place against the wall.

But just as she turned to go back, something niggled at the periphery of her mind — that angry morning almost two months before when Sam and Conner rode their skateboards on the walkway beside her house. They didn't have their shoes on that morning, either. Barefoot.

She stopped with a lurch in the middle of the driveway. *Now why was that?*

There's no such thing as a coincidence.

Maybe it wasn't that they didn't *find their shoes. Maybe they* couldn't *find their shoes.*

She ran back to the lab, grabbed a sterile plastic container and a brand new narrow paintbrush, and ran outside to the middle of the driveway again. Looked right. Looked left. Still no one around.

She casually sidled up to the Hackett's front door and tossed the paintbrush onto their front porch. *Whoops. How did that happen?*

She bent over to retrieve the brush and at the same time, lifted the end of the mat. A section of debris from one side of the covered area, the area that was most used, was brushed into her waiting container. She screwed the lid back on. Placed the mat perfectly back into position. Ran back to her lab.

The largest stones and debris were removed and three samples were prepared in distilled water from the dirt that remained.

According to her textbook *Forensic Biology in a Nutshell*, diatoms could be quite resistant to the elements. But their only possible source could be a moist medium. Definitely not a dusty gravel driveway or a cement walkway.

She crossed her fingers.

She said a little prayer to Frances Glessner Lee.

She looked into the eyepiece and turned the focus knob.

And there they were.

Chapter 65

The SD card where Kate had so carefully loaded up the photos of Julie's earring was sitting on top of the computer.

She slid it into the card slot, then clicked the icon that appeared on the screen.

Yes, the images were still there, along with the four high resolution jpg files she had already sent to Jay Blackfoot.

She ran through the shots she took at the back of Penmarvian. At a spot very close to where Hugh MacKenzie had been sitting in his wheelchair, a view of the train bridge peeked out from between the branches.

That must have been where he'd seen the man and the woman, Kate thought. But exactly where was that spot on the bridge? She searched for something that might distinguish that particular location, then found it. It was a section of tracks with a safety platform on the south side of the bridge. And a rod forming part of the metal railing. Slightly bent.

She had missed that in her first set of photos. Maybe they were at the wrong angle. Maybe she had been so unnerved by her near miss with the train that she had overlooked it.

She wondered if that was the location from which Julie had plummeted.

Maybe there was other evidence she'd missed at that location. Was it worth taking another look?

She so wanted the answer to be no. But she knew it had to be yes.

She now had a sense how Julie's murder could have taken place. But if her hunch was right, she also knew what she could be in for. Trouble that could not be sidestepped, no matter what.

She would have to return and walk that damnable train bridge once again.

She composed a quick email, attached the pertinent new pictures, and sent it all to Jay Blackfoot.

"Jay, I have more information that may interest you. Julie was having an affair with a young male coworker at the store. Could be important. Let me know if this goes anywhere with the crown attorney," she wrote. "In the meantime, I'm going back to the bridge to take another look at what I think is another crime scene. This morning. Wish me luck. May need backup."

She cc'd it too. Just in case there was hope.

To Kowalchuk.

She waited. Waited some more.

No response, of course.

She sighed impatientily, switched off the computer, and dusted off her two hands.

Here goes nothing.

Chapter 66

Kate gathered together a kit in the lab room. Into her knapsack went a magnifying glass, a sterile plastic container, a small knife, latex gloves, a new one-inch wide paint brush, and a plastic bag. She switched the long lens on her Nikon for a 100 millimeter telephoto macro lens, reducing the weight by a pound, and slipped the camera into the knapsack along with binoculars.

She donned nylon ripstop pants and a nylon long-sleeved jacket over a coat, pulled back her hair into a ponytail and stuffed it under a baseball cap.

There, she said, looking in the mirror. *As non-shedding and fibre-free as I possibly can be.*

She had checked both the passenger and the freight train schedules through Waterford and determined that the best time would be late morning, when the commuters were gone and the sun would be slightly at her back.

Kate drove straight to narrow winding Portland Street and headed to the top of the hill where the parking lot sat at the Waterford Cemetery. She mulled over the email that had appeared on the screen of her computer just as she was getting ready to go. Jay Blackfoot.

"Kate," the email said. "A lot of things have happened since I last saw you. The crown has agreed to open a case. The OPP will be handling the investigation. They're sending over a forensic team to your location on the river asap. The coroner is conducting a disinterment in the next few days. It's crucial if you get any more evidence, to hand it over to the lead investigator. His name is Inspector Roger Kapoor. I'll be in touch."

Even the police can't do what I'm going to do today, if all goes according to plan, she thought.

She beeped shut the door locks on the Audi and slid the knapsack over her shoulders. The binos were slung separately, crosswise over her chest.

Trepidation assailed her once again, tempered only by a few degrees of confidence that this time, almost certainly, she had all the information she needed for a safe trip along the train bridge.

She had a window of about two hours.

She had a pretty good idea about the distance she needed to cover. About 150 metres. All she needed to do was locate that bent piece of railing.

She walked down Portland Street to where a well-used path led up the bank to the railway track. She scrambled uphill, grabbing shrubs along the way, and within a few minutes, found herself standing on the gravel bed of the tracks.

She took to the tracks, awkwardly stretching her pace to meet every other tie, arriving at the point just before the tracks exited the shelter of the trees. She was facing open air. It felt horribly familiar.

She looked at Willow Street beneath and waited. Soon, two vehicles drove by in opposite directions — a white pickup truck and a Honda CR-V sports utility vehicle. The rear brake lights of the SUV glowed momentarily, and so did the brake lights on the truck.

Uh huh. I think they saw me.

She screwed up her resolve to forge ahead. Just like the last time, she needed to keep her wits about her.

She scanned the tracks ahead to see if the location of the bent railing could be pinned down. Nothing yet.

She listened carefully. No ominous rumbling.

Looking to the left, then the right, she moved ahead and in a minute or two she had passed over Willow Street. There were four safety platforms on each side of the tracks. The bent railing was likely at the last platform on the south side.

She walked quickly to the first platform, and took a minute to breathe. There seemed to be quite few vehicles on the road. That was a concern. Time was of the essence.

She listened closely once again. No rumbling. She skipped the next safety platform and headed to the third one, for expediency's sake. She paused and raised the binoculars to her eyes.

Yes, there it was, surely. The bent railing.

Huh.

She listened. Nothing. No rumbling. No vibration.

The bent rail, about six metres ahead, took a minute of quick walking.

She scanned the railing from top to bottom, side to side. She stopped and shot a series of photos at every angle.

Kate looked over the rail into the water ten stories below.

There didn't seem to be anything obvious.

She scanned the other side of the tracks.

Nothing.

She got on her knees and gingerly crawled her way ten ties to each side of the bent rail.

Nothing. Her knee twinged uncomfortably.

The whole thing may have been a long shot that didn't seem to be panning out.

Just for the heck of it, she pulled out her one-inch wide flat paintbrush and swept the dust off half a dozen ties into her sterile container, depositing it into her knapsack.

She stood up and brushed off her clothes. She would be really glad to make it back to the other side again, and it needed to be done as quickly as possible.

Her head was down when she started back, two railway ties with each long step, carefully watching her footing.

It was when she crossed Willow Street that she looked down at the road and realized a WPD vehicle had parked right under the overpass.

Uh oh. I'm in for it. I better have a really good story.

Her mind was racing. A ripple of fear shot through her belly.

She was still looking at her footing at end of the bridge where it connected with solid ground once again when she noticed there was something that didn't fit with the junk food wrappers, the cigarette butts, the plastic bags. It was shiny and unusual-looking and jammed into the gravel.

What the...

She stopped and crouched over for a closer look. She poked aside the stones, got out her jack knife and pried out an oddly-shaped object. The knife went back into her rear pocket.

It was a silverish dragonfly with wings outspread. Textured, with a scored abdomen, and a solid hard little thorax.

Now fancy that.

She polished up the object a bit with her fingertips and slipped it into her knapsack.

There were steps on the gravel.

"Give me that!"

Kate looked up.

"Give me that thing you just picked up. Now!"

It was Moira, her neighbour. Red-faced and angry.

"Moira. I had a feeling I might meet up with you."

"Just shut your mouth and give me that thing you put in your knapsack or I'll get it myself. It doesn't belong to you."

"You're right. And it doesn't belong to you, either, even though Conner took it from your jewellery box. It belongs to Julie."

"I have no idea what you're talking about. She had nothing to do with it. Give it to me now!"

"I think you do, and I think she had a lot to do with it. I think she had a lot to do with a lot of things."

Suddenly, Moira shot out with both hands and pushed Kate hard in the chest. She fell backwards to the ground, landing on her elbows and her rear end, momentarily winded and caught off guard.

What the hell!

Moira gave a kick and Kate, her bad knee still not working properly, managed to just get out of reach with a rapid backwards crab crawl. Moira advanced and grabbed at the shoulder strap of Kate's knapsack, trying to pull the whole thing off. She was strong enough to do it, too.

"Get the hell away from me," Kate yelled as loud as she could, tussling with Moira's grip. "You're not going to hurt me like you hurt Julie!" She lay back on her elbows and kicked out at Moira's head, grazing her cheek.

"Give it to me or I'll stomp on your head!" Moira reached out.

"Don't you touch me!" Kate yelled as loudly as she possibly could.

Moira looked around with a wild look in her eyes, pulled a heavy stick out of the undergrowth, and brandished it at Kate who tried her best to scramble upright, but couldn't. Her sore knee.

She rolled to one side. Maybe she could divert Moira before she took another swing.

"You washed the Mickey Mouse t-shirt and the jeans but they didn't come very clean, did they? So you threw them out. And no one in your house could wear the red Nike running shoes after you ruined them, could they? They stank to high heaven. Like the river did that morning you jumped in the water."

"Shut up! You're crazy! Give me that dragonfly or else!"

"I knew it was you. Not the boys. They never wore those shoes after you had them in the river. But you left the evidence on your front doormat."

"You're an idiot!" Moira took a step forward and swung the branch, and Kate rolled to the other side, avoiding the strike by an inch.

Yikes!

"Julie knew all about Sam and Conner, didn't she? She didn't die when you pushed her off the bridge. You had to drown her in the river."

Another swing of the branch, forcing Kate to roll again. Moira raised the branch, poised for another blow.

"Moira, I'm warning you. Stop or you'll be sorry."

She raised the branch even higher.

She's not quitting.

Kate whispered the taekwondo oath. *I shall observe the tenets of taekwondo. I shall respect the instructor and seniors. I shall never misuse taekwondo. I shall be a champion of freedom and justice. I shall build a more peaceful world.*

Kate took advantage of the momentum of a rising half-turn to swing around with her good knee to the side of Moira that was unprotected by the branch, and brought her clenched hand back towards Moira's face. At the moment of connection, Kate exhaled with a shout.

"Ki hap!" *The spirit shouts.*

Moira shrieked and put her hand to her suddenly broken nose, trying to stem the bleeding.

Kate half-bounced on the spot, did a full spin, then a high kick into Moira's chest. It would have been the side of her head if Kate's knee had been working properly.

Moira fell to the ground, clutching her rib cage, and groaning.

Kate rubbed her elbows and her rear end. Just bruises and scrapes. Her knee hurt more than ever from that high kick, though.

And just at that moment a uniformed police officer stepped up onto the tracks, both hands clutching his gun in a firing position. A Smith & Wesson revolver.

"Don't move!" he shouted at Kate. "Put your hands in the air! Now!"

Kate slowly raised her hands.

"You're making a mistake," she said. "Moira's the one who attacked me. I was just defending myself." Then she realized who she was talking to. Police Chief Bill Pound. She groaned.

"Shut up," he said. "Take that knapsack off slowly and lie on the ground face down."

"Don't shoot!" she yelled. "Please."

"Shut up for Chrissakes! Get down!"

She slid off the knapsack, set it down. It wasn't easy to find a spot between the rocks but soon she was able to spread out on the ground beside the tracks. She flinched from the stones scratching the side of her face and the dust grinding against her teeth. Pound was enjoying the sight of that.

Out of the corner of her eye she saw him return the gun to its holster. Kate felt a smidgen of relief

Pound picked up the knapsack and gestured with his head to Moira.

"Let's go," he said. "Don't bother with her. We've got everything we need. No one will believe her crazy story anyway."

Moira still couldn't get up off the ground. Pound grabbed an arm and hauled her up, and she complained and groaned. But she wasn't in so much pain that she couldn't think.

"I think we should tie her to the tracks. There wouldn't be anything left of her. People have seen her up here anyway. It would look like an accident."

Kate's heart sank. Her chances for leniency from Pound were pretty much zero.

There was a silence while Pound contemplated the notion.

"Okay. I've got a couple of zip ties. They'll break away on impact. Move over to the tracks face down," he ordered Kate. "Move it! Now!"

"All right," Kate acquiesced. "Just cool your jets. I've got a sore knee, for crying out loud." She crawled over with difficulty and lay spreadeagled on the tracks. The smell of creosote and diesel forced its way up her nose.

"Shut up!"

Pound grabbed her right wrist a little too hard, placed it on the rail and wrapped a zip tie around both. Then he dragged her other hand over and did the same. He pulled to test the tautness.

"Ouch!" Kate said. "That's tight! Couldn't you loosen them up a bit?"

"Shut up before I kick you in the head!" Pound said. "Okay, c'mon. Let's go. Go go go!"

Kate heard the two scrambling down the side of the slope, Moira whimpering and groaning all the way.

Kate lay uncomfortably on the tracks. She didn't have a plan to get out of this one.

What a stupid way to go. Damn that Kowalchuk. If he was doing his job properly, he'd be here by now. Then: *What am I thinking? That guy never does his goddamn job properly.*

She tried yelling but it was hard to make much noise right up against the ground. She let loose with some muffled screeching.

God, I hope someone hears me. What are the chances?

That was when she heard all the yelling. Men.

"Police! Both of you. Put your hands up! Now!"

The tracks began to vibrate ever so slightly and she knew only too well what that meant. Her heart fell.

"Help!" she screamed facing sideways. "Somebody. Anybody. I'm tied to the tracks!"

A faint thundering grew louder. Then louder still.

Kate emptied her lungs with the force of every cell in her entire being, emitting a horrible ear-splitting extended wail.

Heeeeeeeeeelp!

A head popped up over the embankment. It was Kowalchuk.

About bloody time!

"Quick. The ties!" Kate yelled. "There's a knife in my back pocket."

The sound of metal wheels upon metal rails began to fill the air.

Oh my God. Hurry the hell up.

Kowalchuk found the knife right away and cut the plastic binds. Kate rolled over with difficulty.

The squealing became a long drawn-out screeching, then a clacking as the wheels banged over the joint between the land track and the bridge. The front light on the train engine beamed from the other side of the bridge, rapidly moving towards them.

The conductor leaned on the horn.

"C'mon, let's get the hell out of here!" Kowalchuk helped her to her feet and supported her while they both tried to get off the tracks and onto the safety of the grass.

The wind that preceded the locomotive blew Kate's hair to one side of her face, stifling her breath, blinding her, and forcing her to close her eyes. The air left her lungs; things tilted and swirled.

And it was right then that her sore knee decided to fail her.

She fell to the ground and covered her head while the dust and dirt billowed and flew in the air. It was impossible to get up.

Kowalchuk crouched beside her, an arm around her shoulders as she buried her head in agony.

It felt like forever for the freight train's long lineup of tankers, flat cars, gondolas, and box cars to scream by. Finally, the caboose clacked along. The air settled and Kate looked up and watched the train disappear into the distance.

It was the best thing she'd ever seen in her whole life.

"Are you okay?" Kowalchuk said.

"Oh my God," she said while Kowalchuk helped her to her feet. She dragged the back of her hand across her eyes, swiping away tears, dirt, pain, anger.

She fixed her gaze upon him.

"What the hell took you so long to get here? I could have been killed, for God's sake."

"Uh ... well ... "

"Didn't you read my email? Didn't you talk to Jay Blackfoot? Are you cooperating with the OPP?"

"Sort of."

"What's that supposed to mean?"

A pause. Then. "Let me get back to you on that."

She rolled her eyes.

"Just get me back my knapsack, okay?"

Chapter 67

K̲ate looked at the avalanche of press releases from the Waterford Police Department choking up the inbox of her computer.

DEATH OF JULIE CRAWFORD RE-OPENED
SUSPECT APPREHENDED
WATERFORD POLICE CHIEF RESIGNS
BILL POUND CHARGED WITH NUMEROUS OFFENCES
DRUG RING, THEFT OPERATION BUSTED

Well. I guess this means I'm back on the media list again, Kate thought.

The next issue of *The Tecumseh Challenge* would be packed with all sorts of goodies. Her readers would be ecstatic.

But disappointed too. She couldn't tell them the whole story. The details of the case were still being worked out by the Tecumseh OPP.

I wonder what the other media were reporting?

This should be good, she thought.

ATTEMPTED MURDER AT THE TRAIN TRACKS
By Chelsea Darling, Editor

In a shocking turn of events, Waterford's police chief Bill Pound, a 29-year policing veteran, is dealing with several serious criminal charges as the result of a mysterious incident at the CN railway tracks near Portland Street.

A Waterford woman, Moira Hackett, 41, was also charged with the same offences from the same incident. They are attempted murder, conspiracy, breach of trust, and obstruction of justice, and more charges may be laid.

OPP Insp. Roger Kapoor who is conducting the investigation, had very little information to give about what happened but did say that things "are in the preliminary stages." He looked very grave as he read out a short statement from the podium at the Belleview Police headquarters where the OPP have a sub-office. The room was filled with media from across the province.

One person, likely a victim, had non-life-threatening injuries from the incident but police would not identify the person. It didn't seem to be Hackett or Pound.

Pound and Hackett are now in custody at the Belleview courthouse waiting for a hearing.

Few other details were available but *The Reporter* did manage to unearth some additional information.

A photo of the alleged crime scene is shown (above). Thanks to Cheryl Jenkins, who was walking her Briard dog nearby, for alerting *The Reporter* about the location.

A woman in a ball cap was walking down the rail tracks and Cheryl said she saw her in the middle of the train bridge around twelve o'clock. That's when she called the Waterford Police Department to report what was going on. Police also received reports of the woman in the ball cap from several other motorists.

Cheryl said she heard a lot of yelling and shouting and there were several police cars from both the Tecumseh OPP and the Waterford Police Department.

"Oh my God," Kate sighed. "Not 'around.' 'About.' She saw her 'about' 12 o'clock. Actually, 'she saw her about noon' to be exact. And not a 'Briard dog.' Just a Briard. You don't say 'West Highland terrier dog,' right Alfie?" His head jerked up and tilted, and he gazed quizzically at her. She lobbed the newspaper across the room and it floated to the ground not too far away from him.

He watched her watch him, and his ears perked up a tad. Could it be? Maybe it was time for a …

"C'mon, let's go."

Kate put the magic box to sleep, stood up, stretched, and grabbed the leash hanging up in the kitchen. She hooked it onto his collar as Alfred pulled to get out the door.

Police Chief Facing Attempt Murder Charge
By Kirk Steele, Chief Correspondent

Waterford's police chief was hit with numerous charges after an incident involving a firearm at the town's railway tracks off Portland Street. One person was sent to hospital with non-life threatening injuries.

OPP spokesperson Insp. Roger Kapoor said Police Chief Bill Pound was charged with attempted murder, conspiracy, breach of trust, and obstruction of justice.

Waterford resident Moira Hackett, 41, was charged with the same offences.

Both were remanded into custody at Belleview's provincial courthouse awaiting a bail hearing.

In a short news conference this morning, Kapoor said more charges may be forthcoming. He said little else about the reason for the charges, the relationship between the two suspects, or what took place at the scene.

Further details will be published as soon as available.

Police Re-open Julie Crawford Case
By Kirk Steele, Chief Correspondent

Tecumseh County OPP say that the death of Julie Crawford, whose body was found in the Grand River on Aug. 22 is now being treated as a homicide.

At that time, Waterford Police said the death was not suspicious in nature and described it as a suicide.

OPP spokesperson Insp. Roger Kapoor said that Crawford's body had been exhumed last week and re-examined by the provincial coroner's office. He said there was new evidence to show that Crawford may have been the victim of an assault.

More information will be forthcoming.

"Oh for God's sake," Kate muttered. *It was never officially classified as a suicide, Kirk, never. Your friend Chelsea was the one who started that whole rumour.*

This is why people trust the press less and less, she mused. *Cripes, our job is hard enough as it is.*

Oh how I wish I could print the whole story on the front page of The Tecumseh Challenge. *But I can't. As a crown witness, I can't report a single word of it. The best story I ever got in my whole career. And I'm sworn to secrecy.*

She sighed.

It would all come out later, she knew. Much too late for her preference, of course. But what could she do?

Nothing.

In the meantime, she had a paper to run.

Chapter 68

Kate and Dorothy were sitting in front of the picture window at the Riverview, reflecting on the somewhat sombre scene. A chilly breeze blew off the river, whipping freezing rain against the window and leaving a blotchy skin of ice.

Kate had already filled in Dorothy over the phone with most of the essential information. She was dying to hear the rest.

Stavros approached the table.

"Hello, ladies. Celebrating today?"

"Yeah," Kate said. "I'm celebrating not getting killed."

"Eh?" Stavros said.

Dorothy tsked. "Did you hear what happened to Kate? She was attacked."

Stavros bent over to look at Kate's scratched face.

"What the fuck happened to you? You look like you got run over by a train or something."

Kate nodded. "Good guess. I got run over by my neighbour Moira. Who is now in jail I hope. With the police chief."

"Actually, I heard they gave Moira bail," Dorothy piped up. "And Pound. He was suspended with pay. An absolute disgrace."

"Eh?" Stavros said.

Kate gave a rundown of the encounter, but not exactly why. Only that she hadn't been getting along with her neighbours.

"People are frickin' crazy in this town," he said. "Crazier than I even thought."

"And if it wasn't for her, nothing would have been done about Julie. And now look," Dorothy said.

"Dorothy!" Kate admonished. "I can't talk about that."

"Huh?" Stavros' eyebrows yanked up. "Julie? I thought it was suicide." He took an uninvited seat at the table.

"No. It was murder. And that's all I'm saying," Kate said.

"C'mon," Stavros said. "You can tell me. I won't tell anyone."

Kate didn't laugh out loud. But she did shake her head.

"She's a hero," Dorothy said.

"I'm no hero," Kate said. "I did what anyone would have done if they had known what I had known."

"What you did was amazing, girl," Dorothy said. "Above and beyond the call of duty. Thanks to you, Julie's family will get peace of mind. Those two little girls will get some justice."

"What happened?" asked Stavros.

"Julie's real murderer will stand in front of a judge," Kate said.

"Really," Stavros said. "Okay, I won't ask more nosy questions. Lunch is on me today, ladies. For both of you. Julie was a nice woman. She had a nice personality. She was very classy. She didn't deserve to die. You are my guests today."

Kate and Dorothy smiled. "Well, thank you," Kate said. "Much appreciated." He nodded at Francesco to get cappuccinos.

"I got to check something in the kitchen." Stavros said, pulling away and lining up the front of the chair against the table edge with practised precision. He disappeared into the back and the pair heard his low murmur in the kitchen.

"Okay, great," Dorothy said. "So Kate. What happened exactly? I read the stories in the paper, but I'm sure there's lots they left out."

Kate looked in the direction of the kitchen. Nothing. Safe to talk.

"Yeah," she said quietly. "Like Waterford's chief of police is a crook. His kid robbed the Southern Fried Chicken store and he quashed the investigation. Plus the kid was part of a drug ring, breaking into houses, trafficking, theft. Along with Moira's kids. How handy that she worked at police dispatch. No wonder there were so many robberies in town and none of them solved. She was the lookout for them all. And Pound swept all of it under the carpet."

Dorothy was wide-eyed.

"Julie knew too much. She was close to Conner, and Conner was involved. And when she threatened to spill the beans, Julie had to be eliminated. By Moira. With Bill Pound's blessing."

"Holy geeze. When you've got stuff to report, you've *really* got stuff to report."

"Yeah. I heard from Jay Blackfoot. The coroner said that Julie's hyoid bone was broken. It's a small bone in the neck area. A fracture like that only happens from being strangled. Plus there was evidence of water in her lungs, which means she drowned. And Moira was there when that happened."

Kate described the shoes she found at the side of the Hackett's house and the diatoms from the river. Charlie Pound's van, and people constantly picking up drugs at the Hackett's house. The Southern Fried Chicken robbery and Charlie Pound using his dad's Smith & Wesson. Sam skateboarding early in the morning, every morning, including the morning of the murder. Conner at work at Stavros' restaurant after being dropped off by Moira who drove his truck. The red running shoes, the skateboards with no diatoms, and finally, the Hackett's front door mat with a ton of diatoms — that confirmed it was Moira, not the boys, wearing those shoes.

"But I thought you said Mr. MacKenzie said it was a guy. With red shoes."

"Mr. MacKenzie was helpful. But after talking with him at Penmarvian, I realized his eyesight was not the greatest. Moira is a pretty big woman. She probably looked like a guy from where Mr. Mackenzie was sitting. He was mistaken."

"Oh."

"But he had good information, he saw the red shoes, and that sent me to where I needed to go."

"Yeah, the train bridge. Where all hell broke out."

"I didn't like being bait, that's for sure. But I had to. I was banking on the chance that someone would see me on the bridge and report it to police. Which is exactly what happened. It went through dispatch. Moira got the call and freaked out, and instead of relaying the report to patrol, she told Pound. Then they both went out to investigate. But other people reported it after that, and that's when Kowalchuk went to check it out."

"You took a big chance, setting yourself up like that." Dorothy shook her head. "You put yourself in danger."

"It was a calculated risk."

"And what about when Pound had you on the ground with a gun pointed at your head? How the heck did you think you'd get out of that calculated risk?" Dorothy tsked.

"Yeah, that was a bit unexpected. But I was counting on Jay Blackfoot catching my email in time. I wasn't a 100 per cent sure though. Kowalchuk just happened to hear me yelling from the tracks, and believe me, I made sure that I was yelling a heck of a lot, so that everyone, and I mean everyone, could hear me. Thank God Blackfoot got Tecumseh OPP involved. They showed up just in the nick of time."

Francesco came back with two plates, both extra large: one carried a quiche and a salad, and the other smoked salmon for Kate.

"Hah," Stavros said, suddenly appearing at the side of their table. "I could have told you Pound was a crook."

Kate and Dorothy exchanged glances. Kate surreptitiously felt under the tabletop and kicked Dorothy in the shin. Was there a microphone wired there somewhere? Dorothy gave her a look and valiantly tried not to crack up. Her mouth was full of Greek salad. What a mess that would have been.

"And the mayor knew something too," Stavros continued. "He asked the OPP to come down for a visit. Remember I told you they met in my back room?"

"Yeah," Kate said. "I thought something was up. It was strange that the OPP came and offered to police Waterford completely out of the blue. Seemingly uninvited by council or anyone else."

Stavros bent over and took a close look at Kate's plate.

"The guys in the kitchen sure put a lot extra for you, Kate. Jesus Christ, that's enough to feed three people. Let me go talk to those guys. I'm gonna go bankrupt for sure."

Kate wanted to laugh, but she couldn't. She was too busy shoveling mouthwatering forkfuls of tender smoked salmon into her mouth, each with a carefully measured morsel of lettuce, a sliver of red onion, and a crumb of goat cheese. A perfectly balanced symphony of flavour.

"Mmmmm," she said. Plus something that sounded like: "Thish ish dlishush." She devoured her food then carefully touched her mouth with her linen napkin.

"This calls for another cappuccino. Stavros," Kate called out. "Can I get another cappuccino?"

"And is it still free?" she deadpanned.

Dorothy chortled.

The Faema was already steaming and frothing away.

Chapter 69

The council chambers were full to bursting and there was an air of importance, of things finally being settled, as officials bustled around the room and found their seats.

Mayor Bywater gladhanded amidst the crowd, calling out greetings, and feigning pretend shock at seeing old faces again.

"Wilbur Thompson. How the heck are you, young man? And how is Joannie? I hope she is well after that hip surgery." And Wilbur, who was still actually a bit raw from an unhappy council decision in the not-too-distant past, awkwardly grinned and nodded and called out: "She's fine, thank you, Mayor. Hello!" in a similar jovial tone, along with his seat mate with whom he had been, before they were somewhat rudely interrupted, immersed in conversation.

Kate had pored through the agenda ahead of time, as usual, and wasn't surprised in the least to see the recommendation at the top of the list: "Whereas the Council of Tecumseh County has conducted a study of policing options; and whereas council and staff have examined the two policing options of the Waterford Police Department and the Tecumseh County Ontario Provincial Police respectively; and whereas council has received comments and input from the public regarding their needs and wants, be it resolved that the Council of Tecumseh County accepts the proposal for contract policing with the Tecumseh Ontario Provincial Police and agrees to enter into an agreement immediately.

"And that the Council of Tecumseh County requests the Ministry of Correctional Services and the Ministry of the Solicitor General of Ontario approve a Police Service Delivery Proposal for the policing of the Town of Waterford by the Ontario Provincial Police.

"And that the Mayor forward a letter to the Minister of the Solicitor General of Ontario to initiate the process necessary to accomplish the transition in the community of the Town of Waterford. And that the Ontario Civilian Police Commission be requested to hold a disbandment hearing for the Waterford Police Department, our existing police service, as soon as possible."

Mayor Bywater tapped the gavel. "Good evening, ladies and gentlemen. Welcome." He waited for seats to be taken, jackets to be draped on chairs, and the general sound of buzzing to subside.

Pete stared at Kate's scratched-up face and poked a finger at her. *What happened?* he mouthed.

Kate rolled her eyes and shook her head. *Later,* she mouthed back.

"Thank you, everyone, for attending this evening. I think it will be an important night, and a night that I do believe will mark a historical turning point for the town of Waterford."

There was nodding from the audience.

"But first I would like to acknowledge on behalf of our council and citizenry the terrible tragedy that has befallen one of our local families. Police are now saying the Crawford family — can I say that?" he said, turning to the CAO, then without waiting for an answer, continued, "… has lost a loved one by the hand of another person in the Grand River here in Waterford. We know that murder in Waterford is exceedingly rare and we are thankful for that. But at the same time, we extremely regret that this has occurred. And that during the course of this event some of our citizens have suffered," — and here he gave an almost imperceptible glance in Kate's direction — "and that it has touched many people in unfortunate and may I say life-changing ways. Our thoughts and prayers go to the Crawford and the Hamilton families.

"Now," and there was an uncertain pause, "we find that we have lost our police chief too and that is a regrettable and unfortunate thing as well." There was a titter from the audience. The mayor glanced at the CAO who returned a tight-lipped meaningful glance.

"And at this point, that is all I am at liberty to say," he concluded in a hurry.

"And with that…" he took the gavel in hand and gave a sharp bang, eliciting a jolt that almost ejected a few audience members out of their chairs, "… I now call this meeting to order."

This time around, the crowd was much subdued without the presence of the chief haranguer and trouble-maker — Moira Hackett. Some of her cronies lined the seats of the front row in the room, sullen, somber, dissatisfied.

Kirk and Chelsea were already deep into a private discussion, murmuring, and annoying those sitting in the row immediately adjacent. A few of the crowd members swiveled around and gave them the stink-eye until the commentary fell away.

"Council," the mayor said, "before you is the recommendation. Who wishes to put the motion on the table."

He nodded at the ring of councillors. "Councillor Popowich. Thank you. Seconded by Councillor Chang. Discussion. Councillor Cleghorne."

The four reporters simultaneously began to clack away at their keyboards.

"Yes, Your Worship." She rose to her feet. "I would just like to say that first and foremost, I feel that council has been short-changed by the recent unfortunate turn of events," she began. "It's a shame that our police chief isn't here to defend his police force. I feel they are good men and women and they deserve to carry on."

Councillor Popowich began to fidget with irritation almost immediately.

"Yes, Councillor Cleghorne," Bywater said. "The issue has already been thoroughly aired by both sides. Could you please keep your comments directly related to the motion on the table."

"Yes, Your Worship. I am, Your Worship," Cleghorne responded. "As I was saying, it's been an unfortunate turn of events. The WPD have given us good solid service over the years and I think they would continue to do so, given the chance. I feel that one bad apple shouldn't spoil the whole barrel."

Chang's hand elevated. "Mr. Mayor." He nodded a go-ahead. "Mr. Mayor. I do believe that with the police chief indicted on serious criminal charges, that is surely a significant event. In the meantime, there is confidentiality and we can't comment on any aspect of the situation."

"Yeah," Terryberry said without rising from his chair. "Who knows how far the rot has gone."

A buzz went around the room and there was a hysterical giggle or two. The entire semicircle of councillors shot up their hands to speak.

"But …" Chang's hand went up again to halt the noise in the room and Cleghorne's impending conniption fit. "At the same time, I realize that's a topic of discussion behind closed doors. We must deal with the information we have at hand right now. That is our obligation and our duty."

Bywater nodded, vastly relieved that the comments had, for once, veered away from perilous territory. "Yes. Thank you, Councillor Chang. You are absolutely correct. Councillor Biggar."

"Yes, Your Worship." He rose to his feet with not a small display of pomp. "My family has lived in this town for more than a hundred years."

Pete gave Kate a ridiculous grin. See?

"And I want to say I am extremely disappointed in the recommend-ation. I will definitely be voting against it."

"Against," the mayor intoned. "Duly noted."

"Wait," Biggar continued. "I haven't finished."

Someone exhaled loudly.

"I am extremely disappointed that the long and illustrious history of the Waterford Police Department may be coming to an end."

The mayor shifted in his chair. "Well, we don't know that yet, do we Councillor Biggar. A lot of things need to happen first. And not in the least, we still have to vote on the recommendation, which I hasten to add, is before us now."

"Yes," he continued. "But nevertheless I can see the writing on the wall. Those of us who have defended Waterford and its values all these many years, we're outnumbered by those on council who don't seem to care about tradition or the town of Waterford. And it's a huge shame. It casts a bad light on our council. We don't seem to respect and honour our history around here. And respect the men and women who have toiled and worked so hard."

"Hear, hear," someone called out from the audience.

"We don't want the OPP," someone else yelled out.

Bywater gave the gavel one sharp bang.

"Order! I won't have people yelling from the audience. I just won't have it. It's against the rules of order and I just won't have it. All right. Next. Councillor Popowich. Oh. Councillor Biggar. Are you finished?"

"I guess so," he muttered. He plunked back down onto his chair dispiritedly.

Popowich leapt to his feet. "Mr. Mayor, I disagree in the strongest terms with Councillor Biggar's portrayal of the rest of council not caring about tradition or the town of Waterford."

Biggar crossed his arms.

"This is not a matter of being loyal to one part of the county or another. It's a question of getting the best value for our policing dollar. And notwithstanding the fact that our police chief is in some legal trouble and is no longer part of the picture ..." he faltered, searching for words that would evade thorny issues.

"I just want to say that councillors cannot, cannot make this issue a personal one, or a territorial one, or a historical one, or anything else. It is exactly just what it is. We have to vote according to the information before us. According to the staff report and to the full and detailed presentations given by each party in the competition. That's what I'm going to do and that's what I hope each and every person that sits around this table is going to do."

Cleghorne's arm shot into the air. The mayor raised an eyebrow in her direction. "Yes, Councillor Cleghorne. A rebuttal. A short one, if you please."

"Mr. Mayor, I wanted to continue from where I left off. You cut me off. I wasn't finished."

There was muted groaning in the room. As one, the press corps stopped typing and went to surf the internet.

"Councillor Cleghorne. Please. All right. Go ahead. But I just ask that you be succinct."

"I'd just like to say — just because this issue is so important, that's why we should look at all aspects, and that includes tradition and history." She droned on for the next ten minutes.

Kate grabbed her camera, left her chair, and positioned herself at the side of the chambers behind a row of staff.

She looked around the room.

OPP Superintendent Don Pearcy and Inspector Roger Kapoor were sitting off to one side in their full dress uniforms. A suitcase on wheels stuffed with paperwork was at the ready in case there were any last minute questions. Both men looked tired, but confident.

On the other side of the room sat the now-acting police chief Johnny Grimaldi, and Kowalchuk. They were surrounded by a group of a dozen or more men and one woman in WPD uniform, a show of solidarity. They knew what they were facing, and it didn't look good, but they had not given up yet. The vote was still to come. And most of the audience was on their side.

Kate went to the front corner of the room standing off to one side behind the mayor's podium and tried to gather as much of the crowd into her camera view as possible. There was such a variety of emotions on display: nervousness, sadness, anger, conviction, resolve. She wanted to capture it all. She took a few test shots to adjust the white balance, then released the shutter.

She peered into her display to see the result. Not bad. Maybe a few more shots would do it. She raised the camera to eye level, looked through the viewfinder.

All she could see was a dark blob covering the entire scene.

Whaa?

Chelsea Darling was standing right in front of her, blocking her camera and stealing her shot. Her flash went off once, twice, three times. Her Hollywood-style red hair billowed through the air as she pranced back to the media table.

Kate's jaw dropped. Off to one side she could see Pete having a laughing fit. Kirk steadfastly ignored the whole thing.

Thankfully, the audience and councillors were too focused on the discussion to pay any attention.

Kate rolled her eyes, thought of some defamatory things she longed to say, then made her way over to the other side of the room. She began to plan a replacement shot.

She leaned against the doorframe that led to the outer meeting rooms and bided her time.

"I think we've heard from every councillor at least two or three times on this matter," said the mayor. "Does anyone else have any other points to make that haven't been made already?"

"This has been discussed to death," said Councillor Terryberry.

"Let's call the vote already, for Pete's sake."

"All right. A recorded vote?" Nods all around the horseshoe.

"All in favour of the resolution. Please stand."

Three councillors stood: Chang, Popowich and Terryberry. Stapleton counted with a finger and checked off the names on a list.

"Against." Pickett, Biggar, and Cleghorne rose from their chairs. Another count by Stapleton.

"It's tied three three," she announced. There was utter silence.

"Right. I will cast the deciding vote. And I vote in favour of the resolution," Mayor Bywater said getting to his feet. "In favour of the OPP."

The room erupted into cries of "no" and "it's wrong" and "shame."

And this was the moment Kate chose to snap her camera shutter, capturing the outrage and the anger.

The mayor took his seat again. "There's one more thing," he said. "And I think everyone will want to hear this."

He nodded at Pearcy who made his way to the podium, going the long way around the audience and avoiding as many people as possible.

He stood at the lectern. "Thank you, Mayor Bywater. I want to thank the council of Tecumseh County for this decision and this opportunity to serve the community."

Loud groans and derisive catcalls came from the audience.

"Silence," Bywater called out. He banged the hammer. "I apologize. Please proceed." He nodded at Pearcy.

Pearcy held up a sheet of paper and read: "At this time, the Tecumseh OPP would like to invite members of the Waterford District Police to apply to join the new force. After a suitable training and transition period, we would like to hire several new members, officers who are qualified and knowledgable. Please contact Inspector Roger Kapoor at our detachment, who will assist you with any questions."

There was a shocked silence, then the entire audience got to its feet and erupted in cheers and clapping.

"Finally, some good news," somebody said.

"Why didn't they say that in the first place," another complained.

"Who cares. Count me in," another said.

"That's the best thing I've heard all year."

The man who had called Kapoor a racial slur only a few weeks prior was now shaking his hand and thanking him.

Pearcy was having a hard time making his way back to his seat, with all the hand-shaking, back-clapping, and hurrah-ing going on in the room. Kate took another series of photos and returned to her seat, noting, with not one iota of guilt, Chelsea's expression of annoyance.

Mayor Bywater opened a desk drawer, pulled out a handkerchief, and mopped his brow.

"I now call for a recess," he announced, and struck the gavel. "Twenty minutes."

"I think we're gonna need it," Terryberry hooted.

Chapter 70

Kate decided to head over to the parkette to get some fresh air.

The breeze held a noticeable chill and she buttoned her wool coat, pulled down a hat over her ears, and felt for the gloves in her pockets. She glanced at the sky, luminous with stars. Soon there would be a full moon, perfect for the last of the migrating birds — the raptors, the swans, the cranes, the last shorebirds.

She walked to the edge of the paving stones to where the light reflected off the balustrade, and leaned over on her elbows.

There was none of the roar and odour from that night three months ago when the river had been running high and the Cambridge sewage treatment plant had overflowed. Instead, the water gurgled quietly, choked with rotting leaves and leaving the frosty air tinged with the smell of peat.

She would miss all her songbird friends, long gone now. Winds from the north had lifted the passerines off the ground, propelling them southwards, and they wouldn't be back until next year.

Birds used the stars to navigate, the sight and smell of watercourses snaking along the countryside, the look of the land as it glistened in the moonlight. They called out to one another within their flocks, asking and answering, reassuring and encouraging their fellow family members, mates, and travelers to move south, relentlessly south. There was an air of both determination and desperation about their journey.

It was imperative to avoid all the man-made impediments they might strike during their trek — tall buildings, hydro towers, the dazzling lights of airports, lighthouses, and office buildings. It was all they could do to ride the wind and avoid any obstructions at the last minute, close their eyes to the confusing blinking lights that blinded them from below and ahead, the roar of wind turbine blades that blocked their sense of where lay the Great Lakes, that ominous and most intimidating of natural bodies that would drown them in mere seconds if they mistakenly dropped too low or flew too slowly.

They were on a perilous journey, one that took grit and resolve and an overwhelming, irrefutable sense of something better ahead, not unlike the journey of life itself.

Kate tilted her head and listened carefully for tiny chirps and calls overhead, marveling at the courage of the creatures that might neverthless still be passing by using the Grand River as a pointer south.

She heard steps behind her and once again, found herself whirling around to face whoever was making their way down the parkette towards her.

And just like the last time, again it was a tall figure, and as he passed under the light she could see that it was Kowalchuk. She drew herself in, turned around, and was silent.

"Hello, Kate," he said, leaning on the balustrade beside her. "It's a cold night, isn't it."

"Uh huh," she said, noncommittal.

There was a period of uncomfortable quiet then suddenly the wind blustered through the trees and swept up the dust from the far corners of the cement platform, wildly blowing it around.

They both drew back, waving at the air in front of their faces, then settled back onto their elbows, mirroring each other's pose.

The faintest high-pitched staccato of a lesser yellowlegs sounded above them. Variations echoed at some distance away. Kate looked up and tried to make out the shapes of the birds, but couldn't.

"Sounded a lot like a lesser yellowlegs, didn't it?" Kowalchuk said. "Or was it greater yellowlegs?"

There was a pause. "Lesser," Kate said perfunctorily.

Another pause.

"I wanted to apologize," Kowalchuk said. "I know I was uncooperative that day when you came in and showed me the photos. That was unfortunate. But I have an explanation."

Another pause. "Whatever," Kate said. "I'm sure you had your reasons. Pound put pressure on you. Et cetera, et cetera."

"I know you're disappointed."

"Integrity is a perishable commodity," Kate said. "Once lost, can never be retrieved."

Kowalchuk raised his eyebrows and made a face. "Yeah, but doesn't saving your life count for something?"

Kate glared.

A completely illogical syllogism and wholly unrelated.

She turned to face him. "Look. You did more than ruin my day, that afternoon we had our meeting. A huge injustice was taking place, never mind something that broke the law and violated the oath you swore when you took your job. And you did nothing."

"Whoa. Wait a minute. I didn't know Pound was involved in all that stuff. I just thought he was mad at you because of that article you wrote."

"I don't know if I believe that," Kate said. "Anyone can tell when things don't smell right. The Southern Fried Chicken thing was a major screwup, and you knew it. And Pound was in charge. And you never wondered why there were so many unsolved break-ins in town? You didn't know about Pound's kid or why Moira and Pound had a relationship or Moira's connection to the Crawfords?"

"There might have been signs," Kowalchuk said slowly. "We did get a tip from the public. A white truck near the crime scene with a distinctive licence plate and a man and a woman in the front seat. But I was told it didn't pan out.

"Look, I was away a lot. And I don't really hang out with the other officers. Haven't for years. I'd been looking after my dad every spare minute I had before he died. It was a lot of pressure. I didn't have much down time or patience or private life any more. It took a toll on my marriage. I went through a divorce. And people were complaining about me at work. I was facing dismissal. I had to toe the line."

"So you were afraid to lose your job if you didn't become just as evil as those people."

A silence.

"I guess that's what it amounted to," he said. "I guess I can see that now. I regret that. I'm sorry. I know what you're going to say.

Everyone makes choices. I made some bad ones, I guess. And I do apologize for what I put you through. And anyone else."

"You know, I don't care so much about me. You should really apologize to Julie's family."

"I did. I have. Personally, the other day. I felt very bad. Truly."

"What did they say?"

"They were very gracious. Accepted my apology. Very nice people."

"Did you apologize alone?"

"Yeah. The department is going to craft a formal apology soon. That is, when things settle down with the transfer over to the OPP. I'm working on the wording with Kapoor."

"Right," Kate said.

Another long silence. Then a call from above. A series of loud peep-quacks and an answering rapid krik krik krik.

"Huh. That sounded like a duck," Kowalchuk said. "But I can't think of which one."

"Green-winged teal," Kate said. "I'm going back to the meeting."

"Wait," Kowalchuk said. "Friends?" He held out his hand for a shake.

Kate paused. Cynicism, outrage, and disgust were the emotions that still occupied her thoughts. Not forgiveness. Not at all.

"Let me get back to you on that."

She turned and trudged back to the council chambers.

Chapter 71

*H*oc oppidum condidit. This town founded by.

Kate took in the seven-foot high obelisk that marked the final resting place of Hiram Capron, the founder of Waterford.

It was a bright sunny day at the cemetery, but chilly too. A wind from the north hinted at wintry days that were yet to come.

Capron was Waterford's first reeve, way back in 1850.

I wonder what he would have thought about all these council shenanigans going on now, she thought to herself. *Probably not surprised in the least. Probably people weren't much different one hundred and fifty years ago*

She sat at a nearby bench. The same bench where Julie must have sat more than once.

Blackfoot had let Kate know that the evidence gathered from Julie's disinterment had been processed by the crown attorney. The case was gathering steam and would soon be setting its first court date.

Julie. I hope this is what you wanted.

For Kate there were still so many unanswered questions. So many things that still troubled her.

She looked at the stem of the American Columbo, now a broken dried-out stick that was almost imperceptible from the fall's dead asters and thistles.

A tiny creature was foraging on the ground, sorting through the leaf litter.

Kate sat perfectly still. Sure enough, a preoccupied white-throated sparrow came closer, then closer yet, and scoured the ground not far from her feet. She watched it make a tiny hop from front to back, then a jab with its beak. Hop-step-jab, hop-step-jab. Tiny bits of things were kicked away.

Kate admired its persistence. It gave a couple of forceful flicks and that was when she noticed a silvery glint on the ground.

The bird flew, but not before Kate visually fixed the location. She walked over to the spot, and bent over to look.

Nothing. She scanned the ground. She got down on her hands and knees and pushed aside the loose dead leaves.

There. There it was. A small circular object. A ring of some sort.

She picked it out of the dirt and polished it with the finger of her glove, feeling the bumps that were the settings for precious stones. She held it in front of her eyes and it was silverish. She looked more closely. She was aghast.

Kate slid the ring into her pocket, and returning to the bench, sat for a few minutes and stared into space. She raked her hand through her hair a few times.

She shook her head, mumbled something incomprehensible, and dropped to her hands and knees once again.

She brushed aside the leaves that had fallen around the bench, making a small pile off to one side, and conducted a spiral ground search, carefully examining everything within a three metre radius of the bench until she found what she wanted. The butt of a cigarillo. She squinted at the tiny writing on the label encircling the plastic holder. "Whiskey tipped."

The wind rose to a sweeping updraft as she walked to her car. She glanced up at the sky with the leaves swirling overhead then floating down to the ground. She fingered the ring in her pocket and pulled it out once again.

It was a vintage platinum wedding ring with nine diamonds on top, engraved with a pattern of orange blossoms on the bottom.

Julie's wedding ring. The one she said she never took off.

Kate knew it. She just knew that she'd been right all along. And so had Hugh MacKenzie.

And she had been only half-right about Moira.

She needed to check the results of one of her investigations.

And conduct another.

But she was certain what she would find.

Chapter 72

Kate pushed open the door and at the same time, the wind from the street blew in a few errant leaves. A bell tinkled.

Things were in disarray at Marshalls Mens Apparel. The carpeting was stained. There was barely enough stock to cover the display tables. Clothing was jumbled on the shelves and left out, unfolded, sometimes in a pile.

A door opened and a thin man with eyes like recessed shadows, stepped out of the back room.

He was dressed in autumn tweeds and corduroys yet the clothes hung on his frame like rags on a scarecrow. The jacket drooped over his bony shoulders and there wasn't much to fill out the rear end of his pants. His skin tone was grey, his face worn and lined. He looked sixty, but he was actually forty-five.

He had not been living a hardscrabble life on the streets. He was the owner of a once-successful men's clothing store in downtown Waterford and his name was Marshall Crawford.

It took but a moment for Marshall to register who had just walked into his store. His face darkened with dislike.

Kate went to the counter and deliberately set the ring on the glass surface.

"I found this at the cemetery yesterday," she said. "I wanted to give you a chance to explain."

Marshall stared at the ring, then at Kate.

"It's Julie's wedding band," she said with emphasis.

"Maybe. So what." He moved as if to slide the ring off the counter and into his hand. Kate blocked him and put the ring back into her pocket, startling him.

Bullies are always shocked when people stand up to them.

"I found it on the ground near Julie's favourite bench at the cemetery," she said. "Maybe you can tell me why that ring was there."

"How the hell should I know?"

Kate gave him a long look. "I think you do know. I'm giving you one chance to tell me what happened before I take this to the police."

"Why don't you just give me that ring and get out of here. That ring is mine. It belonged to my great-grandmother. That's a family heirloom."

"Listen. I'm going to make this clear. I knew Julie. She loved that ring. She would never have taken it off unless there was a really really good reason."

"I haven't a clue what you're talking about."

"I think you do. I think you know perfectly well why that ring was on the ground. I think Julie deliberately took it off when you argued with her in the cemetery that day."

"What day?"

"That day in August you turned off the store sign at seven in the morning and went with your sister Moira to find Julie. To have it out with her. Both of you. You knew what the result would be."

"If you don't hand over that ring I'm calling the cops. Now."

"Okay. We'll just wait for them right here, won't we. And we can both tell them our stories."

Marshall didn't budge an inch. Kate knew he wouldn't.

"I want to tell you something. I did some tests on your front door mat here at the store. It's full of things like sand and bits of leaves. But there was one American columbo seed there from the cemetery. And traces of anthracite coal dust. Diesel. Iron. Rust. Creosote. All the things you find on the bed of an old railway track, and only on the bed of an old railway track. Just like the one that crosses the Grand River. Just like at the spot where Julie bent the safety rail and fell from the bridge."

"So what. I already told you. I've been there a lot. I like the view. So did Julie. That's why she jumped."

"She didn't. She was pushed. I think you know that."

"Yeah? Prove it."

"Someone saw you there wearing your red shoes."

"A lot of people have red shoes. You can't prove I was there."

"Yes, I can. Or rather, a man named Hugh Mackenzie can. Plus a couple other ladies. They were walking their Briard early in the morning when they saw you get into Moira's truck, and they left a tip with the police. Who could forget that licence tag? MFKR."

"You're lying."

"You conned everyone. You even conned me for a while. You had your sad little story. You had all those photos ready. You manipulated Chelsea like a puppet master. She ran your story verbatim. But you weren't so innocent, were you? That fat lip the day I came by to get the photo said a lot. Julie fought hard before she died."

"You're a fucking idiot," Marshall said. "I knew that from day one. Miss know-it-all poking her nose into everyone's business. Why don't you just leave things alone? Believe me, it would be a lot better for you if you did."

He glared at her menacingly.

"Tell me something. When Julie threw the ring in your face and threatened to take away the kids, did you hit her then? Or was it when you chased her onto the train bridge?"

That was like waving a red flag at a bull. He hurled himself over the counter but Kate was ready. She grabbed his closest outstretched arm and twisted, bringing him hard to the ground on his shoulder before kicking him in the brachial nerve. He grimaced in pain. Before he could think twice, her foot landed hard in his solar plexus and he doubled over in agony.

But only for a minute. Marshall seemed possessed with a superhuman energy. He dragged himself to his feet and lunged at her again, almost catching her off guard. Kate dodged behind a display table and he came at her from the front. She threw a pile of folded sweaters in his face, then as he tangled with the wool, pushed the table into him and ran off to one side, behind a mannequin.

He slowly got to his feet and staggered towards the mannequin.

"Julie deserved everything she got," he said, walking slowly towards Kate. "She was a phony little big mouth goody two shoes. She was a hypocrite. Screwing her own nephew."

"You didn't have to kill her."

"I didn't. Moira finished her off. Nice and clean."

"I thought so. How handy for you. Your sister took care of your problem. All the women in your life take care of your problems."

Kate switched to the other side of the mannequin.

"That insurance money. Did it all go to drugs? Every last penny? A never-ending stream of drugs for that never-ending habit you have?"

He was getting close.

"You're a disgusting human being. Everything precious in life — destroyed. Drugs, drugs, and more drugs. You are truly the ugliest person I ever met."

He charged.

Kate grabbed the mannequin, and just when Marshall was about to enter her circle of vulnerability, she gave the heavy dummy a mighty shove in his direction, knocking him off balance. She kicked him hard in the knee cap, and he yelled in pain, hopping to one foot. She ran for the door.

He threw himself at Kate, grabbing at her clothes, her hair, anything, trying to pull her to the floor. Marshall was still taller and heavier, and fast on his feet. There was a desperate scramble.

Kate jabbed her elbow into his eye, and a knee in the groin, then she let out with a series of sonkal knifehands on the side of his throat. He recoiled in pain, then as he straightened up, she pulled her fists close to her body and with the force of momentum, executed the bandae dollyeo chagi, a hard spinning wheel kick. It connected with his head with a thump and sent him flying into a nearby chest of drawers, knocking him out cold.

She bent over with her hands on her thighs and caught her breath. She waited for her heart to slow before going to her knees and saying a little prayer.

Thank you God, Allah, and the Divine Being for watching over me.

And for finally healing her right knee. It was clearly fully operational.

"Whew," she said, straightening her clothes and putting herself back together again. "That was exhausting."

"Peace, joy, serenity," she murmured. All things in their rightful place.

She rolled Marshall over, put his hands together behind his back, grabbed a nearby tailor's measuring tape, and knotted it tight around his wrists.

She walked to the phone and dialed the police.

This time, she knew help would be on the way.

Chapter 73

"**C**ome on, I did not have a crush on him. I just admired him a little bit."

Kate and Dorothy were at the Riverview, and Kate was filling her in on Marshall's arrest and detainment without bail.

"Yeah, maybe. But as it turned out, he was the worst of the bunch. He sacrificed everything he had for drugs. Which Sam and Conner supplied him with whenever he wanted. And in return, he turned a blind eye to all their 'deliveries' in town, breaking into homes in the middle of the day and ripping people off. They had quite a system going."

"But not enough. The Southern Fried Chicken store robbery was their undoing."

"Yeah. I still can't believe Conner and Charlie Pound had the nerve to come back and order food there a few days later. And Chuck Ferretti recognized him."

"And Bill Pound did nothing, of course."

"And that sent a red flag to the mayor who sat on the Police Services Board. No wonder he cast the deciding vote on the policing thing. It was probably the last straw."

They both dug into their plates. Stavros had been generous once again, piling high their plates in the kitchen. And this time, no complaints.

"You know something, Kate," Dorothy said between mouthfuls. "This crime fighting thing. It's a bit dangerous, naturally," she winced a little. "But I think it suits you. Maybe you should seriously consider dropping the newspaper business and going into the private eye business. There's probably more money in it." She chuckled.

Kate nodded. "There's more money in just about everything compared to the newspaper business."

Thoughtful.

"But you know, what would my readership think? What would they do if I was gone? They'd just read pap. Junk. No one really cares enough to put work into the newspaper business these days. If I didn't do it, no one would. And the people of Tecumseh County would never really know what was going on in their community."

Dorothy touched the corner of her mouth with a napkin.

"I suppose you have a point there. I for one, love reading your little newspaper. *The Tecumseh Challenge.* That's exactly what it is. A challenge to all those who hold power, to wield that responsibility seriously. Or else." And she made a slicing motion across her throat. "Kate Messenger will be on your case."

Kate laughed and nodded. "Yeah. The paper truly is a challenge."

Dorothy looked over at her, sensing what she was about to say.

"For oh so many reasons. So many many reasons."

"You wouldn't even know where to begin."

"I wouldn't even know where to begin."

They both laughed, and Stavros looked over from the the bar with a quizzical expression.

"Frickin' women," he muttered. "They should be doing my job. See what hard work *really* means in this world."

Kate and Dorothy looked at each other in amazement and burst out laughing once again.

And as they shook their heads and finished their meals, Kate glanced through the window beside their favourite table in the restaurant and caught the extraordinary image of a lone bald eagle drifting by, following the Grand River south to Port Maitland and the open vistas of Lake Erie, the warm storm-prone body of water that discouraged avians from crossing to the south by its very existence, its far away horizons, its deceptively shallow waters and suddenly cloud-filled skies.

The eagle would make a sharp right and capture the updrafts along the cliffs of Lake Erie to the flats of Amherstburg where it would enter American territory over a short and narrow river called the Detroit River, only two kilometres wide at Grosse Ile, and five kilometres wide at the renowned Lake Erie Metropark and the Point Moillee State Game Area.

From there it would round the shoreline and fly south once again, in the leeward crest of the Allegheny flyway, the sheltered swift-moving current of northwest winds that swept migrating birds towards better weather and a better life on the wetlands and in the tropical forests of Central and South America.

Far from the bitter winds that would begin to plague the people of Tecumseh County.

About the Author

C.P. Avis is a journalist, artist, and bird-lover
living in southern Ontario, Canada.
This is her first novel.

www.cpavis.com

On Facebook: search for CP Avis

Give a review on Facebook and Amazon

www.ingramcontent.com/pod-product-compliance
Lightning Source LLC
Chambersburg PA
CBHW031604240626
47153CB00002B/638